he dragon stood on ITs back legs. "I will return at the nine-o'clock bells tonight. As soon as His Lordship's guests arrive, remain with him." IT flapped ITs wings. "Do not let him out of your sight. Trust no one. Keep him safe."

How could a girl keep an ogre safe?

IT circled above me. "You can shout. A person half your size can shout. Act!"

GAIL CARSON LEVINE

A TALE of TWO
CASTLES

HARPER

An Imprint of HarperCollins*Publishers*

Thanks to all the creative writers who posted title
possibilities to my blog. Special thanks to
April Jo Ann Mack for the actual, final, *ta da!* title.
Thanks to Renée Cafiero for the many fixes to many books.
Such security you give me!
And thanks to David Macauley
for his crystal clear book *Castles*

A Tale of Two Castles
Copyright © 2011 by Gail Carson Levine
For information address HarperCollins Children's
Books, a division of HarperCollins Publishers, 195 Broadway, New York,
NY 10007.
www.harpercollinschildrens.com

Library of Congress Cataloging-in-Publication Data
Levine, Gail Carson.
A tale of Two Castles / Gail Carson Levine. — 1st ed.
    p.   cm.
 Summary: Twelve-year-old Elodie journeys to Two Castles in hopes of
studying acting but instead becomes apprentice to a dragon, who teaches her
to be observant and use reasoning, thus helping her to uncover who is
plotting against the ogre Count Jonty Um.
 ISBN 978-0-06-122967-1
 [1. Apprentices—Fiction. 2. Dragons—Fiction. 3. Reasoning—Fiction.
4. Kings, queens, rulers, etc.—Fiction. 5. Mystery and detective stories.
6. Fantasy.] I. Title.
PZ7.L578345Tal 2011
[Fic]—dc22   2010027756
                                                                           CIP
                                                                            AC

Typography by Andrea Vandergrift
16 LP/BR   10 9 8 7 6 5 4 3 2
❖
First paperback edition, 2012

To David, to whom I cannot dedicate too many books

mansions

Owe Street

town wall

south gate

menagerie

Jonty Um's castle

ogre's farm fields

Owe Street

Street

Cane

lair

king's castle

N

KINGDOM
OF
LEPAI

CHAPTER ONE

other wiped her eyes on her sleeve and held me tight. I wept onto her shoulder. She released me while I went on weeping. A tear slipped into the strait through a crack in the wooden dock. Salt water to salt water, a drop of me in the brine that would separate me from home.

Father's eyes were red. He pulled me into a hug, too. Albin stood to the side a few feet and blew his nose with a *honk*. He could blow his nose a dozen ways. A honk was the saddest.

The master of the cog called from the gangplank, "The tide won't wait."

I shouldered my satchel.

Mother began, "Lodie—"

"*E*lodie," I said, brushing away tears. "My whole name."

"Elodie," she said, "don't correct your elders. Keep your thoughts private. You are mistaken as often—"

"—as anyone," I said.

"Elodie . . . ," Father said, sounding nasal, "stay clear of the crafty dragons and the shape-shifting ogres." He took an uneven breath. "Don't befriend them! They won't bother you if you—"

"—don't bother them," I said, glancing at Albin, who shrugged. He was the only one of us who'd ever been in the company of an ogre or a dragon. Soon I would be near both. At least one of each lived in the town of Two Castles. The castle that wasn't the king's belonged to an ogre.

"Don't finish your elders' sentences, Lodie," Mother said.

"*E*lodie." I wondered if Father's adage was true. Maybe ogres and dragons bothered you *especially* if you didn't bother them. I would be glad to meet either one—if I had a quick means of escape.

Albin said, "Remember, Elodie: If you have to speak to a dragon, call it *IT*, never *him* or *her* or *he* or *she*."

I nodded. Only a dragon knows ITs gender.

Mother bent so her face was level with mine. "Worse than ogres or dragons . . . beware the whited sepulcher."

The whited sepulcher was Mother's great worry. I wanted to soothe her, but her instruction seemed impossible to

follow. A sepulcher is a tomb. A whited sepulcher is someone who seems good but is, in truth, evil. How would I
know?

"The geese"—Mother straightened, and her voice
caught— "will look for you tomorrow."

The geese! My tears flowed again. I hated the geese, but
I would miss them.

Mother flicked a gull's feather off my shoulder. "You're
but a baby!"

I went to Albin and hugged him, too. He whispered
into my hair, "Be what you must be."

The master of the cog roared, "We're off!"

I ran, leaped over a coil of rope, caught my foot, and went
sprawling. Lambs and calves! Behind me, Mother cried out.
I scrambled up, dusty but unharmed. I laughed through my
tears and raced up the plank. A seaman drew it in.

The sail, decorated with the faded image of a winged
fish, bellied in the breeze. We skimmed away from the
dock. If fate was kind, in ten years I would see my parents
and Albin again. If fate was cruel, never.

As they shrank, Mother losing her tallness, Father his
girth, Albin his long beard, I waved. They waved back and
didn't stop. The last I could make out of them, they were
still waving.

The island of Lahnt diminished, too. For the first time it
seemed precious, with its wooded slopes and snowy peaks,

the highest wreathed in clouds. I wished I could pick out Dair Mountain, where our Potluck Farm perched.

Farewell to my homeland. Farewell to my childhood.

Mother and Father's instructions were to apprentice myself to a weaver, but I would not. *Mansioner.* I mouthed the word into the wind, the word that held my future. *Mansioner.* Actor. Mansioner of myth and fable. Mother and Father would understand once I found a master or mistress to serve and could join the guild someday.

Leaning into the ship's bulwarks, I felt the purse, hidden under my apron, which held my little knife, a lock of hair from one of Albin's mansioning wigs, a pretty pink stone, a perfect shell from the beach this morning, and a single copper, which Father judged enough to feed me until I became apprenticed. Unless the winds blew against us, we would reach Two Castles, capital of the kingdom of Lepai, in two or three days, in time for Guild Week, when masters took on new apprentices. I might see the king or the ogre, if one of them came through town, but I was unlikely to enter either castle.

I had no desire to see King Grenville III, who liked war and taxes so much that his subjects called him Greedy Grenny. Lepai was a small kingdom, but bigger by half than when he'd mounted the throne—and so were our taxes bigger by half, or so Mother said. The king was believed to have his combative eye on Tair, Lahnt's neighbor across the wide side of the strait.

Queen Sofie had died a decade ago, but I did hope to see the king's daughter, Princess Renn, who was rumored to be somehow peculiar. A mansioner is interested in peculiarity.

And a mansioner observes. I turned away from home. To my left, three rowers toiled on a single oar. The one in the center called, "Pu-u-u-ll," with each stroke. I heard his mate across the deck call the same. Father had told me the oars were for steering and the sail for speed. The deck between me and the far bulwarks teemed with seamen, passengers, a donkey, and two cows.

A seaman climbed the mast. The cog master pushed his way between an elderly goodman and his goodwife and elbowed the cows until they let him pass. He disappeared down the stairs to the hold, where the cargo was stored. I would remember his swagger, the way he rolled his shoulders, and how widely he stepped.

The deck tilted into a swell. I felt a chill, although the air was warm for mid-October.

"Go, honey, move. Listen to Dess. Listen, honey, honey." A small man, thin but for fleshy cheeks and a double chin, the owner of the donkey and the cows, coaxed his animals into a space between the bulwarks and the stairs to the rear upper deck. He carried a covered basket in his right hand, heavy, because his shoulder sagged. "Come, honey."

His speech reminded me of Father with our animals

at home. *Good, Vashie,* he'd tell our cow, *Good girl, what a good girl.* Perhaps if I'd repeated myself with the geese, they'd have liked me better.

The elderly goodwife opened her sack and removed a cloak, which she spread on the deck. Holding her husband's hand, she lowered herself and sat. He sat at her side on the cloak. The other passengers also began to mark out their plots of deck, their tiny homesteads.

I wasn't sure yet where I wanted my place to be. Near the elderly couple, who might have tales to tell?

Not far from them, a family established their claim. To my surprise, the daughter wore a cap. In Lahnt women wore caps, but not girls, except for warmth in winter. Her kirtle and her mother's weren't as full as mine, but their sleeves hung down as far as their knuckles, and their skirt hems half covered their shoes, which had pointed toes, unlike my rounded ones.

The cog dropped into a slough in the sea, and my stomach dropped with it. We rose again, but my belly liked that no better. I leaned against the bulwarks for better balance.

My mouth filled with saliva. I swallowed again and again. Nothing in the world was still, not the racing clouds nor the rippling sail nor the pitching ship.

The son in the family pointed at me and cried, "Her face is green wax!"

My stomach surged into my throat. I turned and heaved

my breakfast over the side. Even after the food was gone, my stomach continued to rise and sink.

Next to me, a fellow passenger whimpered and groaned.

I stared down at the foamy water churning by, sicker than I had ever been. Still, the mansioner in me was in glory. Lambs and calves! I would remember how it was to feel so foul. I wondered if I could transform my face to green wax without paint, just by memory.

The cog rose higher than it had so far and fell farther. I vomited bile and then gasped for breath. The bulwarks railing pressed into my sorry stomach.

The person at my side panted out, "Raise your head. Look at the horizon."

My head seemed in the only reasonable position, but I lifted it. The island of Lahnt had vanished. The horizon was splendidly flat and still. My insides continued bobbing, but less.

"Here." A hand touched mine on the railing. "Peppermint. Suck on it."

The leaf was fresh, not dried, and the clean taste helped. "Thank you, mistress." My eyes feared to let go of the horizon, so I couldn't see my benefactress. Her voice was musical, although not young. She might be the old goodwife.

"I've crossed many times and always begun by being sick." Her voice lilted in amusement. She seemed to have found respite enough from her suffering to speak more than a few words. "I've exhausted my goodman's sympathy." She sighed. "I still hope to become a good sailor someday. You are young to travel alone."

Mother and Father didn't have passage money for more than me. "Not so young, mistress." Here I was, contradicting my elders again. "I am fourteen." Contradicting and lying.

"Ah."

I was tall enough for fourteen, although perhaps not curvy enough. I risked a sideways peek to see if she believed me, but she still faced the horizon and didn't meet my eyes. I took in her profile: long forehead, knob of a nose, weathered skin, deep lines around her mouth, gray wisps escaping her hood, a few hairs sprouting from her chin—a likeable, honest face.

"Conversation keeps the mind off the belly," she said, and I saw a gap in her upper teeth.

The ship dropped. I felt myself go greener. My eyes snapped back to the horizon.

"We will be visiting our children and their children in Two Castles. Why do you cross?"

She was as nosy as I was! "I seek an apprenticeship as"—I put force into my hoarse, seasick voice—"a mansioner."

"Ah," she said again. "Your parents sent you off to be a mansioner."

I knew she didn't believe me now. "To be a weaver," I

admitted. "Lambs and calves!" Oh, I didn't mean to use the farm expression. "To stay indoors, to repeat a task end-lessly, to squint in lamplight . . . ," I burst out. "It is against my nature!"

"To have your hands seize up before you're old," the goodwife said with feeling, "your shoulders blaze with pain, your feet spread. Be not a weaver nor a spinner!"

Contrarily, I found myself defending Father's wishes for me. "Weaving is honest, steady work, mistress." I laughed at myself. "But I won't be a weaver."

The boat dipped sideways. My stomach emptied itself of nothing.

She gave me another mint leaf. "Why a mansioner?"

"I love spectacles and stories." Mansioning had been my ambition since I was seven and a caravan of mansions came to our country market.

Then, when I was nine, Albin left his mansioning troupe and came to live with us and help Father farm. He passed his spare time telling me mansioners' tales and showing me how to act them out. He said I had promise.

"I love theater, too," the goodwife said, "but I never dreamed of being a mansioner."

"I like to be other people, mistress." Lowering my pitch and adding a quiver, I said, "I can mimic a little." I went back to my true voice. "That's not right." I hadn't caught her tone.

She chuckled. "If you were trying to be me, you were on the right path. How long an apprenticeship will you serve?"

Masters were paid five silver coins to teach an apprentice for five years, three silvers for seven years. The apprentice labored for no pay during that term and learned a trade.

"Ten years, mistress." Ten-year apprenticeships cost nothing. Our family was too poor to buy me a place.

The cog dipped lower than ever. I sucked hard on the mint.

"My dear." She touched my arm. "I'm sorry."

"No need for sorrow. I'll know my craft well by the time I'm twenty-two . . . I mean, twenty-four."

"Not that. In June the guilds abolished ten-year apprenticeships. Now everyone must pay to learn a trade."

I turned to her. Her face was serious. It was true.

The boat pitched, but my stomach steadied while a rock formed there.

CHAPTER TWO

"What will you do?" the goodwife asked.

"I will think of something." I sounded dignified. Dignity had always eluded me before. I excused myself from the goodwife's company and found a spot on the deck closer to the cows than to the human passengers. My curiosity about them had faded. I removed my cloak from my satchel, spread it out, and sat.

If our farm weren't so out of the way, we'd have learned the apprenticeship rules had changed and I would still be home. I'd probably have stayed on Lahnt forever.

Word might reach Mother and Father in a few months or a few years. When they found out, they would be wild with worry.

I hadn't enough money for passage back, nor did I want

to return. I would send word as soon as I was settled. No matter what, I would still be a mansioner.

Perhaps a mansioner master or mistress would take me as a fifteen-year apprentice. No one but me would give free labor for fifteen years. Who could say no?

My mood improved. Curiosity returned, and I watched the people on deck. The rowers rested their oars when the cog master's attention was elsewhere. The oddly clothed mother and daughter were squabbling. The goodwife had recovered from her nausea and joined her husband. I liked best to watch the two of them. Sometimes she leaned into his shoulder, and he encircled her with his arm. Her expression showed peace, eagerness, and patience combined. If I were ever to play a wife, I would remember this goodwife's face.

Night came. I curled up, hugged my satchel close, and wished desperately for home. But why wish? I mansioned myself there, under my woolen blanket in my pallet bed on a floor that didn't roll, with Albin only a few feet away and Mother and Father in their sleeping loft over my head. Yes, that was their bed groaning, not the mast.

Soon I was asleep. In the morning I felt myself a seasoned mariner.

At intervals the animal owner walked his beasts around the deck. "Come with Dess," he'd say in his sweet voice. "In Two Castles Dess will buy you fine hay, feed you fine grass. How happy you will be."

I decided that he and the goodwife were the most worthy passengers on the cog.

Master Dess's heavy basket turned out to contain kittens. He'd reach in for one at a time, stroke it from head to tail, and speak softly to it. Early in the afternoon of the second day, when even the gentle breeze died away, the cog master let Master Dess release them all.

The seven kittens, each striped black and white, burst out to chase one another between legs, around the mast, up and down the deck. A kitten played with the end of a coil of rope, batting it to and fro. The tiniest one climbed the rigging to the top of the mast and perched there for half an hour, lord of the sea. My heart rose into my throat to see it, so tiny and so high.

On its way down, it lost its balance and hung upside down. Frantically I looked around for something to help it with—a pole, anything. No one else was watching, except Master Dess and the goodwife, whose hands were pressed to her chest.

An oar might reach the kitten. I rushed toward the rowers just as the kitten scrambled upright and minced down the mast with a satisfied air. I returned to my cloak. Soon after, Master Dess collected that kitten and its mates.

When they were all in their basket, the goodwife came to me, bearing a small package wrapped in rough hemp. I jumped up.

"May I sit with you?"

I made room for her and she sat, tucking her legs under her. She placed the package in her lap.

What a pleasure to have her company!

"May I know your name, dear?"

I could think of no harm in telling her. "Lodie. I mean, Elodie."

"And I am Goodwife Celeste. My goodman is Twah."

"Pleased to meet you." I rummaged in my satchel. One must show hospitality to a visitor, even a visitor to a cloak on the deck of a cog.

She was saying, "You and I both feared for that brave kitten." She paused, then added, "Have you heard of the cats of Two Castles?"

I shook my head, while drawing bread and cheese and a pear out of my satchel. With the little knife from my purse, I cut her chunks of the bread and cheese and half the pear.

"Thank you." She tasted. "Excellent goat cheese." She unwrapped her own package.

"Cats in Two Castles?" I said to remind her.

"The townspeople believe cats protect them from the ogre. There are many."

"Many cats or ogres?" How could a cat save anyone from an ogre?

She laughed. "Cats." Her package held bread and cheese, too, and a handful of radishes.

We traded slices and chunks, observing custom, according to the saying, *Share well, fare well. Share ill, fare ill.*

Goodwife Celeste's cheese wasn't as tasty as mine, but the bread was softer, baker's bread. I wondered where my future meals would come from, once my food and my single copper ran out.

Goodwife Celeste returned to telling me about cats. "You know that ogres shift shape sometimes?"

"Yes."

"Cats know they do, too. The cats sense that an ogre can become a fox or a wolf, but they're not afraid."

Our cat at home, Belliss, who weighed less than a pail of milk, feared nothing.

"They're aware that an ogre can also turn into a mouse." She finished eating. "More?" She held out her food.

"No, thank you." I offered her more of mine, too, and she said no.

As I wrapped my food and she wrapped hers, her sleeve slid back. A bracelet of twine circled her left wrist. Were twine bracelets the fashion in Two Castles? She probably wouldn't have minded if I'd asked, but I didn't want to reveal my ignorance.

"Can an ogre shift into any kind of animal?" I said. "A spider or an elephant?"

"I believe so."

"Can an ogre shift into a human?"

Her eyebrows went up. "I doubt it." She returned to the subject of cats. "A cat will stare at an ogre and wish him—*will* him—to become a mouse. They say one cat isn't enough, but several yearning at him, and the ogre can't resist."

I pitied the ogre. "Is that true?"

"Many believe it. What's more, people train their cats. They don't train them to try to make an ogre become a mouse. It is in the cats' nature to do that, and the ogre must cooperate by giving in. But folks train cats to perform tricks and to stalk anything, including an ogre. Some make a living at cat teaching. With the flick of a wrist . . ."

She showed me, and I imitated her—nothing to it.

"With this gesture, anyone can set a cat to stalking."

"If there were no cats, what would the ogre do?"

"Nothing, perhaps. Or dine on townsfolk."

My stomach fluttered. "Does he live alone, or are there more ogres in his castle?"

"Alone with his servants. Count Jonty Um is the only ogre in Lepai. Likely there are others in other lands."

"He's a count?" You couldn't be a count unless a king made you one or made one of your ancestors one.

"A count."

"What happened to the rest of the ogres in Lepai?"

She turned her hand palm up. "I don't know. They may have become mice and been eaten. And ogres sicken and die, just as people do."

How lonely I would be if I were the only human. "Mistress? What about dragons? Are there many? Are any of them noble?"

"Just one in Two Castles, and IT is a commoner. Dragons don't generally dwell near one another." She straightened her left leg. "My old bones don't like anything hard."

I wished I had a cushion for her. She was so nice. I thought of Mother's warning, but Goodwife Celeste couldn't be a whited sepulcher. We had been together all this while, and she had done nothing to raise my suspicions.

"Beyond Two Castles," she continued, "Lepai has a few dozen dragons, here and there."

"Do people protect themselves from the dragon, too? Not with cats, with something else?"

"No. Everyone is used to IT. IT's lived in the town since IT was hatched a hundred years ago."

"So old?"

"IT is in ITs prime."

We fell silent. I leaned back on my arms and looked up at the blue sky. Summer weather in October. No clouds, only a breath of a breeze. How safe I felt, like a twig floating in a quiet pond.

Goodwife Celeste picked shreds of cheese and bread crumbs off her lap in a housewifely way. She walked to the bulwarks, tossed them over, and returned to me. Back at my cloak, she knelt. "Crossing is a holiday. For a few days

17

we're as safe as the kittens in their basket." She gestured at the cog around us.

I had been thinking exactly the same thought!

"I'm sorry I won't be able to help you in Two Castles."

That startled me. I hadn't thought of asking for aid.

Was she telling me in a roundabout fashion of her own troubles? Were she and her goodman too poor to feed themselves, or were they in some other sort of difficulty?

She put a gentle hand under my chin. "You have a determined face. Nothing will easily best you." She stood. "My goodman may well be wondering what we had to gossip about for so long." She left me.

That night, when I curled up on the deck, worries came and refused to be pretended away. The mansioners would not take me. I would starve. In the winter I would freeze, fall ill, die. Mother and Father would never know what had become of me.

CHAPTER THREE

he weather remained uncommonly warm. The cog master complained about the still air and our slow progress. I feared we would arrive after Guild Week, and then what would I do?

We'd set out on a Sunday, the only day the cog left Lahnt. Masters in Two Castles began seeing boys and girls on Monday, and by Friday all the places would be taken.

At noon on Tuesday I lunched on the last pear, the end of my provisions. By nightfall the wind freshened, although the air remained warm. When I awoke the next day, I sensed a change in the motion of the cog. The troughs weren't as deep, the crests not so high. I rushed to the foredeck.

An uneven triangle broke the horizon. Our cog now

sailed amid fishing boats, a whale among minnows.

I folded my cloak and pushed it into my satchel with my spare hose, chemise, and kirtle—my entire wardrobe, except for the clothes I wore and the shoes on my feet. My hand encountered the only other item, a list in Mother's small, neat writing on a sheet of parchment. I took it out.

HALF DOZEN RULES FOR LODIE

1. *Be truthful.*
2. *Act with forethought, not impetuously. Your mother and father depend on your safety.*
3. *Neither stare nor eavesdrop.*
4. *Do not interrupt or contradict your elders or finish their sentences or think you know more than they do.*
5. *Do not befriend anyone until you are certain he or she is worthy of your trust. Beware the whited sepulcher.*
6. *Know always that you have our love.*
7. *Be generous (an extra, generous rule).*

I patted the page seven times before returning it to my satchel.

Half the morning passed as we drew closer to land. From behind, the other passengers pressed against me, as impatient as I. I touched my apron and felt the familiar bulge of my purse. The stink of fish assailed my nose.

I took in the tiers of houses ahead, a few built of stone,

most of wattle and daub—clay and wood. Above town, on the right, a cluster of towers poked the sky. To the left, barely cresting the hilltop, were the tips of more towers, the other castle. Which was king's and which ogre's, I had no idea.

What I sought most I didn't see—the mansioners' wagons or at least the three pennants: the pennant that showed a laughing face; the one with a weeping face; and the one with a hushing face, a finger over the lips. No mansions, but the entire town could not be on view from here.

The cog master shouted instructions to his seamen. Passengers called to people waving from the dock. Someone touched my elbow. I turned.

The goodwife held a bundle of black-and-white fur. "Here. I bought you a kitten. It's good luck to bring a cat to Two Castles."

"Thank you, but—"

"You can leave it on the wharf. No cat starves here."

The kitten was asleep and didn't waken when Goodwife Celeste handed it over. It filled my two hands but weighed almost nothing, its ears huge, its pink nose tiny. I knew from the white left ear that this was the kitten who had climbed the rigging.

"Thank you, mistress."

"You're welcome. I hope to see you in the mansions someday soon."

"Do you know where they are?"

She pointed upward. "Beyond the town. See, there is King Grenville's castle." Her finger moved rightward to the jutting towers. "The mansioners are east of his castle and"—her finger shifted to the left—"east of his menagerie." Left again. "They are northeast of Count Jonty Um's castle, which is farther south but less than a mile from town."

"I see. Thank you."

She smiled and threaded her way back to rejoin her husband.

Farewell, my only friend, my kind friend who cannot help me any longer.

My stomach growled despite the fish stench. The cog bumped against the pier, causing the kitten to waken and squirm in my hands.

"Be still," I whispered. "I'll set you free soon enough."

As if it understood, it quieted and peered out at the world of solid land.

A seaman lowered the gangplank. I hung back and let the other passengers descend first. The girl in the odd apparel and her family were embraced by another family. Travelers were passed from hug to hug. Seamen rushed by me, joking to one another.

If anyone awaited me, this would be less an adventure. I remembered Albin's wisdom: A mansioner is always alone. If a hundred people had come to meet me, I would still be separate.

The goodwife and her goodman set off together into an alley. I wondered why no one had been here to greet them.

The kitten sniffed my wrists. I followed the last passenger and stepped onto the pier. How unaccustomed my legs were to a floor that didn't move. I wondered if seamen ever fell land-sick after weeks at sea.

I set the kitten down between an empty bucket and a mound of fishnet. "Be well. Live a happy cat life." I touched its nose. "Bring me luck."

It mewed briefly, then fell silent. I walked the length of the pier to the wharf. Where the two met, I stopped.

To my left a woman hawked muffins out of a handcart. My mouth watered, but I didn't go to her. I was sure to find better if I waited.

In a doorway a man and a woman sat on stools mending nets. Nearby a fishing boat lay upended, its owner busy applying oakum and pitch.

Stalls lined the wharf and people ambled along, stopping to examine the wares or to buy.

The women were clad as the mother and daughter in the cog had been, in narrow kirtles with long sleeves and long hems and with colored aprons tied round their waists. As at home, the tunics of the men ended just below their knees, revealing a few inches of their breeches. Everyone—men, women, and children—wore hoods or caps that tied under their chins.

I tugged on my sleeves to make them seem longer. I am a mansioner in costume, I told myself, not outlandish, not a bumpkin.

Two dogs chased each other to the edge of the water and back again. On the pier, a plump black cat with a white tail ambled to my kitten and began to lick it all over. Other black-and-white cats sunned themselves here and there on the wharf. If this had been a town for yellow cats, my kitten might have been snubbed.

I heard applause.

Mansioners? Here?

Three young women and four in middle age stood in a loose row on the wharf, backs to me, blocking the reason for their clapping. When I reached them, I saw two black-and-white cats at the feet of a young man perhaps seven or eight years older than I.

Yellow hair flowed from his cap down his sturdy neck. His skin seemed to glow. Large gray eyes, fringed by thick lashes, and curving lips might have made his face feminine but for the strength of his jawline and chin. Powerful arms pulled tight the sleeves of his frayed tunic. His hands and bare feet were long and graceful. The bare feet, the hollows in his cheeks, and his worn tunic bespoke desperate poverty.

Twisted around the fourth finger of his right hand was a ring of twine, knotted in front where the jewel of a silver ring would be. Goodwife Celeste wore a twine bracelet. Was this fashion, or did twine-jewelry wearers belong to some confederacy?

The young man's hands described a circle in the air, and the two cats rolled over. The women clapped as enthusiastically as if he'd stopped the sun. I clapped softly.

"Ooh, Master Thiel. Again, if you please."

His name was Thiel, pronounced *Tee-el.*

He bowed, rewarded each cat with a tidbit, then obliged. The cats obliged, too. We clapped again. I touched the purse at my waist—still in place.

Here was a cat teacher, as Goodwife Celeste had said there would be, although he seemed not to be earning much at it. A wooden bowl on the ground held but four tins.

"Mistresses, here is the cats' newest trick." He raised his hands high above his head. The right-hand cat leaped straight up, like a puppet on a string. The left-hand cat licked its paw.

"Tut, tut." Master Thiel crouched. He rewarded the cat who'd leaped and snapped a finger against the other cat's scalp, chiding it in cat parlance, I supposed. The cat shook its head and became attentive again. This time when the young man raised his hands, both cats jumped.

More tricks followed. The cats waved, shook his hands, and even leaped over sticks held a few inches above the ground.

My stomach rumbled. I wrenched my eyes away. Across

from where I stood, a broad way marched straight uphill. Chiseled into the stone of the corner house was the street name, Daycart Way. This seemed the likeliest route to food and mansioners.

I set out, my satchel slung across my chest. People strolled on my right and left. A boy herded three piglets. Children and cats and dogs chased one another. The dogs came in every size and color, but the cats were always black and white. I watched my feet to avoid the leavings of the animal traffic—not merely dogs, cats, and piglets, but also donkeys and the occasional horse, bearing a burgher or a person of noble rank.

At the first corner, I came upon two more cat teachers, these hardly older than I. They practiced just the rolling-over trick. I wondered if Two Castles boasted a guild of cat teachers. These two might be apprentices and the young man on the wharf a journeyman.

I angled close to the merchants' stalls at the edge of the avenue. If I had been rich, my fortune would soon have been spent. The first table I passed was spread with belt buckles, most iron, but a few brass and one silver, the silver one hammered in the shape of a rose. How Father would cherish such a buckle.

In the next stall a knife-and-scissors sharpener sat at his wheel, waiting for custom. "Sharp scissors and knives!" he cried.

Beyond him a shoemaker shaped leather on a last. Shoes stood in double file up and down the table at his elbow. Mother might express wonder that the natives of Two Castles had such pointy feet.

How I wished they could be here, saying whatever they really would say, wanting whatever they really would want.

In the shoemaker's shop, which opened behind the shoemaker's chair, his goodwife sat on a bench while a boy and a girl near my age stood and addressed her. From the attitudes of the two—leaning forward from their waists— they were vying for an apprenticeship. I supposed both had the necessary silvers.

I heard a voice I knew coming from behind. "Step lively, my honeys, my cows, my donkey. Come with Dess."

Next I passed a table heaped with leather purses and touched the lump in my apron where my linen purse hung. A leather purse never needed darning or leaked its contents. I had double backstitched mine before leaving home.

My feet refused to pass by the next stall, a clothes mender's. On her table were neatly sorted piles of chemises, kirtles, aprons, tunics, breeches, hose, garters, capes, hoods, and caps, all in linen or wool. Of course everything had belonged to someone else, and likely death or poverty had brought the goods here to be repaired and made ready to wear again.

Rich folks' new garments were soft. Poor folks' garments became soft after long use. At the beginning they were stiff enough to stand unaided. My grandmother first wore my chemise, which now slid against my skin as gently as rose petals.

From behind the table, the mending mistress disputed with a goodwife over the price of a cloak. The mending mistress's right shoulder sloped upward. The goodwife had a hairy mole above her upper lip. A cat prowled in and out and around the legs of the table.

An orange kirtle caught my eye, pretty, adorned by three wooden buttons at the neck. I held it up. Narrow with long sleeves. Fashionable. I folded it again. My copper wouldn't be nearly enough.

Closest to me on the table were the caps. I moved two aside to reach a madder-red one, faded to the same color as my kirtle. A copper might buy a cap. If they were here, Mother and Father and even Albin would tell me to keep my coin, which would doubtless buy me food for several days. But I wanted a cap. Wearing a cap, my head at least would belong in Two Castles.

A cap might help persuade a mansioner master to take me, while a bareheaded girl would be turned away.

The mending mistress and the goodwife agreed on a price. When the goodwife paid, her sleeves slid back and I saw no twine jewelry.

The mending mistress scratched her chin as the cat brushed against my leg, back and forth.

"I have a copper." I held up the cap.

Her hand dropped from her chin, and her lips turned from down to up. "Ah. Are you an apprenticeship girl?" She emphasized her consonants and drawled her vowels long enough for me to think the next letter impatient. Two Castles talk, I supposed, and wondered if I could imitate it.

I nodded.

"Have you settled your place yet?"

I shook my head.

"Which one are you trying for?"

"I'm going to be a mansioner." I spoke my consonants decisively and stretched my vowels.

She looked puzzled.

I must not have done it right. I repeated myself more slowly, even harder on the consonants, even longer on the vowels.

"No matter," she said. "A cap will keep you cool in summer, warm in winter. Not that one." She took the madder cap from my hands. "It won't show off your pretty face."

I wished I could subtract her lie from the price of the cap. I wasn't pretty. My eyes were too big, my eyebrows too thick, my mouth too wide, my jaw too pronounced. *But* if you were in an audience, even standing behind the

29

benches, far from the mansion stage, you would still be able to make out my features. At that distance, the distance that mattered, I was pretty.

I tried the accent again. "Mother tells me my eyes are the color of moss."

Perhaps that was better—or not. She said nothing, but picked through the caps, discarding half a dozen until she found the one she wanted, a woad-blue cap, hardly faded, the color of a bright blue sky, with cunning scallops along the edge. "Here. Let me tie it on you." She did so. "Hmm." She pulled two forehead curls from under the cap. "Ah. You are fetching."

No, I wasn't. The cat mewed, probably agreeing with me.

I abandoned the accent. "Will there be enough left over to buy my luncheon?"

"I will give you back five tins, young mistress."

In Lahnt five tins would buy two meals at least.

The second rule on Mother's list warned me not to be impetuous.

Mother, I'm not. I need a cap! "My coin is hidden." I half turned from the mending mistress and hunched over, so she wouldn't see, as if my purse held jewels.

When I straightened, I held out the copper. The cat leaped up. Its paw batted the coin from my hand.

CHAPTER FOUR

dived after the coin, but the cat took it in its teeth and scampered into the crowd. I shoved people aside and gave chase. A streaking cat with a coin in its mouth should be easy to spot.

But there was no streaking cat.

I stood still in the middle of the street and looked about. A cat sunned itself on a windowsill, its mouth empty. A cat crossed an awning pole, its mouth empty. A cat washed itself in a doorway. I wished I'd noted the robber cat's markings when I'd had the chance.

I returned to the mending mistress.

"Did you get it?"

"No, mistress." I took a deep breath for courage. I had never spoken to an adult as I was about to. "Your cat owes me a copper." Another breath. "Or you do."

"The cat wasn't mine." She entered the shop behind her.

Parley ended?

But she returned with a fat cat in her arms, all black except for a white patch on its back. "I'm sorry, young mistress."

She could have ten cats. But I could prove nothing against her. Still, I wanted someone to blame. "What kind of cats live in Two Castles?"

"Here we have thieves of every sort. You should have been more careful."

More careful? My ears grew hot. It was my fault? More careful than bent over, hiding my purse? No one had warned me of animal robbers.

"I can't give you a cap."

My ears were going to catch fire. I untied the cap, dropped it back on the table, and walked to the next stall, a tallow candlemaker's. Now I had no money for food.

"Honey! Girl! Wait for Dess."

I turned.

Master Dess and his beasts had progressed as far as the shoemaker's stall. He waved to me. "Too bad. I saw the cat. Terrible bad." He toiled upward, his cows at his side, his donkey lagging. "Come, honey."

"You saw?" I said as he reached me. We hadn't exchanged a word on the cog, but in this town of strangers he felt like family.

"What a shame." Letting go of his animals, who didn't budge, and putting down his kitten basket, he opened his cloth purse. "The goodwife gave me three tins for your kitten. Here they are, maybe not the same three tins." He took my hand and put the coins in it. "I have your kitten again. It's an even exchange."

"Thank you!" The exchange wasn't even. I hadn't returned the kitten or paid the tins. "You're very kind."

He hefted his basket and opened it. Only three kittens remained, one with a white ear. It extended a paw at me. "She knows you."

I touched the pink nose.

"You should have her. Everyone has a cat. I'll give her to you."

"I have no way to feed her."

"Too bad! Cats must eat." He closed the basket and resumed his upward trek.

People must eat, too. If I were one of Master Dess's animals, I would have no worries.

I started back downhill, hoping to question the cat teachers. But when I reached the corner, the two of them were gone. I wondered if they might have sent a cat to rob me and left when they had my coin. On the wharf, the young man had also departed.

Had they all been in league? Perhaps they'd noticed my capless self and singled me out as easy prey.

But my thieving cat had been under the table when I arrived.

I looked out at the strait, where cloud reflections moved across the water. White fishing boat sails bit into the bottom of the sky.

No more dallying. First food, whatever three tins would buy, then the mansioners. I headed uphill again. A grand lady outstripped me on a palfrey. I saw her and her mount only from behind: the lady's straight back, her bright green kirtle, the dark hair spilling from her cap down her shoulders, the horse's dappled rump, and its tail braided with scarlet ribbons.

How lovely it would be to ride, especially to ride to a castle or a burgher's house, where a big meal was laid out for me.

I wished this were a food vendors' street. Nothing sold along Daycart Way was edible.

Behind me, coming from farther down the hill, a bass drum of a voice boomed, "Make way! Make way!"

The crowd fell silent. Was King Grenville passing by?

The throng closed around me and pushed me until my back pressed against a vendor's table. A woman and I were separated by her five young children, who leaned into her skirt and mine. Because the children were shorter than I, my view wasn't completely blocked by the adults surrounding them.

"Make way."

My neighbor, the mother, whispered, "Turn into a mouse."

The ogre! My breath stuck in my throat. If he plucked me for his cauldron, what could I do?

"Very thin here," I squeaked. "Not worth the trouble."

The voice roared, "I want no broken bones or flattened heads."

Flattened heads! Had that happened?

"Ogre coming. Dog coming."

I heard the full, echoing bark of a big dog.

Count Jonty Um's voice gentled to a rumble. "Hush, Nesspa."

He smelled like a clean ogre, perfumed with cinnamon and cloves, pounds of them. As he climbed farther up the hill, I began to see him. First came a thatch of black hair, cut so haphazardly that his barber was blind or couldn't keep his hands from shaking. Like me, the ogre wore no cap. Next came an ear as big as a slice of bread. He turned his head my way.

He was a young man ogre! Shrunk down, he could have been anyone. But as himself, he was eleven feet tall or more, puffed up as a pudding. His face might have been pleasant if it hadn't been so red with anger or blushing. He had round cheeks, level eyebrows, a square chin, brown eyes, and freckles across the bridge of his nose.

"Freckles," I murmured. I wanted to yell to Mother and Father across the strait. Freckles on an ogre!

Sweat lines streaked his forehead and cheeks. "Make way!"

An angry voice rang out. "We're crushed, Count Jonty Um." The voice paused. "Begging your pardon."

The crowd squeezed closer. Behind us, the table fell over. The ogre drew almost even with me so I could see down to his chest. Of course his dog remained out of sight.

His tunic, dyed a wealthy deep scarlet, was silk. A silver pendant on a gold chain hung around his neck. The pendant and chain together probably weighed ten pounds and would be worth a hundred apprenticeships.

He passed on. People spaced themselves apart again. Someone complained that Count Jonty Um strolled only at the busiest time of day.

Behind me a familiar voice spit out, "Monster!"

The mending mistress's table lay on its side. Piles of clothing had slid to the ground. I righted the table and began to pick up garments.

She took a tunic and attempted to brush it clean while making a sound of disgust in her throat.

I tried the accent again. "What a pity!" I folded hose for her.

"Don't think you can pretend to help and make off with a cap."

I raised my empty hands. My voice rose, and my attempt at an accent vanished. "As if I would! Lambs and calves! The ogre has more manners than you!" I moved away.

Her indignant voice followed me. "You compare me to an ogre? How is that for manners?"

I felt my face turn as red as Count Jonty Um's had been. People gave me a wide berth.

One could speak however one liked to an unknown young person with no coppers in her purse. In a mansioner's play, the impoverished unknown woman was often a goddess in disguise. If this were a play, the goddess (me) would transform the mending mistress into stone or into a deer. I grew more cheerful.

The ogre could actually shape-shift into a deer. How curious that he went about the town in his own form. If he turned himself into a cat, everyone would love him.

Might he have done so earlier? Could he have been the one to take my coin? Might his wealth be cat plunder?

Noon bells rang from the direction of the king's castle, joined in a moment by more distant ringing. Then other bells tolled closer by, sounding from somewhere in town, likely the Justice Hall. Last came the harbor bells, chiming out across the strait.

I stopped my climb to listen—bass bells, tenor bells, bright soprano bells, all in harmony—pealing and pealing, calling to anyone with ears, but saying to only me, *Two Castles, king's town, big town, thief town, stay, Lahnt girl, stay.*

Or maybe they said, *Starve, Lahnt girl, starve.*

The bells faded. I continued on my way.

CHAPTER FIVE

A market square opened before me, more crammed with stalls and people than the street had been. The odors of sweat and spoiled eggs hung over all, but they were redeemed by the aroma of baking bread, roast meat, and the faint but heady fragrance of marchpane—sugared almond candy.

What would three tins buy?

Nothing, it seemed. A muffin cost four tins, and I couldn't wheedle down the price. My nose drew me to a man frying meat patties over a brazier. Though he had no customers, he still wouldn't sell me a quarter patty.

The marchpane perfume grew stronger. An old woman walked by, carrying a tray of the candies.

I hurried after her and tried again to speak with the

heavy consonants and dragged vowels of a Two Castler. "May I see, Grandmother?"

"What's that?"

I repeated myself without the accent.

"Looking's free." She held the tray out.

Each candy was cunningly fashioned as a fruit or a flower, the tulip looking just like a fresh bloom, the pear green but for a hint of pink. The tiniest candy, a strawberry one, would probably cost more than a copper.

I had tasted marchpane once. I'd found a marchpane peach on the ground at the Lahnt market. It was grimy and partially flattened where a shoe had trod. Father saw me pick it up. He took it, brushed off the dirt, kept the flattened part for himself, and gave the rest to me.

"Don't tell your mother," he'd said, and I wasn't sure if he thought she'd disapprove or if he didn't want to share three ways.

The marchpane mistress moved away. I followed as if on a string. Perhaps I would have died of starvation in the marchpane mistress's shadow if I hadn't tripped over a cat, who *mrrow*ed in protest. Jolted out of my reverie, I looked about and saw, just a few yards away, an enormous reptile's huge belly and front leg.

A dragon!

I skittered backward. People filled in between IT and me. Conversations continued. The smell of rotten eggs all but overpowered me.

If others weren't afraid, neither was I, despite the tingle at the nape of my neck and my breath huffing in and out. I sidled closer.

A little clearing surrounded the dragon. I hovered on the border, as close as I dared, midway between head and tail. ITs long, flat head faced forward, so I felt free to inspect. IT stood on stumpy legs. The tip of ITs tail, which was as long as the rest of it, curled under a dye maker's table.

Poor creature, to be so hard to gaze upon. Imagine being covered in brown-and-orange scales except for a wrinkled brown belly that hung almost to the ground. ITs spine crested at half the height of a cottage, and ITs claws ended in long, gray talons. The wing facing me was folded, but judging from the rest, that was probably hideous, too.

ITs head thrust aggressively forward, hardly higher than my own. The head thrust seemed masculine. Was IT a *he*?

Wisps of white smoke rose from ITs half-closed mouth and ITs nostril holes. A pointed yellow tooth hung over ITs orange lip. ITs long head rounded at the snout. The skin about ITs eyes puffed out.

The cat between me and IT licked a paw.

At my elbow a goodwife said, "My achy knee augurs rain."

Her goodman laughed. "Your achy knee sees clouds."

IT turned ITs head and stared at me. ITs eye, flat as a coin, glowed emerald green. I felt IT take stock of me, from my overwide, too-short kirtle and round-toed shoes to my bare head and my smile, which I maintained with *good dragon, nice dragon* thoughts. IT faced away again. I resumed breathing.

A line of men and women stretched away from IT, waiting their turn for something. Two baskets rested by ITs right front leg, one basket half full of coins, the other holding wooden skewers threaded with chunks of bread and cheese.

Third in the line was Master Thiel, the handsome cat teacher from the wharf. Draped around his neck, a cat lolled, as relaxed as a rag. Might this cat have robbed me, taught by his cat teacher?

The cat had a black spot above his left eye. Three big spots dotted his back. His legs were black to the knees, as if he wore boots. The rest of him was snowy white. Copper-colored eyes, the hue of my stolen coin, examined me examining him.

Barely opening ITs mouth, the dragon spoke in a nasal and hoarse voice. "Step up, Corm."

A stoop-shouldered man at the head of the line dropped coins into the coin basket and took a skewer, which he held out boldly. "I've waited long enough, Meenore."

IT had a name, Meenore, a nasal name. Sir Meenore? Lady? Sirlady? Master? Mistress? Masteress?

"Everyone savors my skewers." IT opened ITs mouth into a singer's round O and blew a band of flame, which engulfed the food.

The man danced backward. "Toasted, not cindered, if you please."

Enh enh enh.

Dragon laughter! The corner of ITs mouth curled up in a grin that reminded me of our dog Hoont at home, when I pulled her lips back toward her ears.

The flame shortened and lightened from red to orange. The fat in the cheese spit and crackled. How rich it smelled!

After a minute Meenore swallowed ITs flame, revealing the bread and cheese, toasted golden brown, beautiful.

Master Corm blew to cool his meal. I licked my lips. He put the skewer to his mouth and pulled off the first morsel with his teeth. Oh! Even untasted it tasted good.

Next, a boy tugged his mother toward the basket. The mother took two skewers.

"Can I, Mother?"

She gave him the coins, and he dropped them one by one into the coin basket. Ten *clink*s. Five tins for a skewer. Too bad for me.

Although he begged, the mother wouldn't let her son

toast his own skewer. When the food was cooked, the two moved off.

A fine drizzle began to fall. The cat teacher stepped up.

I wanted to ask him if cats were ever taught to steal, but my tongue turned to wood, a doubly timid tongue: afraid to draw ITs attention again and bashful about addressing this perfect young man.

Clink clink clink clink. Only four tins! Maybe I could get by with three.

Meenore swallowed ITs flame. "The price is *five* tins, Thiel. Pay up or leave the coins as tribute." *Enh enh enh*.

The cat purred.

Master Thiel bowed with a dancer's grace. "Apologies. My fingers miscounted." His voice was as gentle as a gemshorn, the shepherd's horn that calms stampeding sheep.

Four coins, five, an easy mistake. His purse jingled as he pulled out another tin. Lambs and calves! Bare feet, hollow cheeks or no, he was far richer than I.

"Make way!" Count Jonty Um emerged from a side street into the square.

Silence fell. The crowd parted. I backed away. The waiting line spread out. Only Meenore remained motionless. The cat on Master Thiel's shoulders stood up, back arched.

The count's dog, a Lepai long-haired mountain hound, pranced along, taking no notice of the cat but frequently looking up at his master. Though big as a wolf, his head came only to Count Jonty Um's knees. He was a beauty, with a coat of golden silk and a regally large head matched by a big black nose.

The count approached IT. "Three skewers, if you please."

What about everyone on line? That was no true *If you please*. Clearly an ogre did what he liked, no matter the inconvenience to small folk.

"It isn't fair!" burst out of me.

The silence seemed to crystallize.

Enh enh enh, IT laughed, possibly in anticipation of seeing me squeezed to death in one enormous hand.

Count Jonty Um turned and lowered his gaze until he found me. "I am unfair?"

I attempted a Two Castles accent again. Perhaps he wouldn't hurt me if he thought I had parents here. "*It* isn't fair." Not you.

"Meenore unfair?" he roared.

I was still alive. "Not IT." I gestured at Meenore. The accent came and went. "It."

Enh enh enh.

The ogre looked puzzled.

"Er . . . ," I said. "Others were ahead of you."

"Oh. I apologize. Thank you for telling me." How stiff he was. There was no feeling of gratitude in his voice, but he stepped back, three giant steps. "Proceed."

In continued silence, the people in line eased back into

their places, the man who had been at the end treading on the heels of the fellow in front of him to avoid closeness to the ogre. I realized that everyone would have preferred Count Jonty Um to go first and leave.

People resumed their strolling and buying, while giving the ogre a wide berth. At the head of the line, Master Thiel took his skewer from the basket.

Meenore said, "Young Master Thiel, I commiserate with you on the death of the miller."

Count Jonty Um boomed in, "I am sorry for your loss."

A polite ogre.

"Thank you." Master Thiel nodded at the dragon but not at the ogre. "My father will be missed. He had many . . ."

His father, dead? How he must be grieving. I thought of Father, and my eyes smarted.

"Missed by you most of all." *Enh enh enh.*

How could IT laugh? What a churlish dragon!

Master Thiel answered with dignity. "Masteress, my good father had confidence in my abilities."

Ah. A masteress.

Master Thiel continued. "My father believed—"

His cat jumped from his shoulder and strolled off. "Pardine!"

The cat didn't return. I knew I should leave, too. The sooner I found the mansioners, the sooner I might eat. But ·

so much drama was passing here and the food smelled so tasty that I remained rooted in place.

Master Thiel held his skewer out. In a moment it was done. He stepped aside to eat. Masteress Meenore swallowed ITs fire and turned my way, which brought that smoking snout uncomfortably close.

I stood my ground.

"I commiserate with your loss, too, girl from the island of Lahnt."

CHAPTER SIX

"y loss?" Had Mother and Father died, and IT could divine their deaths?

"You are a thief's victim."

I felt weak with relief. But how could IT tell I'd been robbed? "How can—"

"Simple." IT raised ITs voice. "Gather and hear. Masteress Meenore, finder of lost objects and people, unraveler of mysteries, will now exhibit, gratis, ITs skill at deduction, induction, and common sense, which in other circumstances would cost ITs customary fee."

Luckily no one stopped to listen. The ones on line had to hear, which was bad enough.

Count Jonty Um blared, "A demonstration. I will enjoy this."

"Your Lordship," IT said, "my demonstrations are always enjoyable if one is not their object."

The object today would be me!

IT continued. "You may ask the guests at your coming feast to recount my many other displays of intellect, which will entertain everyone." IT swiveled ITs head toward me. "What is your name, girl of Lahnt?"

I didn't have to tell! I hugged my satchel as if it could protect me. "Unravel the mystery of my name, if you can, Masteress Meenore." My legs tensed to run from ITs flame.

Enh enh enh. "The girl from Lahnt is clever, hasty, brave, and lacking in respect for her elders."

IT described me exactly as Mother would! Might IT be a mother, a *she*?

"Great faults and perhaps greater virtues," IT said.

Mother would not have agreed about *greater virtues*.

"Your name is of no consequence. You started your journey with something in your purse that you considered valuable. Whatever it was, was taken. In your distress you forgot to tuck your purse away afterward, evidence of the theft."

I pushed the purse under my apron.

Master Thiel, who'd finished eating, spoke. "Perhaps no one steals on Lahnt, so she didn't anticipate her danger." He smiled at me, showing pearly white teeth.

"Few do steal at home, Master Thiel." I smiled back,

a fourteen-year-old's smile, I hoped, perhaps even a fifteen-year-old's.

"If no one steals *there*," IT said, "more reason for caution *here*. Despite the theft, her purse still contains coins, four or fewer tins."

Could IT see through cloth? I asked, "How do you conclude that, Masteress?"

"Next in line," IT said.

How rude, to ignore me! How interesting!

Leaning heavily on a cane, a tall man hobbled forward. His payment tinkled into the basket. "I like my cheese well done, Meenore."

Instead of flaming, IT said, "By hiding your purse now, girl, you revealed that you still have something in it, which I had already surmised."

"I am waiting," the lame man said.

"You are safe in your guess, Masteress Meenore," Master Thiel said, laughing charmingly. "She will hardly show us what her purse holds."

Indeed, I wouldn't. I was glad to have Master Thiel on my side.

The lame man held out his skewer.

"My customer waits. I will explain my conclusions in a moment." Masteress Meenore toasted the food, to my eyes less thoroughly than IT had the other skewers. IT was eager to prove ITs brilliance. "She needn't open her purse for me to know the contents. If she—"

"More flame, Meenore."

IT toasted the skewer again and then continued. "If she never had more coins, the few she has now would be precious to her, and the purse would have been hidden from the start."

The lame man spoke while chewing. "How do you know she has fewer than five coins?"

"Surely Master Thiel must have come to the same conclusion as I," Masteress Meenore said.

Master Thiel shook his head, smiling.

But I knew, and I wished I'd departed the moment I saw IT. Rather than be shamed, I would shame myself. "Masteress Meenore observed me counting the tins as they dropped into ITs basket. If I had five coins or more, I would have joined the line. If I had no coins, I would not have bothered to count."

"Ah," IT said. "The girl without a name has inductive and deductive talents herself. She is poor and starving, from the way her eyes have dwelled on my excellent skewers. I have now explained in full."

I hurried away before I could see Master Thiel's pity. As I went, I made myself chuckle instead of weep. Good luck to bring a kitten to Two Castles? What would ill luck have been?

The drizzle increased to a light rain. Above the market, the stalls and the crowd thinned. A lark sang from its perch on an iron torch holder. I couldn't help wishing the bird roasted and set before me.

The upper half of a tower showed beyond the end of the way. I had almost reached the top of town, and soon I would see the castle whole.

Here the homes belonged to wealthy burghers. The houses were taller, as befitted their owners' elevated rank, with an extra story for servants.

The midafternoon bells chimed, muted by the rain. At the next corner I found a well. The water smelled sulfurous, but I drank anyway. The Two Castlers seemed healthy enough, and the water made my belly feel less empty. I rinsed my hands and face and neck, braided my damp hair, and tucked the braid into a knot at the back of my neck.

Then I looked down at myself. The hem of my kirtle was gray from the cog's bilgewater, and gray stains splashed up my apron. My apparel was unfashionable and, of course, I lacked a cap. What would the mansioner master make of me?

I heard a strange call that rose and fell, high-pitched, low-pitched, and bubbling. The sound troubled me until I remembered the king's menagerie.

The rain became heavier, and the air began to chill. I hurried, pressing my satchel against my chest. I could have put on my cloak, but then it would be wet, too.

If I was near the menagerie, I was on my way to the mansioners. Soon I reached the final row of houses, then behind them, kitchen gardens bordered by the town wall, much too high for me to climb. But here, at the top of Daycart Way, was the south gate, open and unguarded in peacetime.

I stepped through. Daycart Way became an oxcart road that soon forked. The right branch led to King Grenville's castle, which was so close that I could see the shape of a head in the outer gatehouse window.

According to Goodwife Celeste's description, the left-hand road would take me to the mansioners. I started up it. On either side of me, a meadow of late-blooming golden patty flowers glistened up at the wet sky.

Perhaps the mansioners were enjoying a snack and I might be invited to join in—join the troupe and partake of the meal.

The road was turning to mud. I avoided the wheel ruts and stepped from one higher, dryer patch to another. A wooden enclosure, taller than I was, lay ahead on my right, likely the menagerie, because I heard the eerie call again.

I reached the enclosure, which abutted the road. The gate stood open. I would have liked to glimpse a few of the creatures, but the view within was blocked by evergreen shrubbery trimmed in the rough shape of a bull.

After the menagerie, the road forked again. To my right it wound upward, likely leading to the ogre's castle. Straight ahead, perhaps a quarter mile off, five theatrical mansions stood in a row, appearing from here as boxes painted in rain-dulled hues: at the head of the line, purple for ceremonial scenes, then green for romance, black for tragedy, yellow for comedy, red for battles. From the side of the purple mansion, the mansioners' pennants hung limp in the rain. When the troupe traveled, the mansions would be hooked together and pulled by oxen, a stirring sight with the pennants in the lead.

Rain had probably ended rehearsals, but someone must be there, I thought, to keep watch. Better to arrive when the place was quiet, and the master or mistress would have time for me.

What would I do if I were turned away? I was already half starved. How would I keep from starving completely?

I wouldn't be turned away. I would say how hard I'd labor, how far I'd traveled, how much I loved the mansioners' tales, how I'd practiced them at home.

Might I start with a meal? Porridge would do.

Thunder growled in the distance. I felt something pass overhead and smelled rotten eggs.

Masteress Meenore landed between me and the mansions. Steam rose from ITs nostrils. *Enh enh enh.* "Here is the clever girl who will not reveal her name."

My heart skipped beats. It was one thing to be near a dragon in the midst of a throng, another to be alone with IT. I ran around IT, hoping to see someone, hoping IT wouldn't pursue.

CHAPTER SEVEN

"So you wish to be a mansioner." I heard the rustling of ITs wings as IT caught up with me. "Perhaps no one has informed you that the free apprenticeship has been abolished."

"I know."

Was IT going to the mansions, too? Might IT put in a good word for me? Or reveal me as the bumpkin victim of a thief?

IT spread a wing to shelter me from the rain, an unexpected kindness. I looked up and stopped hurrying to stare. IT halted, too.

The wing was a mosaic of flat triangles, each tinted a different hue, no color exactly the same. Lines of sinew held the triangles together, as lead holds the glass in a stained-glass window. The tinted skin, in every shade of pink, blue, yellow, and violet, was gossamer thin. I saw raindrops bead on the other side.

"My wings are my best feature." ITs voice took on a sweeter, lighter tone than I'd heard before.

A lady dragon?

"You cannot see until I fly, but the wings are not identical. The pattern and arrangement of colors differ."

"It's beautiful, but . . ."

"But what?" ITs smoke tinged purple.

"Can't a branch poke through? Wouldn't an insect bite tear your skin?"

The smoke bleached to white. "The skin is as thin as a butterfly's wing yet strong enough to turn aside the sharpest sword."

The pride in ITs voice made me smile. Then I wondered if IT was ashamed of the rest of ITself, and that made me want to pet IT.

I set off again, staying within the shelter of ITs beautiful wing. As we walked, the rain waxed into a downpour. I wondered what time it was. Near dusk, I guessed.

IT craned ITs head toward me. "You will offer yourself for a longer free apprenticeship." IT must have seen my surprise, because IT added, "First I used inductive reasoning, in that you are headed for the mansions and you have no silvers and you attempt an accent not native to you. The rest is deductive. What can you offer but lengthy labor and talent, if you really are talented? The mansioner master is called Sulow."

"Do you know him well?"

"Without exception, I know people better than they think. Most I know better than they know themselves."

"Is he a kind master?"

Enh enh enh. "Try your Two Castles accent on him."

I couldn't tell if this was good advice or the opposite.

"Your robber was a cat, was it not?"

"Yes."

"You wonder how I know."

I was sure IT would tell me.

"You are a sensible girl, aside from desiring to be a mansioner. You would not have let a human thief near you."

"Thank you." I wished Mother could hear someone call me *sensible*—without knowing the someone was a dragon.

The road ended in mud and patches of grass. We approached the mansions from the rear. Each one was a huge rectangular box on wheels, though the wheels had been stopped with chunks of wood. During performances and rehearsals, the front long side of the mansion would be taken away, revealing the mansioners and the scenery. I heard no voices and guessed that the boxes had been shut against the weather.

Cats huddled under every mansion, waiting for fairer

weather or for a hapless field mouse.

"If he is here, Sulow will be in the yellow mansion."

Yellow for comedy. I wondered what that might signify.

We circled the mansion. A procession of jesters had been painted on the outside: juggling, beating drums, playing flutes, turning somersaults. Rounding the corner to the front, we found the door open just a crack.

Masteress Meenore folded ITs wing. I was soaked instantly.

The drenching gave me inspiration. Every year I had seen the mansioners of Lahnt perform *The Princess and the Pea*. I had tried the princess role at home, and Albin said it was my best. Now here I was, sufficiently bedraggled for a dozen true princesses.

I spoke the princess's first line soundlessly because my voice had fled. My knock on the door was a whisper tap.

But after a moment the door creaked, and I heard, "Meenore?" in the round, sonorous tones of a mansioner.

I didn't trust IT enough to attempt an accent. "Throw wide the castle doors"—by lucky accident, I sneezed three times as the door finished opening—"to admit a young princess of exalted lineage."

A man of middling height stood in the doorway. He was thin, but with a moon face, flat nose, tight mouth, and shrewd, heavily lidded eyes that slid past me. "Go away, Meenore. I haven't reconsidered."

"Wait!" I cried.

"Sulow," IT said, catching the door with a claw, "have I asked you to reconsider?" Raindrops sparkled in the red glow of ITs nostrils. "Here is an aspiring mansioner."

Master Sulow's eyes took me in at last. Puzzlement or annoyance creased his brow. "Yes?"

I spoke in a rush. "I seek an apprenticeship, a fifteen-year, *free* apprenticeship. I will labor harder and longer than—"

"There are no free apprenticeships. How old are you?"

Be truthful, Mother said. "Fourteen."

Enh enh enh.

How I hated IT!

"Your name?"

"Lodie. I mean, *E*lodie, Master Sulow."

"Can you wield a paintbrush?"

Be truthful. "Certainly."

"A needle?"

That I could. "Yes."

"You would toil without a tin for fifteen years, until you are twenty-seven?" His lips twitched. "Unpaid, unheralded for such a span of time?"

"If I will be a mansioner at the end of it, gladly."

"Then you may audition for me."

Perhaps the kitten had been lucky after all. Apprentice mansioners didn't usually audition, since they wouldn't be acting for years. I reasoned that Master Sulow must have a particular role in mind.

"Come in." He backed away to let me in. "I have another guest, Young Elodie. Master Thiel here wants to be a mansioner as well, along with his cat."

Did Master Thiel love mansioning, too? Were we kindred souls? I mounted the two steps and stood just inside the door.

Master Sulow sounded exasperated. "His cat! Without apprenticing, either one of them. And Meenore wants to sell ITs skewers at my entertainments."

Two tallow candles cast a dim and smoky light. Master Thiel sat on a bench, his long legs extended, his features vivid in the candlelight and shadows. What a mansioner hero he would make! He rose and bowed when I entered, spilling Pardine from his lap.

I curtsied—not a quick bob down and up, as Mother had taught me, but the elaborate reverence I'd learned from Albin.

"We meet again," Master Thiel said.

"Indeed," I said with all the stateliness I could muster.

A bowl full of apples rested on a low table. I forgot Master Thiel and mansioning. In my state I might have traded my future for those apples.

Behind me, Masteress Meenore said, "Sulow, have you been engaged to mansion at the count's feast?"

He answered, "I have, though I'd be happier if His Lordship watched in the form of a pig. A pig doesn't pretend to be more than a beast."

"I know a few humans," IT said, "who combine pig, snake, and vulture without the excuse of shape-shifting."

Master Thiel said, "Bring a cat for safety, Sulow."

"I will. And a mansioner learns to protect himself in a thousand battle scenes, isn't that so, young mistress?"

I started out of my apple reverie. "Yes, master." Surely he would offer us apples. Hospitality demanded that he must.

IT said, "Give her an apple, Sulow. I doubt she's eaten all day." IT hadn't given me a skewer, but IT had been selling them, so hospitality didn't apply.

Hospitality seemed not to apply here, either. "If she becomes my apprentice, she may have more than an apple, but nothing until then." He took my elbow and guided me past the beautiful apples, until I was backed against the wall opposite the door. "Stand here." He seated himself on a stool across from Master Thiel. "Excellent."

Masteress Meenore continued to watch from the doorway. The floor and the space around me were bare of props and scenery.

Master Sulow said, "What is your favorite part to perform?"

"Do you know *Pyramus and Thisbe*, Elodie?" Masteress Meenore asked. "I relish a good Thisbe."

I nodded. I adored that play. It always made me weep, and I had the words by heart, although it wasn't Albin's favorite of my pieces. He said I was too young for it. "After your heart has been broken," he always said, "you can play Thisbe."

"Yes," Master Sulow said, smiling for the first time. "If you know the role of Thisbe, that is my choice, too."

Master Thiel said, "Nothing represents true love more forcefully." He held up an apple. "Do you mind, Sulow?"

Master Sulow laughed. "You'll have it anyway."

Why could Master Thiel have an apple and not I? I wanted to wrest it from his hand and gobble it up.

Controlling myself, I said, "May I do Thisbe's last scene?" This was the most powerful moment, when she grieves over Pyramus's body.

"By all means. I will establish the mood." He threw back his head and roared, a lion's roar, convincingly enough to make my heart race.

Oh, excellent! I clapped, which made a wet sound.

Then I kept my hands together and lowered my head, to concentrate and become my role, but the apples filled my mind. Albin said inspiration could come from any source. I wanted an apple as much as Thisbe ever wanted Pyramus.

Master Sulow coughed.

An apple would be my Pyramus. I whispered, "'O Pyramus? Is that you?'" I heard the genuine longing in my tones. I imagined an apple withering to an inedible core and wailed, "'O, O my love.'" I dropped my voice to a murmur. "'My heart, my darling.'" Tears ran down my cheeks, real tears. "'O Pyramus . . .'" O Apple. "'. . . do you yet breathe?'" Do you yet have pulp and juice? I crouched. "'What do I see? O!'" O! My apple core! "'My bloodied shawl! My love, O my love, my love, O my love, have you . . . died . . .'" Have you shriveled? "'. . . for love of me?'"

I dared say no more. I could hardly speak for sadness. I stood and curtsied.

Master Sulow shook his head, as if shaking off a vision. Master Thiel applauded. Masteress Meenore said, "Mmm. Hmm. Mmm." Had I managed to surprise IT?

Master Sulow picked up an apple, which he pressed into my hand. I bit into it. No fruit had ever tasted so sweet. Thisbe's tears still flowed as I chewed. He'd said he'd give me an apple if I was to be his apprentice. I would be a mansioner. I had performed better than ever before. Master Thiel had clapped. They'd all liked it. I swallowed. "Thank you, master. I'll toil and—"

"You earned your apple, but three paying apprentices began their service yesterday."

I paused, the apple at my mouth. Had I heard right? He'd promised.

"You should take her," IT said. "You won't easily find her like."

"Meenore, do I tell you how to deduce or induce or whatever? The three I have are trainable. They'll do." He took my elbow and walked me to the door. "I have no need of a fourth."

CHAPTER EIGHT

The door squeaked shut behind us.

"He never wanted an apprentice," I said, my elation seeping away. "He knew all along. Did you know?" I finished the apple except for the stem and seeds. I was still hungry.

"How could I?"

IT was the masteress of knowing everything.

"I do know Sulow likes his silver."

Liked money more than an apprentice who could turn herself into Thisbe. Some of my happiness came back. "Masteress Meenore, I was a fine Thisbe, wasn't I?"

"More than fine. I did not expect it."

Another realization struck. "He didn't expect it, either.

He wanted to laugh at me." Oh. I turned on IT. "And so did you!"

IT exhaled blue smoke.

I stamped away and started back toward Two Castles. I had no idea what I would do when I got there or how I would keep myself alive. Fear as well as hunger stabbed my belly. I could *be* a tragedy, not merely portray one.

The rain had lightened, but twilight was falling, and the air had turned winter cold.

Masteress Meenore landed at my side, radiating heat. I supposed IT had a home with food and a bed, if dragons slept in beds. Why didn't IT go there?

"Masteress Meenore, where may I find the nearest other company of mansioners?"

"In Pree. A month's march, and the road is unsafe."

Perhaps a caravan was going there, and I could travel along as someone's servant.

"The master in Pree isn't as welcoming as Sulow." *Enh enh enh.* "I don't see why you want to be a mansioner, Lodie—"

"*Elo*—"

"*Lodie.* Do not correct your elders. I prefer *Lodie*."

"Elodie is prettier."

"That may be. Why would you prefer to be a mansioner when you might be a dragon's assistant?"

"I've always hoped . . ." ITs words penetrated. "Your

assistant? Or a different dragon's?" What would a dragon's assistant do?

"I will not pay you much. I am stingy."

The evening bells began to chime. *Pay pay pay pay.*

I liked the sound, but I grew frightened. Would I go to ITs lair? Would chunks of me be on ITs skewers tomorrow?

IT sniffed. "I will withdraw my offer, if you think *that* of me."

Could IT read my mind? "I didn't say anything!"

"Precisely."

I had hesitated, so IT knew. IT waddled several yards away. I missed ITs warmth.

"What will my duties be?"

IT reared onto ITs back legs and spread ITs wings without flying. "Back away."

I did, and quickly.

IT spewed a jet of flame, burnishing the yellow meadow and rusting the charcoal sky. "You will proclaim my powers of deduction, induction, and common sense." IT came down heavily on ITs front legs. "And you will thread my skewers, carry my baskets, assist me with my many responsibilities."

Proclaiming sounded well. A mansioner might proclaim.

"We will try each other out to see if we suit."

I nodded.

"If I find you wanting, I will not keep you."

If I found IT wanting, I wouldn't stay.

But where would I go?

"Twenty tins for the month. I will feed you, and you may live with me. That is my offer."

I hardly heard the sum. As soon as IT finished speaking, I demonstrated my proclaiming ability loud enough for the moon to hear. "I will serve you, Masteress Meenore, with dedication, with enthusiasm, and with whatever art nature has bestowed on me."

IT smiled, showing every pointy yellow tooth in ITs mouth.

"Is there food at your house?"

"At my lair. Bread and cheese, which you may toast. Sundry victuals."

The idea of food more substantial than an apple weakened my knees. I stumbled, then caught myself. At home my family and I would have shared four meals since I'd last eaten more than the apple.

"Masteress, would you pay to post a letter from me to my parents, to let them know I'm safe?"

"One letter. The scribes are all knaves: twenty tins to write a letter, twenty-five for posting, five for a small sheet of parchment, ten for a large." IT snorted. "Ink is free."

"Masteress Meenore, I can write my own letter."

IT exhaled blue smoke. "You will still need parchment and the posting fee." After a pause IT added, "I failed to deduce that you can read and write."

Not many could. "My mother taught me." To take my mind off home, I thought about my salary.

A hundred tins to a copper, fifty coppers to an iron bar, four iron bars to a silver. Many lifetimes before I earned my apprenticeship.

"Lodie, walking is not my preferred mode of travel. Return to the town gate, then follow the high street, Owe Street, west to the end. There is my lair. I will be waiting with your supper."

"How will I recognize your"—I gulped—"lair?"

"You will. Be alert as you go. When you reach me, tell me what your senses perceived. Mysteries abound in Two Castles. As my assistant, you must learn to notice them." IT stood on ITs back legs and lifted in two great wing strokes, ITs wing colors muted by the dusk, ITs body in flight powerful and sleek. In a moment IT rose higher than the tallest castle tower, caught a wind, and glided away.

The rain had all but stopped. I pulled my cloak out of my satchel and wrapped it around me.

Mysteries abound. I reviewed the mysteries I had already encountered: the thieving cat; barefoot Master Thiel and his jingling coins; the polite ogre hated by all; no one at the dock to meet Goodwife Celeste and her goodman, who had come to see their children; even Master Dess, who seemed perfect enough to be a whited sepulcher; the dragon willing to hire an unknown girl. An abundance.

Soon I reached the menagerie fence. I ran my fingertips from one upright log to the next, rough to the touch. I smelled wet earth, damp fur, and the rust of raw meat—some animals' feed, I hoped. My eyes sharpened as the dark deepened.

Again I heard that rising and falling call, which jangled even more eerily in my ears now that it was night. I would have been terrified if not for the protection of the fence. Any animal that escaped its cage would still be contained.

Then my hand encountered air. The gate hung open.

I fled. Although I heard nothing behind me, I didn't slow for a full five minutes. I was lucky not to slip in the mud. Finally I stopped to quiet my breathing. The open menagerie gate—one more mystery.

In this setting I could truly be Thisbe, out at night to meet my Pyramus, who would look very much like Master Thiel. I could indeed see a bloodied lioness and bolt, leaving behind my veil, if I had a veil.

Torchlight and candlelight twinkled in the town to my right and the castle to my left. Torches flanked the nearby castle gatehouse. The drawbridge was up for the night.

I took the final fork. Below the town's gate, a figure approached, striding toward me on Daycart Way.

In the daylight, thieves. At night, murderers?

A few houses remained, and he might yet enter one of them, but I couldn't wait. I darted to the town wall and stood with my back against it, hoping to disappear into its shadow.

The figure, a man, passed through the gate.

Mrrow? from near my feet.

The man halted.

I cursed Two Castles for its cats. My muscles tensed with fear.

"Who goes there?" His voice was sharp, challenging.

The cat rubbed my legs.

The man waited. I waited. The cat leaned into my calf.

Finally the man continued, and in a minute I saw him by castle torchlight. It was Master Dess! Master Dess, without his cows and donkey, but still with his kitten basket.

I almost called to him. Now that I was ITs assistant, I could return his three tins. But his voice had been so harsh, I didn't dare.

He knocked twice on the gatehouse door, then pounded—*bang! bang! bang!*—then knocked twice again. A signal?

The drawbridge dropped to let him cross. I remained where I was until he must have reached the castle. The cat made tiny noises, washing itself.

I left it behind. As I followed Owe Street west, I caught a whiff of spoiled eggs. The odor grew with every step.

The street ended at a structure such as I'd never seen before, as big as four houses and twice as tall, with a roof that reminded me of interlaced fingers, pointing upward. The fingers, made of tree trunks, twisted and curved, lashed together by iron bands. Smoke filtered in wisps between the fingers and rose in a thicker plume from a chimney on the other side of the edifice. The walls were made of wattle and daub, as an ordinary cottage would be.

The shape of the building was a rough circle, ringed at regular intervals by rainwater vats as high as my shoulders. The wooden door, big enough to admit a dragon, stood open.

ITs lair. I waited in the shadow outside for a long minute before crossing the threshold.

CHAPTER NINE

asteress Meenore faced me from halfway across the single enormous room, where stench seemed to have replaced air. I swallowed repeatedly and tried not to gag.

"Do you like my perfume?" The smoke from ITs nostrils changed from white to blue.

Blue smoke meant shame!

I begged my eyes not to water, but they watered anyway. Should I lie?

IT would know.

Soften the truth?

IT would know.

"Do you like it, Lodie?"

I breathed deep without choking. "Like it? Enh enh enh."

Enh enh enh. Enh enh enh. Enh enh enh. "My odor is terrible. But you will get used to it, Elodie."

Ah, Elodie. I shrugged off my cloak and hung it on a hook by the entrance. The lair was warm even with the open door.

"You would like to eat." IT lumbered to the fireplace, which was set into the wall across from where I stood.

How strange, a fireplace in a dragon's lair.

Wood had been laid, but there was no fire. Above the hearth, a cauldron hung on an iron rack from which also dangled a stew pot, a soup pot, and sundry long-handled spoons. To the left of the hearth sat the basket of coins and the basket of bread-and-cheese skewers. I crossed the room to lay my satchel down by the baskets.

Masteress Meenore breathed flame on the hearth logs. I took a skewer and held it out to the fire. The scent of bread and cheese improved the air.

When the skewer was toasted, I blew on it to cool it, although I could hardly wait. A human-sized bench and a tall three-legged stool were drawn close to the fire. I sank onto the bench. The bread tasted as sweet as a scone, and the oozing cheese was sharper than any I'd ever sampled.

Masteress Meenore—my masteress!—took two skewers between ITs right-claw talons. IT lowered ITself until IT reclined facing the fire, leaned on ITs left elbow, and thrust the skewers up to ITs wrist into the heart of the fire.

I gasped, although a dragon wouldn't burn. After a minute or two, IT pulled the skewers out and devoured them entirely, bread, cheese, and wood.

"The skewers are pine. I enjoy the resin."

What else did IT like the flavor of?

In ITs uncanny way, IT answered my thought, "I prefer cypress wood, but the boatwrights take it all. I will not eat oak under any circumstance. I dine also on what humans eat and pebbles when I feel too light. On occasion I swallow knives, but they do not sit well." IT cooked and ate two more claws-full of skewers, then belched. ITs smoke shaded blue again. "Pardon me."

I nodded and tucked away three more skewers myself.

IT rose. "I shall return shortly." When IT moved, I saw that ITs belly had covered a huge trapdoor. "Do not take a single coin from the basket while I'm gone. I will know."

"I'm not a thief!"

"And do not open the trapdoor." IT clumped outside.

Without ITs presence and despite the fire, the air chilled. I drew my cloak around me again and approached the trapdoor. The wood was heat-blackened but firm when I touched it. The handle was a ring of iron.

I was not a mistress of deduction or induction, but I needed neither to guess what lay below: ITs hoard. Every dragon was reputed to have one. I might be standing on wealth enough to buy the ogre's castle.

ITs wealth, not mine. I returned to the fireplace bench, sat with my back to the fire, and surveyed the lair.

Light came from the fire and the dozen torches that were spaced around the edge of the room. With IT gone, I could smell the greasy torch rags.

The walls were hung with painted cloth so faded I couldn't make out what had once been depicted. Masteress Meenore's heat had baked the dirt floor as hard as pottery.

If the fireplace was twelve o'clock, eight to ten o'clock was occupied by a high table pushed against the wall. A long bench hid under it. Mother said you could learn a household's character from its table. I rose and went to this one. The wooden tabletop, which sagged in the middle and was worn and scratched, came up to my chin.

I saw a jug, half a wheel of yellow cheese, two loaves of bread, an orange squash, a small salt bowl, and a big double-handled bowl that held a spoon and a knife. The bowl was common green pottery, the spoon wood, the knife handle wood, too—a poor folks' bowl, poor folks' cutlery.

At eleven o'clock along the wall was a heap of large tasseled pillows. The tassels lay in my hand as smoothly as silk. The pillows might have been worth a silver or two if their linen hadn't been so worn. But though worn, they were unstained. I lifted one to my nose and smelled rosemary.

Across the lair, at three o'clock, stood a double-doored cupboard. I hadn't been forbidden to open it, so I concluded I was supposed to. The contents were a stack of folded lengths of linen, clean but threadbare; sundry bowls of the same quality as the one on the table; a row of four pottery tumblers; a small pile of cutlery; four sheaves of unused skewers tied with thread; and a little box, which proved to contain knucklebones.

Nothing more. IT might have warned me away from ITs hoard to make me think IT rich, while in truth the hoard was home to a few starving mice. Or IT might be fooling me twice.

Unbidden—unwelcome—a mansioners' tale came to mind, the tale of Bluebeard. What if the hoard contained the bones of dozens of Masteress Meenore's assistants?

I stood over the trapdoor. Open it? Run?

I knelt and grasped the iron ring. And there I stayed, uncertain. I wanted to be a dragon's assistant if I couldn't be a mansioner for now, and I needed food and a place to sleep.

And IT interested me. And no one feared IT. I stood up.

The trapdoor opened. I jumped back.

IT heaved ITself up onto the floor. "Lodie of Lahnt, if I had found you below, I would have tossed you out. If I had found you napping at the fireplace, I would have tossed you out, too. I want neither a thief nor an assistant who lacks curiosity."

I returned my cloak to the hook at the door.

"So, what have you learned about your masteress?"

Imitating ITs way of speaking, I said, "I used my powers of induction and deduction to conclude there is an outdoor entrance to the hoard."

"What else?"

"I cannot tell whether or not you are rich. All depends on what lies under the trapdoor."

"Well done, Elodie."

I was Elodie when IT was pleased with me.

"Your home is scrupulously clean." I may have brought in a louse or two, a flea or three, but none had preceded me.

"Yes. I will tolerate you for the night, but you must bathe in the morning. I will burn your clothes."

My clothes that Grandmother had worn or Mother and I had made? I rushed to my satchel and hugged it. "I'll wash everything."

"Twice. No, thrice. And scrub!"

I nodded, lowering the satchel. IT stretched ITself along the floor, ITs snout near my feet, ITs eyes fixed on me. I yawned.

"You are sleepy."

O masteress of deduction! I nodded.

"Then tomorrow you may tell me what you observed on your way to me, and tomorrow night, when you are clean, you may sleep on pillows. But now it is the floor for you. I suggest under the table. I am a restless sleeper."

Don't crush me! I barricaded my dirty self behind the long bench under the table. The clay floor was even harder than the deck of the cog. I fetched my cloak and my satchel, layered everything for cushioning, and stretched out on my side, back to the wall, my head sticking out beyond the bench, so I could still see into the room.

IT went to the cupboard, then sat on the floor with the box of knucklebones in ITs claws. Hunching over, IT spilled them out. One of the bones, the jack, was yellow, according to custom. The others were their natural ivory. IT tossed the yellow bone into the air, picked up another bone, and caught the yellow one in the same claw, in one deft move. On the next throw, IT picked up two bones.

Oh, Father! Dragons play knucklebones!

Knucklebones was a popular girls' game. I had played a thousand times. Did this make IT female?

"The dragon claw is as nimble as the human hand, Lodie."

The knucklebones tip-tapped the floor. My last awake thoughts were: Here I am, full belly, bedded down near a dragon. Father, Mother, you would wring your hands. How lucky I am!

CHAPTER TEN

woke once during the night and heard a distant lion's roar, probably from the menagerie. Or from the town, with the menagerie gate open. Not from Master Sulow, because the mansions were too far away for the roar to carry.

Perhaps the ogre turned into a lion at night and terrorized the town. I moved closer to the bench. The lion would hardly attack a dragon in ITs lair, would he?

Masteress Meenore lay on ITs back. ITs legs, loosely bent at knees and elbows, bobbled in the air, in the manner of a dog completely at ease.

In the morning I awakened to chill and silence. At home in Lahnt, Father used to build up the fire before waking me. He'd kiss my ear or my forehead or my nose, whatever part of me I'd left out of my blanket.

Hugging my cloak around me, I stood and went outside. Sunny day, cold air, November in October.

IT was breathing fire on one of the outdoor rainwater vats behind the lair. IT swallowed ITs flame. "Fetch the stool."

I did.

"Your bath is ready. Here." IT opened ITs claws to reveal a milky brick of soap.

At home we saved our soap for laundering. "But—"

"Use it. While you bathe, I will scour the lair." IT left me.

I placed the stool and climbed up. The water seethed and smelled like year-old eggs, but when I put a toe in, the toe liked it, hot, not scalding. And I was first in for once—Father, Mother, and Albin hadn't taken their baths before I had mine.

Sloshing and sizzling sounds emanated from the lair. I pitied my dying fleas. In a few minutes IT emerged with a cloth in ITs claws. "I will return shortly. You have been generous with your filth . . ."

Filth seemed too strong for truth.

". . . and now I must bathe, too." IT draped the cloth over the edge of the vat. "When you are entirely clean, wrap yourself in that. Then launder your clothes, not omitting your satchel itself, until they are also entirely clean."

"Yes, Masteress."

"I have heated that, too." IT pointed at another steaming vat. Then IT flapped ITs beautiful wings and headed south.

I wondered where IT bathed and wished I could watch.

While IT was gone, I washed my things, rubbing cloth against cloth until my arms ached. When IT returned, IT steamed everything dry in a trice.

A Lahnt proverb goes, *Love your lice. Only skeletons have none.* But here I was, louse free and still breathing.

Inside the lair, IT seated ITself by the fire and took a clawful of skewers. "Did you sleep well?"

I took a skewer, too, and sat on the fireplace bench. The skewer basket was almost empty. "I was awakened once by roaring from the menagerie lion."

IT clucked ITs tongue, and the orange in ITs scales deepened to scarlet. "This is the sort of pronouncement my assistant must not make."

What had I said?

"Suppose there were no lion in the menagerie, and someone from the town heard you assert there was, and moreover that you heard it roar." IT waved the skewers. "Your nonsense would—"

"But it did roar. It's not—"

"Do not interrupt your masteress."

I blushed. "I'm sorry. But I heard it."

ITs scales dulled. "You may say 'I heard a roar from the direction of the menagerie.' You can be certain of nothing more."

I grew afraid. "Was it the ogre?"

"You may probe the possibilities." IT put the skewers in the fire. "But you must not draw unwarranted conclusions."

"Then might it have been Count Jonty Um?"

"Indeed. He is capable."

I shuddered.

IT removed the skewers and ate one.

"*Was* it the count, Masteress? Do you know?"

"Not of a certainty. Nor a likelihood. I have never known His Lordship to shift into a lion, and I have known him since his infancy."

My heart lifted. He seemed a decent ogre; I wanted him to be a good one. "Why is he so disliked and feared?" My heart prepared to sink. "Does he turn into something else, or eat people?"

IT raised ITs eye ridges. "Many who neither shape-shift nor eat people are disliked and feared. Our king for one."

A perfect example. On Lahnt no one liked him. I waited for an answer about Count Jonty Um eating people, but none came, so my fear remained. I toasted my skewer. "Are there any lions nearby that are not in the menagerie?"

"Perhaps. The menagerie houses none. The last lion in the environs of Two Castles was killed a year before my birth. King Grenville wants to procure one for his zoo, but he refuses to pay full price."

What could I have heard? I began to eat.

IT ate a skewer uncooked and went to the table. "The day is passing. Nothing done, nothing earned. Fetch a sheaf of skewers."

IT meant the skewer sticks, which I took from the cupboard, and IT set me to cutting bread into cubes. I had to stand on the bench to be tall enough.

"Now tell me, what did you see on your way here last evening?"

As I cubed, I told IT about the open menagerie gate. "I heard calls from inside." I imitated the rise and fall of the creature's voice.

IT said the cries came from an animal called a high eena.

"Masteress, a man was leaving town, Master Dess from the cog. He brought a donkey and two cows and a basket of kittens over—"

"His appearance?"

I described him and told what had happened outside the town gate. "When he knocked"—I rapped the bench—"on the gatehouse door, the guards raised the drawbridge without seeing who he was. His knocks were"—I stopped myself—"may have been a code."

IT scratched around ITs ear hole and looked unconcerned.

"What if there's a plot against the king?"

The noon bells pealed. Testily IT blamed me for the lateness of the hour.

What if IT was part of the plot?

We pushed cheese and bread onto skewers in silence. After a few minutes, I called up my courage and asked if I might write and post my letter home.

IT put down ITs skewer and waddled to the trapdoor. "Follow me, Lodie." IT pulled the door open.

I didn't move. Did IT plan to kill me before I could write to Mother and Father?

CHAPTER ELEVEN

rom halfway in, IT swiveled ITs neck and grinned back at me before disappearing down the stairs.

I stood at the top and saw a light spark on far below. The glow brightened. IT was lighting torches.

"Come!"

The stairs were stone blocks wedged into the earth. Follow IT or leave ITs service.

IT could have murdered me last night. I stepped cautiously and continued downward into a chamber almost as high and big as the one above, empty but for three large baskets beneath a table and four stacks of books on top, a fortune in books. I had never seen so many gathered together.

IT stood on the far side of the table. I approached, curious about the books but most eager to see inside the baskets.

They brimmed with coins, mostly tins but also coppers, several iron bars, and a sprinkling of silvers. I had never seen a silver before. The coin turned out to be smaller than a copper, much smaller than a tin, no bigger than one of my teeth, such a little thing to be worth a year of an apprentice's labor.

I wondered if the baskets held coins to the bottom or were only a layer hiding something else underneath.

"In a century of industry and thrift, a dragon can amass wealth." IT pulled out the baskets and thrust a claw into one after another, churning up the contents. Coins spilled onto the floor. "No bones of bygone assistants."

I blushed.

IT sat back and rested a claw on a stack of books. ITs smoke turned gray; ITs eyes paled. In a dire and doleful voice, IT said, "I cannot read."

I didn't know how to soften ITs sorrow. I ventured, "Few people can."

IT snapped, "Is that supposed to comfort me?"

I tried again. "Your vocabulary is big."

"And varied and excellent. I astound my hearers with the erudition of my speech." IT opened the top book to the middle and passed a claw across the page. "But I cannot decipher the merest word." IT took the book.

I followed ITs tail back up to the lair, where IT set the book on the bench by the fireplace.

"Nothing read, nothing learned. We will not starve if we have a holiday. Read to me, Lodie."

IT had said I could write to my family, but I didn't want to remind IT. I lifted the book onto my lap. Lambs and calves, it was heavy, both thick and wide, covered in bumpy orange-brown leather that reminded me of ITs scales.

IT stretched out with ITs long head at my feet. ITs smoke rose in spirals. I wondered what spiraling smoke meant.

"Begin."

I opened to the first page. "Masteress Meenore, this is a book about vegetable gardening."

"Mmm. Proceed."

I thumbed through. Each chapter described planting, tending, and harvesting a different vegetable. On the first page an enormous *A* in gold lettering was followed by *corn squash* in smaller black letters. In the corner of the page, with a border of gold dots, was a drawing in green and black ink of an acorn squash.

"Is the gold real?"

"Read."

I began. ITs eyes never left my face. If my mouth hadn't been moving, I would soon have been asleep. IT didn't object when I practiced my Two Castles accent, but IT wouldn't let me mansion a cabbage into tragedy or a carrot into comedy.

"Read as the farmer's daughter you are."

If I hadn't been a mansioner as well as a farmer's daughter, my throat would have given out. As it was, I finally had to interrupt myself. "Masteress, I need to drink."

IT accompanied me out to the rainwater vats. I carried a tumbler, and IT held a bowl and the ladle. The changeable Lepai weather had brought more rain, but by now no clouds remained. The air smelled of sweet grass and fallen leaves.

IT lapped ITs water with ITs tongue, as a cat does. When we finished, IT led me back inside. I told myself how interesting endives would be.

But instead IT said we would eat our midday meal. Perhaps in honor of the book, IT roasted the orange squash to have with our skewers.

"Masteress?" I asked over spoonfuls of squash. "Will you plant a garden in the spring?"

"I have no land for a garden." Then IT gave me leave to visit the scribe when I finished eating. "Thirty tins. Do not let any cats get my coins."

I counted out the tins while IT watched me narrowly. When I had enough, I spilled them into my purse, tucked the purse under my apron, and touched the spot.

"Do not touch! You are signaling thieves."

I pulled my hand away as though my apron were on fire. What a bumpkin I'd been.

"While you are out, observe and listen. Smell the air. All your senses are in my employ, Lodie."

On Lair Lane, a shutter slammed shut. A cat cleaned itself in a doorway. I spied four cats. It occurred to me that Two Castles might have not a single mouse.

Roo Street was busier than quiet Lair Lane. At a weaver's stall a man turned over lengths of cloth. I tried out the Two Castles accent I'd just practiced for hours and he simply directed me to a scribe's stall. I skipped across Roo onto Trist Street.

Ahead, outside a jeweler's stall, Goodwife Celeste held a silver bracelet close to her eyes while the jeweler pounded his fist into his palm and disputed with her husband, Goodman Twah.

I'd thought them too poor to buy jewelry.

"Mistress! It's Elodie! From the cog!"

Her hand closed around the bracelet, and she lowered her arm. "Elodie! How nice to see you."

Was it? I'd interrupted something.

"Have you become a mansioner's apprentice?"

I told her about Masteress Meenore.

"The dragon Meenore?"

"ITself."

"Look about for something else, Elodie." She put her

hands on my shoulders, the bracelet hand still a fist. "IT is moody. Today IT may be kind, but tomorrow IT could be angry and do anything. If you stay, be prepared to flee."

To flee, but not to seek her aid.

"Come, Celeste." Her goodman twined his arm in hers. "The grandchildren are waiting. Good day." He nodded at me and at the jeweler.

"Good day!" The jeweler's voice was sharp.

Goodwife Celeste and her husband headed uphill. She still had the bracelet, so her goodman must have paid for it.

I decided to be cautious in ITs company and to continue barricading myself while I slept.

In Romply Alley the scribe's table took up little space between two cheese sellers' booths. The scribe was a tiny woman with a large nose, as if the pungent cheese had directed all her growth one way. "You'd like me to write something for you?"

I said I needed no assistance.

She peered at me through small, red-rimmed eyes. "Remarkable."

Thirty tins bought me postage and a scrap of parchment. I wrote in a cramped script,

Am well, am safe. Many weavers here. A master has taken me for free. Do not miss the geese, but miss you both and Albin. Your loving daughter, Elodie

I wished I'd had room to write *loving* a hundred times. Every sentence was a lie concealed in truth. I wanted to tell them what an adventure I was having, but I had no space and didn't dare.

The scribe waved a fan over the parchment to dry the ink. "You write a fine hand, young mistress. Don't set up in competition with me."

I paid, while watching for thieving cats. The tins changed hands without trouble, and I started back to my masteress. As I turned into Lair Lane, I stopped, then ran into the lair, leaping as I went.

"Masteress!"

IT looked up from ITs game of knucklebones.

"An abecedary of vegetables!" I brushed aside the bones and put the book on the floor under ITs snout. "Look!" I opened to the first page. "*A* for acorn squash." I turned to the end. "*Z* for zucchini. It's an A to Z in vegetables."

ITs smoke grayed.

Gray smoke for sadness, but I rushed on. "Mother taught me to read with an abecedary. I'll teach you. We can start—"

IT sat up. "What did you see and hear and smell in the town?"

"Don't you—" I stopped myself and told IT everything except Goodwife Celeste's warning.

When I finished, IT had me read again until the evening meal, by which time I had progressed as far as *mustard*.

After we ate, IT challenged me to knucklebones. I sat cross-legged on the floor, and IT stretched out facing me with the tip of ITs tail in the smoldering fireplace.

I couldn't win. IT tossed the jack higher and straighter than I did and so had more time to pick up bones. My sole advantage lay in the variations. IT knew none, so I showed IT the ones I excelled at: round the castle, fairy fling, rolling the gnome. But soon IT surpassed me even at these.

And then, in the middle of a game, IT said, "Lodie, three scribes have attempted to teach me to read, and all have used abecedaries. But the letters fly apart. Straight lines curl. Curved lines throb. I know a single letter." ITs right claw drew a circle in the air. "*O*."

"Oh."

"Yes, *O*. The trouble must be in the dragon eye, or in my eyes."

I wasn't convinced IT couldn't learn. Clever as IT was, IT seemed meant to read.

We played a while longer, and then I slept, unafraid, not barricaded. Goodwife Celeste was certainly misinformed about my masteress.

In the morning IT gave me instructions. "Walk through the town and proclaim my powers. You will say"—IT inhaled deeply—"'Today, in Two Castles and only in Two Castles, the Great, the Unfathomable, the Brilliant Meenore is available to solve riddles, find lost objects and lost people, and answer the unanswerable. Three tins for a riddle solved . . .'"

So now I knew what three tins would buy.

"'. . . fifteen tins for a lost object found, three coppers for a lost person found—'"

I blurted, "A lost person should cost more than three coppers." A person!

"What is a person worth, Lodie?"

"Many silvers."

"And if the lost person is the son of a servant, who may never own a single silver, the son should remain lost?"

I blushed. "No. But what if the father or mother may never own a copper?"

"Then we will negotiate. You must also say, 'The fee for answering the unanswerable will be decided between the parties. The Great, the Unfathomable, the Brilliant Meenore may be found in the square. Speak to IT with respect.' Elodie, I charge you: Make the residents of Two Castles take note. This is your most important task. Make them listen."

Or soon IT would find another assistant.

Outside, the morning was as bright and cold as yesterday. I filled myself with enthusiasm and began proclaiming at the top of Lair Lane. "Today," I cried in a burst of awe, "in Two Castles and nowhere else, the Great . . ." A man hurried by, face turned away.

I rushed to the man's other side. "IT is available to solve riddles, find lost"—I wailed *lost* piteously—"objects and—"

The man pressed his cap tight over his ears. "Hush! I know Meenore."

"Sir, but do you know all IT can do? Unriddle riddles, answer—"

"I know what IT does. Every week IT heats water for my household. I pay IT fourteen tins."

"Oh," I said weakly, then rallied. "IT can perform many other wondrous feats." I skipped sideways along with him. "Find anything. *Anything.*"

"If I lose *anything* and cannot find it," he said, stopping to retie his cap strings, "I will seek out Masteress Meenore." He started off again. "Do not pursue me, girl, or I'll call the constable."

I waited until he turned a corner before proclaiming again. I proclaimed on Lair Lane, Roo Street, Daycart Way, and Mare Street along the harbor, but wherever I went, everyone already knew Masteress Meenore. A baker told me that for ten tins, IT started his oven fires when they went out. Weekly, for two coppers, IT boiled the water in the town's wells to purify them.

The midmorning bells were ringing when a smith told me, "IT makes my fire the hottest in Two Castles." He took my forearm in his grimy hand. "IT could be a fine smith if IT didn't have to be Unfathomable. Tell IT Master Bonay says so."

At her place in Romply Alley, the scribe told me that IT had once deduced that her box of quills was hidden under a rock in her garden. "How did IT know?"

I announced loudly, "IT has ITs mysterious meth—"

"Make way! Ogre coming. Dog coming."

The scribe pulled me between her table and one of the cheese seller's stalls.

Count Jonty Um's shadow darkened the alley. His shoulder brushed an awning. He stopped three stalls from me, by a cobbler. "Sit, Sheeyen. A girl turned in here, shouting about Meenore. Where is she?"

My heart rose into my throat as the scribe pushed me forward. I lurched into the street, almost fell, caught myself, and found my face an inch from a fold in the ogre's cloak.

CHAPTER TWELVE

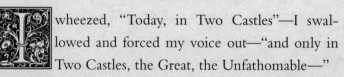I wheezed, "Today, in Two Castles"—I swallowed and forced my voice out—"and only in Two Castles, the Great, the Unfathomable—"

Count Jonty Um boomed, "I wish to speak with IT."

"Masteress Meenore is in the square, um . . . Count Um."

"Count Jonty Um. We will go together." He placed a heavy hand over the crown of my capless head. A finger touched each of my ears. If he pushed down, I'd sink into the street up to my nose.

"Make way," he cried. "Ogre passing. Girl passing."

Everyone stared. The scribe mouthed words at me: *Take care.* How could I take care? The ogre could squeeze my head like a lemon.

Count Jonty Um edged along to avoid upsetting tables

and bringing down displays. He'd captured me, but he took care with the townspeople's stalls. Today's dog, a brown shepherd on a short chain, managed not to knock over anything, either. Gradually my heart slowed to a gallop. Because of the ogre's hand, I feared to turn my head, but I moved my eyes from side to side.

Everywhere, people froze to watch us. I saw pity for me on many faces, but no one challenged him. Cats stared, too, from between their owners' legs, from stall tabletops, from windowsills. I heard hisses.

In the market square Count Jonty Um cried, "Ogre and girl going to the dragon. Make way."

By the time we reached Masteress Meenore, ITs customers had fled. IT swept one wing in front of ITself, then to the side, and lowered ITs head in a definite, almost graceful bow.

Did bowing, rather than curtsying, make IT a he?

I ducked out from under the ogre's hand, and he let me go. IT raised both wings at the elbow, put one back foot behind the other, and dipped, in a definite curtsy.

A bow and a curtsy. He–she–IT.

IT said, "Your Lordship . . ."

Count Jonty Um bowed, too, a quick bend at the waist that meant *I am a count, you a mere masteress.*

"Your lordship has not come for skewers. We will consult at my lair. Lodie will lead you."

"*E*lodie, if you please, Masteress." I wanted the count to know my proper name.

IT took the basket of coins in a claw, leaped into the air, and flew, barely clearing Count Jonty Um's head. IT circled low, twice, three times. Why was IT lingering?

I deduced and proclaimed, "See, one and all, how Masteress Meenore is sought by nobility. IT will answer your questions, too. Schedule your own meeting with the nimble-witted, farseeing Masteress Meenore."

IT flew off in the direction of the lair. I picked up the basket of skewers. "This way, Count Jonty Um."

"Make way!" he cried. He put his hand on my shoulder.

I gathered my courage. "You can let go, Count Jonty Um. I won't run away."

His hand dropped. We left the square, watched by everyone. When we reached a less crowded street, he boomed, "Thank you for telling me to let go. You told me to wait in line, too. I like truthful people, Elodie."

I looked up. The line of his lips had softened, his face was no longer red, and his eyes seemed wider. An easier, more relaxed face made me feel easier, too.

"This way."

A robin landed on his shoulder, ruffled its feathers, and stayed. Cats might hate him, but not all animals. The dog seemed comfortable at his side.

He must have noticed that I was rushing to stay ahead of

him, because he stopped. "You can ride on my shoulders."

What would I hold on to up there? His great ears? What if I fell and pulled an ear off with me, or grabbed his silver pendant and swung from his neck like a bell clapper? "No, thank you."

He reddened again. I had insulted him. He set off at a slower pace, a considerate ogre. I tried to think how to apologize without making the insult worse.

He sneezed hugely. "Sulfur."

The robin flew away.

"We're near the lair." He liked frankness. "Count Jonty Um, I was afraid of falling off your shoulder and pulling your ear down with me."

He began to smile. The smile broadened, mouth half open, white upper teeth shining, bathing me in sweetness.

How changed he was! Almost as if he'd shape-shifted.

The smile faded and his expression dulled again, but I had lost my fear of him.

The lair's doorway was wide enough to admit us side by side. Masteress Meenore faced us from just inside. The count sneezed again.

ITs smoke tinted from white to blue. I deduced IT thought ITs odor had caused the sneeze, as was likely.

"Welcome, Your Lordship," IT said.

"Thank you." He let go of the dog's chain and she trotted away, snuffling the floor.

IT stiffened, meaning, I was certain, that as soon as the dog and the ogre left, the lair would be scoured again. The animal made straight for the fireplace bench, where IT had placed bowls and refreshments—apples, pears, dried dates, and figs.

The count went to the animal. "Shoo, Sheeyen."

She loped to the door and curled up on the threshold.

"May I take your cloak, Your Lordship?" I said, without considering how enormous it was.

He put it in my arms, but I wasn't overwhelmed. The wool was so fine and light that the cloak weighed no more than my own. I folded it and placed it atop the coin basket by the hearth.

IT had moved the table between the fireplace bench and the fire. On the tabletop ITs precious pillows lay in a row.

"Please, Your Lordship, seat yourself." IT gestured at the table. "It is sturdy. You will not break it."

The count sat, his back to the fire, leaning forward, balancing himself so that the table didn't take his full bulk. He sneezed again and blew his nose politely on the sleeve of his tunic, which today was evergreen silk.

Masteress Meenore's smoke darkened to slate blue. IT lowered ITself on ITs haunches between the cupboard and Count Jonty Um.

IT had positioned the stool for me on the ogre's left. I sat. Deftly, IT sliced a pear and an apple and fanned the slices into a circle in an empty bowl. In the center IT placed a fig. The result was a fruit daisy. I had never seen such elegance.

"Partake, Your Lordship." IT gave the bowl to the count and gestured at the other refreshments. "Help yourself, Elodie."

"Thank you, Masteress." And thank you for my name. With my little knife I sliced half an apple and half a pear, some slices almost all peel and others almost all fruit, the peel ones for me, the fruit ones for sharing. As the lowliest here, my portion should be the most meager. I took figs and dates as well, all for sharing. They were delicacies.

Masteress Meenore helped ITself, too. I speared a date with my knife and placed it in the count's bowl. He gave me his fig, which was a kindness.

Mother, Father, Albin! Look! Albin, I will remember this for my mansioning and forever: the smallness of me, the hugeness of them, these two creatures, each with teeth the size of ax blades, sharing fruit, the meekest of food.

Our snack would have been a silent one if not for IT, who held forth on the history of castle building. I learned about the progression from castles on low ground to castles on high, from wooden castles to stone, from few windows to few windows and many arrow slits.

I nodded and said nothing. Count Jonty Um said nothing as well and hardly even nodded. I wished he would speak. I wanted to hear an ogre's thoughts on any subject: castles or cottages or the weather. Or being an ogre. Or shape-shifting. Especially the last two.

But he seemed to live inside a cocoon of silence, the air around him thick with it.

"In sum, the lords of badly defended castles rarely lived to build better ones. Have you eaten your fill, Count Jonty Um?"

He nodded. I hadn't eaten my fill, but I moved the bowls to the floor by the hearth and returned to my seat.

IT held up a claw. "I must have the details, of course, but I know why you've come, Your Lordship. You are in danger."

CHAPTER THIRTEEN

He stood fast. "No danger."

ITs tail tapped the floor, an irritated sound.

After a full minute, during which the count stared over my masteress's head, he sat again. "No danger. Nesspa, my dog, is missing." He gestured at the dog, who still slept by the door. "Sheeyen isn't mine. She belongs to the castle."

And the castle belonged to him. But I understood. Sheeyen wasn't his pet.

"Your missing dog is but one aspect of your danger." ITs smoke tinged violet.

Count Jonty Um folded his arms. "Only Nesspa concerns you."

Masteress Meenore reared up on ITs hind legs. The tail

thumps were louder; the smoke darkened. "I am not a sorcerer, Your Lordship. I cannot deduce from nothing. If you conceal your circumstances, I will return to toasting bread and cheese."

Count Jonty Um stood to leave.

I didn't want him to leave us and perhaps lose his pet forever. "What does Nesspa look like? Is it a girl or a boy dog?"

"A boy. Big, up to my knee. His coat is gold."

"He has a beautiful black nose," I said. "I saw him."

The count crouched almost to my level. "When he sees me, he wags his tail. When he sleeps, he snores, like this." He growled in the back of his throat.

I held my breath. For a moment I thought he was going to turn into a dog, but he sat again and didn't shape-shift.

IT sank back down. "Might he have run away?"

His Lordship shook his head and sat again. "He never has. He is six years old." He paused. "Things have happened, but no danger. Only hatred of an ogre."

I nodded.

"The hatred is nothing new," IT said. "What *is* new?"

"Someone is stealing from me. Not just taking Nesspa." He paused again. I suspected he thought out each sentence before saying it. "Stealing things. Linens, a wall hanging, a harness, three knives."

"Ah," IT said.

"Someone is poaching. Maybe the same person. I don't

allow hunting in my woods. My deer and rabbits used to come to me. Now they're shy. Two mornings ago when I awakened, Nesspa was gone. He always sleeps on my bed."

"A servant?" IT asked.

"They're loyal."

I swear I felt IT think a snort at the certainty. "No one has sent you a ransom note."

"No one." He opened the drawstring on the leather purse at his waist and drew out a silver, which glinted between his thumb and forefinger.

Masteress Meenore ignored it.

"When you find Nesspa, I will give you three more silvers and one for your assistant."

For me? A silver? Two more and I could apprentice.

"My fee for finding your dog is two coppers."

"The silvers . . ."

They both turned to me.

"Never mind." But I wanted my silver.

"If I discover the people or the person endangering you," IT said, "and put an end to your risk, then I will expect payment in silver."

And a coin for me, too. Say it!

IT didn't.

"Why do you say I'm in danger, Meenore?"

"The hatred, which is nothing new, as I said, has always been tempered by fear. Now someone, or more than one, is unafraid. That"—IT spread ITs claws, palms up—"is your danger."

I felt frightened, but I wasn't sure why. How could anyone hurt him?

"Tell me, Your Lordship, what is the reason for tomorrow's feast?"

He looked down at his hands. "I want people to visit me. And His Highness will make an announcement."

My masteress waited in vain for an explanation of the announcement.

His Lordship met ITs eyes. "Most of all I want them to come."

"Ah. Are you permitting your guests to bring cats?"

He reddened and nodded.

Why? Cats *were* a danger.

IT said, "To persuade fools to visit you, you agreed to foolish demands."

What did IT mean?

His Lordship mumbled—actually a quieter roar—"There will be dogs in the hall."

"Naturally. If they may bring a weapon, you must have a defense."

Oh. His guests had refused to come without their cats.

He clasped his hands so tight the knuckles whitened. "I want them to stop fearing me. And hating me. My steward suggested a feast. If they come and are safe, I hope the fear and hate will stop."

But why did they fear and hate him? I had lost my fright by being with him for only a short while.

IT stood. "I will endeavor to find your dog and save your life. Elodie will live in your castle for now, as my eyes and ears."

Lambs and calves! I went to the cupboard for my things.

IT added, "Take care, Elodie. Count, His Majesty and Her Highness are visiting you, are they not?"

"Yes."

Oh no, the king!

"Elodie, His Highness is economical. He has no fear of an ogre and likes the count's wood better than his own to keep him warm, the count's food better than his own to feed his gluttony."

"The girl Elodie is to reside in my castle?"

What was wrong with that?

"Good."

I smiled as I folded my spare kirtle into my satchel. If he liked, I could teach him the mansioner's tales.

He stood. "What will she do?"

"Your kitchen will need extra hands for the feast. Elodie, your hands will do if you can peel an apple, not merely weep over it."

Naturally I could. I drew tight the satchel strings. "But Masteress, the town knows I'm your assistant."

"Tomorrow, as I cook my skewers, I will mention that I let the count borrow you for a handsome sum."

Only serfs could be loaned out, and I was no serf. I hated for the count and the entire town to think me one.

"Your Lordship," IT said, "Elodie must have the run of the castle and your grounds. Let your steward know."

Count Jonty Um took his cloak and pulled it around him.

"Elodie, this is your charge." IT raised ITs snout and blew a long column of white smoke. "Seek the dog, yes. But above all, be alert to danger to His Lordship. Raise the alarm if you are alarmed. Do not hold back."

"What about the poaching?" I asked.

"Leave the poaching to me. And if Nesspa is not inside the castle, I will find him outside."

Count Jonty Um crossed the lair and picked up the end of the dog's chain.

"Farewell, Your Lordship. Elodie, I will come to the outer ward at dawn tomorrow for your report." IT raised ITs eyebrow ridges. "Do you know where the outer ward is?"

"The area between the castle and the walls that surround it?"

"Just so, although these walls are called curtains. Do not disgrace me."

I thought of my disappointing history as a caretaker of geese. And now I was to caretake an ogre!

Outside, clouds had begun to roll in. His Lordship

started down Lair Street, to my surprise. I had expected him to follow the ridge and avoid the bustle of the center of town. After a few steps, he slowed to my pace.

I walked on his right, Sheeyen on his left. The street was deserted here, so he didn't have to call his warning.

"I'm not a serf, Your Lordship."

He nodded.

"Your Lordship?"

He stopped.

"May I ask . . ."

"Yes."

I breathed in deeply. "Why don't they like you?"

He sat on his haunches. I still had to look up to see into his eyes.

"My father was not a kind ogre." He shook his head. "My mother was not kind to people, either. They didn't eat anyone. We don't eat humans. But they liked to frighten when they shifted shape. Fifteen years ago a child died. It was an accident, but it was my father's fault." He watched my face.

I didn't blame the son!

"The townsfolk think I am like my parents. They don't know any other ogres."

So he wanted to show them the difference, and they didn't want to see. I touched his cloak over his knee. "I understand."

We continued on, passing burghers' homes. A young woman with a broom stepped out of a doorway. As soon as she saw me, she hissed, "Save yourself. Run!" and darted back inside.

I reached up and took the count's hand. We proceeded past the next house and the next. A cat crossed the street in front of us, its head turned toward the count. Sheeyen trotted along silently.

"Nesspa would have barked."

The midafternoon bells tolled. The stalls and the throngs began.

"Make way. Ogre and girl."

"Not captive," I cried. "New servant at the castle."

He turned on Sabow Street, which led to the market square. In the square he let my hand go and made purchases—first a string sack, then food and more food: lamb pottage, fish golden with saffron (the rarest spice in the kingdom), boiled eggs, legs of roasted capons, pickled blue carrots, cheese, and bread. How my stomach rumbled.

No one hated him when he opened his purse. People nodded, chatted, thanked him.

My mouth watered. When he stopped the roving marchpane seller, my mouth became almost a fountain. He bought a dozen pieces and paid out two dozen coppers.

With a bulging sack, he started up Daycart Way and resumed his cry of "Make way." He continued blaring until we reached the wealthy homes again and the crowd had thinned to nothing.

We passed through the town's south gate and continued on. To the east, the mansioners' carts caught the light of the setting sun. As we took the north fork, I heard a shout followed by a laugh.

"They're rehearsing." And I am in my own mansioner's tale, I thought, accompanying an ogre to his castle, where the drama will occur.

When we had passed perhaps a quarter mile beyond the fork, with empty, harvested fields to our left and right, the count stopped.

"Your Lordship?"

"Watch. Do not be afraid. Everyone likes this." Eyes closed, he let Sheeyen's chain go and raised his arms in a gesture of command, like Zeus in a myth, calling forth lightning. His mouth widened in a silent scream, and his eyes bulged.

I *was* afraid! Had an arrow struck him from behind? I ran around him. No arrow, but he was clearly in pain. Sheeyen sat on her haunches and howled. I picked up her chain.

He shook from side to side and forward and back, becoming indistinct, a blur of motion—a shrinking blur. He was my height, then smaller, smaller still.

CHAPTER·FOURTEEN

is Lordship's arms fell to his sides. The vibrating slowed and stopped. His cloak and tunic hung in heaps and folds over the narrow shoulders of a monkey, an animal I recognized from an illustration in Mother's only storybook. The monkey was hardly bigger than a fox, his miniature ivory face fringed by coarse orange fur.

He smiled infectiously, showing his teeth and gums. His amber eyes were merry.

I had to smile back.

He removed the count's clothes and shoes while grinning as if at the silliness of lavish attire, or attire at all. When he emerged, I saw how delicate he was—thin arms, thin legs, and a scrawny chest showing through his frill of fur. All the luxury was in his long bushy tail, which curled up at the end. He stood half erect on his two back legs, with one fisted hand on the ground.

I touched his arm to feel the fur, which was as rough as an otter dog's coat. As I stroked, a spark passed between us. The monkey threw back his head and panted, laughing, I thought.

Something had to be done with his clothing. I began to fold each item while wondering how I could fit it all into my satchel and then carry it as well as the sack of food.

I rolled his belt and tucked his purse—still heavy despite all the purchases—between his hose and his tunic. Meanwhile he bounced on his bare feet, chirping like a bird, adding a screech, a *choo*, and a sucking sound.

"I wish I spoke monkey language, Your Lordship." I folded the cloak and added the huge shoes, soles up, to the pile.

The pendant lay on the ground, apart from the rest. I hid it in the toe of a shoe.

Night would fall soon. Were we safe out here, where Two Castles's thieves might kill us for the pendant and the purse? A monkey who took five minutes to transform back into an ogre would be unable to defend us, and one dog wouldn't be enough to hold off a gang.

The monkey sat in the road and pulled apart the strings of the sack.

Sheeyen tried to stick her nose in, but I pulled her away.

"Your Lordship, we mustn't stay here. Robbers and bandits may come."

He chittered and patted the ground next to himself in a gesture that said as clearly as a word, *Sit*.

The monkey was a count. I sat.

No. I was human, and he was a monkey.

The road stretched along a low rise. In two trips, tugging Sheeyen along each way, I carried everything down the western slope to a spot low enough, I thought, that we wouldn't be noticed in the dark. The monkey followed, then sat again, pulling me down next to him. Together, we watched the sunset turn the sky gold and scarlet.

Chirping, he took a packet out of the sack and opened the burlap covering to reveal lamb pottage.

"Sit, Sheeyen," I said.

Pottage was humble food, but delicious: grain mixed with beans, a chopped onion, a little shredded meat, shaped into a ball, wrapped in a square of linen, simmered with other wrapped packages of carrots, celery, beets. At home we'd eat the pottage and vegetables atop a plate of stale bread with broth spooned over. At the end we'd break off pieces of our plates and devour them, too.

Here there was no broth, but the pottage was moist, with more meat than I was accustomed to. The monkey and I shared it, feeding each other by turn, as people do.

He ate daintily but as much as if he were still ogre size. I gave Sheeyen a little at first, too, then ignored her. After a while she lost hope and slept.

"Your Lordship, are you awake inside your present shape?"

For answer he twittered, but his eyes met mine in a way I had seen in no other animal. Perhaps he could understand and remember. I had questions, and I hoped he would answer them when he could speak again.

But before I could say anything, he pulled another packet out of the sack.

Lambs and calves! This was the saffron fish, as golden as if King Midas had touched it. The monkey held a chunk to my lips. I tasted, spat it out, and wiped my mouth on my sleeve. Ugh! Gold itself would taste better. How could people enjoy saffron so much?

The monkey's shoulders shook. He took a great handful of the awful mess and crammed it into his mouth. After he swallowed, he smiled and pointed at his teeth, now dyed yellow.

I couldn't help laughing.

Next he brought out pickled blue carrots. As we ate, the stars and the moon rose. I drew my cloak tight around me. The monkey jumped up, fetched the ogre's huge cloak, and draped it inexpertly over my shoulders, making his panting laugh and ignoring my protests that it would get dirty.

I covered my head with the cloak, which enfolded me, and inside I was as snug as if I were in the lair.

We continued eating. The sack collapsed as its contents slid into our stomachs. In the back of my mind, I was aware of the marchpane still remaining. No matter how much I ate, I would make room for it.

Between bites I spoke. "Pardon me, Your Lordship"—I cleared my throat nervously—"I have a few questions. . . ."

He went on chewing.

I asked about the dog, Nesspa, what his habits were, what he dined on, whose company he kept in addition to His Lordship's.

"My guess is"—I thought aloud, deducing or inducing or using my common sense—"that you don't often change shape, because changing hurts so much." More to myself than to the monkey, I said, "I wonder why you did with me."

He reached across the sack of food and pressed my hand. Had he become a monkey because he liked me, and the monkey would show the feeling more clearly than the ogre could? A lump grew in my throat. Love lay back in Lahnt with my family and Albin. Goodwife Celeste seemed to like me, but she'd as much as told me to stay away. Masteress Meenore appeared to like or dislike me according to my usefulness.

After a moment he let my hand go and fed me a chunk

of bread, which, more than the saffron, told me how it might feel to be rich. If you were rich, you could chew this bread without paying attention to how sweet and tangy it was. You wouldn't close your eyes as I was closing mine and savor each bite, because you could have more whenever you liked.

I returned to my questions. How long could he remain an animal? Forever, if he liked? Or for only a few hours? Did he have to stay shifted awhile before he could switch back? If he changed into, for example, a rabbit or an owl, did other rabbits or owls know he wasn't really one of them? Did he choose the sort of animal he would change into, or did it choose him?

Question everything. Could he get stuck inside an animal? Could magic force him into a shape and keep him in it?

"Is it strange to be yourself again after you've been a monkey?"

When the sack was almost flat, he drew out the small packet and opened it. Marchpane! I made out the shapes—strawberries, roses, tiny apples, daisies.

"May I sample one?" I heard awe in my voice.

He twittered. I took that as consent. If he'd snatched the packet away, I'd have taken that as consent as well and snatched it back.

I picked a rose and nibbled it. Oh, heaven. Father! I'm eating marchpane that no one stepped on.

I held the remainder of the rose out to the monkey, who took it and gave me an apple. Soon we finished the marchpane between us. Despite his ogre's appetite, he let me have most of it. When all was gone, he lay back and stared up at the stars.

"Can you find the constellations?" I lay back, too. "They're all from mansioners' tales, you know." I pointed as I spoke. "There's Cupid as a cherub and Thisbe's apple and Zeus's lightning rod."

The monkey chittered.

I let out a long breath. "Your Lordship, I came here to become a mansioner, and I will still be one someday."

He panted softly, perhaps chuckling at my ambition.

"I will be. Albin says I have a gift, and he mansioned everywhere, before counts and kings, although not King Grenville or you." I was off, telling a monkey about Albin and Mother and Father and Lahnt and the geese, telling him more than I'd told Masteress Meenore, despite ITs endless curiosity.

When my life's story ran out, I just watched the stars and smelled the earth around us until, not meaning to, I fell asleep.

When I woke, I smelled stone and saw darkness. Terrified, half asleep, I raised my arms. My fingers encountered only air. Ah. I had not been entombed. My fingers discovered that I lay on a pallet bed. A woolen blanket covered me from neck to toe. No, three blankets. My nose and ears were cold, but the rest of me was cozy warm. Whoever put me here—the monkey? the ogre? a servant?—had considered my comfort.

My eyes adjusted to the dark. I found my satchel a few inches from my head. Nearby, someone snored a barrel-chested snore. A woman's voice mumbled from a dream.

The room was vast, vaulted, Count Jonty Um's great hall, no doubt. I hadn't been in a castle since I was a baby, when Mother and Father presented me to the earl of Lahnt, but Albin had performed in castles. I had his descriptions to draw on. Although each castle was unique, he said, they resembled one another, like cousins in the castle family.

In the dimness, I surmised I lay among the servants' pallets, with my pallet in the middle of the group. The best places clustered close to the hearth, where a few embers still glowed. Against the opposite wall, another hearth also smoldered. High above us, slitted windows made a dotted line near the ceiling. From my low vantage point, I saw small squares of blue-black sky.

There would be lower, larger windows, too, recessed into the wall of the inner ward, the courtyard at the heart of the castle, but I couldn't see them from here.

My mind refused to return to sleep. The pallet next to mine might be occupied by His Lordship's enemy, the dog thief and poacher. Or the snorer might be the one. Or the mumbler. In some neglected castle nook, Nesspa might be whining and gnawing at the bars of a cage.

What better time than now to look for him?

I rose to my knees and found that I had been sleeping in my cloak. At the foot of the pallet, my shoes pointed away from me. I pulled them on, stood, and threaded my way between the sleepers.

As I walked, the rushes scattered across the floor swished, but no one stirred. I sniffed the air. The rushes had been strewn with bay leaves. How rich! How like a castle!

I paused to decide where to go. During the day, as I'd been told, the emptiness would be filled by trestle tables and benches and bustle. But now the furniture leaned against the wall. Ahead, in a row on a dais, stood three chairs, two human sized, one built for an ogre. Of the two, one chair gleamed silver, the other gold. The third, barely visible in the gloom, was wood.

Three doors always exited a great hall. One, at the end of the wall on my left, would lead to a tower, which would hold a donjon for supplies on the lowest floor and a residence above on the next two stories. The door on the wall to my right would open into the inner ward. The third door I couldn't see, but it should be behind the screen in the corner ahead, and this would take me into the kitchen, across which I would find another door to another tower.

Where to hide a dog? Perhaps in a tower or in the stables.

Statues win no races and find no dogs. I should decide and go.

The towers adjoining the hall would be most convenient to search, but also most dangerous in case I made a noise. I rejected them for now. Tonight I'd investigate the kitchen tower.

I tiptoed behind the screen to the door, which groaned as it opened. I stopped breathing and waited, listening for sounds of waking.

What would they do if they caught me?

Silence. I slipped through and left the door ajar, so it wouldn't groan on my return.

Now I was in a short passageway; castle walls are so thick that rooms are separated by little tunnels. I entered the enormous kitchen, only slightly smaller than the great hall.

Door on my right, but not the tower door. Dimly outlined shapes of tables, stools, benches, buckets. At last, to the left of the sink, the tower door.

I pressed my ear against it. Through the thick wood, I thought I heard a thud and a whine. I pictured Nesspa, hiding from thudding feet, whining in fright.

Of course the explanation was likely more innocent. The castle steward and his family, for example, could live above the donjon. Someone might have risen to use the garderobe and stubbed his toe.

This door opened noiselessly. A stairway rose to my right. Ahead, beyond an open doorway, a light flickered in the donjon. Grain sacks piled twice my height faced me, parted by a narrow aisle. Except for the aisle, the sacks butted one another, leaving not enough room between them for a rat, let alone a big dog.

The donjon wouldn't contain just grain, however. I started down the aisle. After perhaps ten steps, the piles ended, and I saw a candle in a holder on the floor and a monstrous shadow flowing across rows of barrels, the shadow bigger by far than the ogre.

I backed away. Don't hear me! Don't see me! Whatever sort of monster you are, be deaf and blind!

Safely out the tower door, I sped through the kitchen and across the great hall to the servants' pallets, where I turned about, looking for the biggest sleeper.

There. I knelt at his side and shook his shoulder. He rolled over. I shook harder.

He raised his head. "What?" Then he leaped up, tucking his blanket around his waist. He wasn't as tall as he'd seemed from above, but he was muscular, with a hairy chest and a graying beard. He grasped my arm, whispering, "Who are you?"

"Someone is in the donjon."

"By thunder, who are you?"

"The new kitchen maid." I repeated, "Someone is in

the kitchen tower donjon. Or something. It's big."

His grip tightened. "How do you know?"

"I know." What else could I say? "I saw."

He half dragged, half lifted me out of the hall, making much more noise than I'd have dared. No one woke. In the kitchen he took a long knife from a chopping table. "This will do. By thunder, it will do for you if no one's there."

"Hurry!" I said, terrified of whatever was in the donjon and almost as terrified of this man.

But at the doorway he paused, yanked me up to his height, my feet dangling. "The steward hired you? By thunder, I'll—"

"Not the steward." My arm hurt! "The count said more help was needed for the feast. His Lordship brought me."

He let me go. I staggered sideways as he flung the tower door open. I pointed down the grain aisle at the glimmering light. He tugged me along.

I saw the misshapen shadow again. He saw the person making the shadow.

"Your Highness." He dropped to his knees. "Pardon us."

I looked beyond the shadow and saw a tall woman with stiltlike limbs, thin shoulders wrapped in a blanket, thin hands holding the blankets, trailing sleeves, a head in a cap circled by a thin golden crown. I fell to my knees, too. The king's daughter, Princess Renn.

CHAPTER FIFTEEN

"Beg pardon." I bowed my head.

"You have a knife? Against me?" Her voice rose in pitch until it cracked, then started lower and rose until it cracked again. "Enemies from Tair!"

The knife thudded to the floor. "Not from Tair, Your Highness. From right here. She"—he pulled my head up by my hair—"by thunder, she said there was an intruder in the donjon."

I saw the princess more clearly. She had a heart-shaped face, cleft chin, small mouth, and a long, sloping nose. She might have been pretty if her blue eyes had been merely large, but they were enormously large with too much white. If she missed beauty, however, her mouth was sweet and her big eyes full of feeling, both fear and outrage.

"Who are you?"

He pulled back his shoulders. "Master Jak, His Lordship's chief third assistant cook, Your Highness."

Princess Renn's lips twitched in a hint of a smile. She turned to me.

"I'm *Ehh*"—I extended the vowel even longer than a Two Castles person would—"lodie, the new kitchen maid." If they were going to oust me or imprison me, they should know my proper name.

In the silence, I listened but heard no dog whimpers, no scrabbling paws, no panting.

"*Eh*lodie," the princess said, "why did you come to the donjon?"

Feigning innocence, I said in a rush, "I'm the new kitchen maid and I woke and couldn't fall back to sleep and I've never been in a castle before and thought I might look around and I'd heard that His Lordship lost his dog and if I could find it, it would be a fine thing and I came here and I didn't see you, Your Highness, I saw your shadow." I pointed.

The shadow still hulked. Princess Renn was thin, but the blanket expanded her. Her shadow suggested a bearlike creature with a tiny head.

She laughed and held out her arms, making the shadow even bigger. "La! Look at me!"

My shoulders relaxed in relief. Master Jak laughed, too,

although his laughter sounded forced.

"I am afraid myself of myself! Jak, rise! *Eh*lodie, rise! Spread your arms."

Papa and mama and daughter monster shadows filled the donjon. Master Jak's laughter turned genuine.

When our laughter subsided, the princess said, "I commend you both on your courage. *Eh*lodie! To come back after you'd seen the monster! And Chief Third Assistant Cook Jak! To brave the monster with only a knife! Jak, you may return to your well-deserved rest."

But I might not?

Master Jak picked up his knife. As he backed out of the donjon, his eyes were on me, and their expression was not friendly.

"*Eh*lodie, stay awhile. We are both sleepless, and my maid is snoring. I should like company."

How would I be company for a princess, unless she wanted to hear about mansioners' plays or the antics of Lahnt geese?

When the door closed behind Jak, Princess Renn held her candle up to my face. "La! You are a child!"

"Fourteen, Your Highness."

"You are not a minute past twelve." She frowned. "You don't sleep in a cap?"

"No, Your Highness."

"But during the day you wear one?"

127

"No, Your Highness. On Lahnt, where I come from, only married women and men wear caps, except in winter, when we all wear them."

"But you live here now. Are you too poor to own a cap?" She put so much feeling into *poor* that I almost wept for myself.

I shifted from my left foot to my right. Probably everyone who'd seen me since I'd arrived thought of me as The Girl Too Poor to Own a Cap. "I will save to buy one."

"You can have mine. I have others. Here." She raised her hand to her head. I saw a gold ring on her middle finger. As her sleeve fell away, two gold bracelets gleamed in the candlelight. "Hold this." She removed her crown and held it out to me.

I took it. How strange she was. Kind, very kind, but strange.

And the crown was strange in my hands, dreamlike, unexpectedly heavy for such a thin band, only an inch or two wide, without a single jewel. The metal had the sheen of moist skin, the upper rim unexpectedly sharp, the lower smooth. For a mad moment I imagined running off with it.

She donned her crown again and put the cap on me. "You have a small head." The cap's flaps nearly met under my chin. "But you'll grow into it." She inspected me, her face close to mine.

I smelled cardamom oil, the same perfume Mother wore.

Woe invaded her voice. "Oh! It's too fine. They'll think you stole it." She walked in a circle in the small clear space among the barrels. "My maid has several caps, which would do, but I don't want to waken her." She put a hand on a barrel. "Might there be caps in a barrel?"

"They probably hold pickles or some such, Your Highness." The stores were for a siege, and no one could eat caps. I took off the cap, but I wanted it. "I can turn it, Your Highness."

"What?"

I spoke louder. "I can turn it."

"La! I heard you. Turn it?"

A princess wouldn't know what ordinary folk did. "Some people, when their caps are worn, turn them on the other side where the fabric is less used. No one will think me a thief in a turned cap."

"Then I may give you the gift! *Eh*lodie, you are clever." She kissed my forehead.

Lambs and calves!

I reversed the cap and tied it back on.

"Let me." She tied the strings twice more. "There. This is how I tie my cap. Now you will not lose it. I believe in thoroughness. See?" To my astonishment she lifted the hem of her kirtle. "Two chemises underneath. Thoroughness. Now let us search for Nesspa together. For Jonty Um's sake, we'll put our sleeplessness to use. Where shall we look, *Eh*lodie?"

"The stables?" The count had probably searched there—and here—but the dog might have been taken somewhere else first.

"Excellent. The grooms will be asleep. La! Hide an animal among animals, like hiding a ring in a mountain of rings."

Nothing like hiding a ring among rings, but I didn't say so.

She held out her hand. "We'll go there now."

How courteous she was, to clasp the hand of a kitchen maid.

We left the tower. The princess walked with a bounce as we crossed the inner ward and passed between two apple trees laden with fruit.

"He will be so happy if we find Nesspa." She stopped, tugging me to a stop, too. "If we find Nesspa, I want to bring him to His Lordship. I want him to be grateful to me alone."

"Yes, Your Highness." I could give no other answer, although I wanted Masteress Meenore to be known as the finder, through me. "Do you . . ." She seemed friendly enough to answer a question. "Do you hold His Lordship in high esteem, Your Highness?" I wanted to know if anyone did.

"Certainly I do. I esteem him very much!" We walked

again. "He is taller than I, wealthy, with excellent table manners."

So much for true esteem.

"The miller's son, Thiel, is also taller than I and possesses fine table manners, but he isn't wealthy."

My Lahnt table manners might not be good enough for Master Thiel.

"Jonty Um is handsome for an ogre, don't you think? Not so handsome as Thiel, I suppose. Do I esteem Jonty Um?" She raised her arms and twirled, kicking an apple across the courtyard. "Father has betrothed me to him, *Eh*lodie. A king always betroths a princess."

My mouth fell open. Hastily, I closed it. News of the coming marriage had not reached Lahnt. I wondered if it was widely known here and if my masteress knew. Few in Two Castles could be pleased.

We started walking again.

"I shouldn't have told you. It's still a secret. Father wants wealth, a strong arm in battle, a lion if need be, and I like a strong arm, too." She laughed. "And a gentle lion. La! He is lovely as a monkey. I do not fancy him as a bird."

I didn't know what to think. Would they be happy?

We reached a door and, to the side, a descending stairway. I stopped, not knowing which we wanted, door or stair.

"You are ignorant, *Eh*lodie." Her voice was gay. "The stables are below."

Twelve steps down took us to another wooden door. I eased open the bolt, hoping not to awaken any sleeping stable hands. As soon as the door cracked an inch, I smelled the familiar farm odors.

Oh. Hot bran. I whispered, "An animal is ill." Hot bran and something else that smelled sharp and stung my nose.

"La! Very ill?"

How could I tell from the scent of a poultice? "I don't know, Your Highness, but someone is likely to be tending the beast."

I heard voices, one of them a lilting, "Honey, honey." Master Dess!

"What should we do, *Eh*lodie?"

Leave? Sneak in?

Neither. She was a princess and could do what she liked. "Perhaps Your Highness might enter, announce your presence, say you were sleepless, wanted air, and heard voices."

She nodded eagerly. "I can do that."

"You might ask what's amiss. I'll wait a minute and come in after. If anyone notices me, I'll say I lost my kitten and—"

"Jonty Um allows no cats."

Of course not. "Er . . . my pet pig."

"Do you have a pet pig?"

"No, Your Highness."

"Aha! Subterfuge." She flung the door open.

I jumped away from the doorway.

She strode inside.

I peeked in and saw her march through a wide aisle between animal stalls. "What's amiss?" she cried. "I was sleepless, heard voices, and wanted air."

Not quite right, but who would question her?

I slipped in, mansioning myself as a shadow. This end of the stable was in deep gloom, but I saw fireplace glow far to my left, and tallow lamps shed smoky light on a distant stall straight ahead, where two men stood.

"Your Highness?" The speaker wasn't Dess, and his accent was neither Two Castle nor Lahnt. He pronounced his *h* as *ch*, *ch*ighness.

I peered over the gate into the first stall along the aisle, where a sow and her piglets slept, nestled together as neatly as a mended plate. No Nesspa.

Princess Renn cried, "Is one of the beasts ill? Desperately ill?"

Had we happened on another affront to His Lordship, someone injuring one of his animals? The sow grunted in her sleep.

The voice with the new accent said, "Your Highness, a stable is no place for a lady."

"A princess is not a lady." She sounded indignant. "They are entirely different. Who are you?"

"Gise. Head groom, Your Highness."

I shrank into the shadow of the stall as Master Gise advanced toward her. If I moved, he would certainly see me.

"The matter is well in hand, Your Highness. Master Dess, the animal physician, is tending the beast."

Master Dess, the animal physician?

Of course he would be. Perhaps he'd been on his way to a sick animal when I'd seen him outside the king's castle.

"I should like to observe, now I'm here."

"As you wish, Your Highness."

They started off. I waited a minute or two before moving. Then I followed, peeking into horse stalls, cow stalls, and another pig stall as I went.

But if Nesspa were here, he would bark or whimper, unless he was asleep or unconscious. Or dead.

Princess Renn and Master Gise walked toward the lamplight, past a corner stall and the intersecting aisle.

"Sickness or injury?" the princess asked.

"Flying goat spiders, Your Highness," Master Gise said.

"On a goat? I must see."

I reached the corner stall. As I turned left toward the firelight, I knocked over a broom, which landed with a soft thud. I froze, my heart booming in my ears.

"What was that?" Master Gise said.

"La! I heard something fall over."

Was she addlepated? Did she want me caught?

"I'll go and see," Master Gise said.

I eased open the next stall I came to. Crouching, I backed in with my eyes shut, as if I'd be unseen if I couldn't see.

"It must have been only a mouse," she said. "No need to go."

"I'll be just a minute."

"Stay, Gise. I need you to hold her head. There, honey."

Thank you, Master Dess.

"The bites are blue and green and puffed, like moldy bread." Princess Renn's voice quivered. "The pitiable, hapless goat."

I opened my eyes and turned to see what animal I had joined. No beast, but a man sprawling on his side across the hay.

He lay with his back to me, his shoulder inches from my thigh. I had been lucky not to bump into him. He didn't stir, quite a sleeper to slumber through the dropped broom, Master Dess's visit, and the princess's up-and-down voice. Could he be . . . ?

I knelt over him. His chest rose and fell. Drunk, perhaps.

As I rose, I saw him better: golden hair bronzed by the darkness, firm jaw, muscular arm. And on his finger, a ring of twine.

Master Thiel?

CHAPTER SIXTEEN

Yes! Master Thiel. How sweetly he slept, as deeply as a child.

Was he one of the count's grooms, or did he have no other place to lay his head? My heart went out to him if he had no home.

My heart went out to him if he had a dozen homes. Quietly, I left the stall.

"Do you treat Jonty Um when he is ill?"

"Princess, His Lordship is not a beast."

"He is tended by Sir Maydsin," Master Gise said, "as you and your father are."

"La!" I heard embarrassment in her voice. "I meant when he is a beast. Have you ever tended him when he was a monkey?"

"No, Your Highness. Hush, honey. I meant *hush* to the goat, Your Highness."

Where might Nesspa be hidden? And if I found him, what would I do?

"What are you putting on her?"

"Bran, Your Highness."

If it was just bran, what was that sharp smell?

I entered a large open area. Ahead, on the outer castle wall, firelight cast a red glow and provided faint illumination. My view of the fireplace itself was blocked by carts and trestles topped with harnesses and saddles. This would be the likely spot to hide anything.

The princess's voice twanged. "Why is she rolling her neck so?"

"There are many bites, Princess. She is very sick."

A thorough search would take hours. I began by peering into the blackness under the nearest cart, but seven snoozing dogs could be there and I wouldn't see them.

I tiptoed to the fireplace and saw the expected: three stable hands sleeping on their pallets. Mustn't wake them. I picked my way silently between two of them and found the poker. But on my return, I accidentally tapped a slumberer's shoulder with the toe of my shoe.

Luckily, he faced away from me. He rose groggily on one elbow. I stopped breathing.

For a full minute he didn't move, but then he rolled

onto his stomach, and I tiptoed away.

I used the poker to probe gently under a cart. No Nesspa, so I climbed into the cart itself, which turned out to be a bench wagon for bringing guests to the castle. I felt beneath the benches. My fingers encountered no animals, but they brushed against a morsel of fabric, which I picked up. By feel it was a pouch, holding nothing heavy, perhaps holding nothing. Still, its owner might want it. By feel again, I opened my purse and stuffed it in. In the morning I would try to find the owner.

As I climbed out of the cart, I heard a bleat and then a groan from deep in the stable.

"Alack! Is she dying?"

No one answered. Then, finally, Master Dess said, "The goat is dead."

Poor creature.

"Dead? Deh-eh-eh-d!" Princess Renn wailed.

A horse neighed. I groped under another wagon, then climbed in and explored. The cart was empty but for a thin layer of straw.

"In the morning," Master Gise said, "I will have the carcass removed and inform His Lordship."

"Dead people are called *remains*," the princess said. "Why should a beast be called a *carcass*?"

It did seem unfair. I hoped Nesspa wasn't a carcass. I looked under an overturned wheelbarrow. Nothing.

"Princess," Master Dess said, "in death the goat will be treated with respect. I swear to it."

They were silent until Master Gise said, "You should return to your apartment, Your Highness."

Her voice rose. "*Should?* I think I should stay with this goat and mourn her death. You both may go."

Lambs and calves, she was good! Presence of mind, Father would have said. Master Gise and Master Dess would leave, and she and I could search together, but I'd have to warn her about waking Master Thiel and the stable hands.

"Your Highness, Master Gise lives here, and I will sleep here as well tonight."

They would pass me on the way to their pallets! I crept toward the aisle of stalls. I had to get out, and quickly.

"Then I will stay only a minute or two and let you have your rest. Will you join me in an *Eh*lodie—oh! I meant *eulogy*—to these remains."

Did Master Dess know my name? I couldn't remember.

I tiptoed by the carts as fast as I could go.

"We must leave this life"—her voice rose on *leave*, a signal for me, as if I needed one—"all of us, whether goat or grasshopper, child or chicken, person or panther, human or heron. . . ." She was entirely carried away. I hoped she would continue until I escaped.

While she named more pairings, I reached the middle

aisle we had entered through and worked my way past the stalls. As I went by, I peeped into Master Thiel's stall for a second glimpse of him. The stall was empty. I halted, squinted, looked away and back again. Still empty.

". . . and even an ox or a camel or a bumblebee may be mourned. La! Perhaps not so much a bumblebee."

Had I looked in the wrong stall? No. There was the broom I'd knocked over. Had I imagined Master Thiel?

"The goat will surely be mourned. Maker of goat's milk, giver of goat cheese, happy in life, she deserves these few words in her memory."

I neared the doors.

"Now, masters, I will let you finish the night in sleep."

I was out. I flew up the stairs and waited for her in the inner ward.

What would I do if Master Gise or Master Dess decided to escort her to the donjon?

She came out alone. "Was I not quick-witted to secretly tell you to leave? Did you find Nesspa?"

I nodded, then shook my head. "I may have missed him in the dark."

She patted the top of my cap. "You did your best." She yawned. "I shall continue the search tomorrow. Go to your bed, *Eh*lodie, and I will go to mine."

I went to my pallet but not to instant sleep. A servant nearby moaned from a dream. At home, Albin was a quiet sleeper. The cottage was small, cozy. I would be tucked into bed, a pallet there, too, nestled in our little house tight against our mountain, thrice snug and sheltered.

And thrice loved.

I rolled onto my side. What had I learned tonight?

That the princess was kind and gave away caps and was going to marry an ogre despised by her subjects. That Master Thiel and Master Dess could pop up anywhere. That Master Dess was an animal physician. That a dog was not easily found. That, so far as I could tell, I had discovered nothing to help my masteress deduce or induce and nothing to keep His Lordship from harm.

CHAPTER SEVENTEEN

Awareness of the meeting with my masteress must have awakened me while my fellow servants still slumbered. My eyes felt gritty from too little sleep. I sat up and straightened the princess's cap, sliding the bows from my left ear to my chin.

The fire had died down to nothing. I placed my satchel under my mattress and tidied the blankets over the lump. The pallet would be stacked, but I didn't know where, so I left it. I owned nothing to interest a thief.

Hugging my cloak, I exited into the inner ward. At the well I splashed my face, although a little water wouldn't pass for cleanliness with IT. Then I ran through the postern passage, an arched tunnel to the postern door, which opened onto the west side of the outer ward.

Dawn hadn't yet come, but the growing light revealed a fishpond to my right and a double row of fruit trees along the outer curtain, the castle's outermost wall.

Where would IT land? Each side of the castle was a quarter mile long. Had IT come down already on the other side? IT wasn't in the sky, and I might be expected to deduce where IT would land. *Enh enh enh.*

I smelled not a whiff of spoiled eggs. I started toward the back of the castle, reasoning that IT would be unlikely to land in front, where the gatehouses were and where guards might come swarming out.

As I rounded the tower, I saw ahead three fenced-in herb and vegetable gardens. Along the inner curtain bloomed Lepai rosebushes, which can flower through a light frost.

Ah, there IT was, flying from the west. IT sailed over the outer curtain, then wheeled to and fro just as the sun rose.

"Masteress!" I cried.

The tip of ITs tail flicked, in recognition of me, I supposed, but IT continued to fly, swooping here and there. When ITs face turned toward me, I saw a wild grin.

IT landed in the middle of the ward with ITs right claw outstretched. ITs left claw held three filled skewers.

I heard a terrified *yeep!* As I watched in horror, IT raised a fat brown hare to ITs flame. A minute later, IT held out the roast.

"Would you like a haunch, Lodie?"

I shook my head and kept half the ward between IT and me.

"Then come and eat your skewers. Breakfast will be gone by the time you return indoors."

I rushed close for the skewers—uncooked—then backed away.

IT sat, placed the hare on ITs thigh, and carved the meat with ITs talons.

"Are you the ogre's poacher?" I blurted.

ITs smoke blued. "I induce and deduce flawlessly, but occasionally I forget common sense. I should have let the rabbit live." IT devoured ITs meal quickly, bones as well as meat. "I am no poacher"—ITs smoke whitened, ITs discomfort over—"not since I gave up catching and toasting young maidens." *Enh enh enh.*

I smiled, although I imagined a squirming, shrieking girl in ITs claws. My fear of IT surged back.

"Lodie . . . come closer." IT held my gaze.

I went, but slowly.

"Answer me. Even if you are a budding mansioner, I will know if you are lying. Do you believe I might roast a person?"

I swallowed. I wished Goodwife Celeste had never frightened me.

ITs smoke was bright pink, ITs scales red. "Angry as I

am right now, am I flaming at you?"

I shook my head.

"I could broil you and eat you, and your parents would not know and no one here would care. . . ."

His Lordship might care. "You told me to doubt everyone."

"Yes, but test your doubt. You slept in my lair unharmed for two nights. And during one of those nights, you were grimy and flea ridden. Awareness of your dirty state troubled my sleep."

When I'd been awakened by the roaring, IT had been soundly asleep.

"Yet I did not harm even a lobe of your ear. Alas, you are almost as filthy as before, for all that you now have a cap." IT lowered ITself onto ITs belly, keeping ITs head high. "Tell me what has happened and what you have learned."

The most important news first. "Her High—"

"Wait." IT lumbered to the outer curtain at the end of the herb gardens.

I followed, munching on bread and cheese, no longer afraid.

"The castle has ears, but the outer curtain is deaf. Now, speak."

"Princess Renn is to marry His Lordship."

"Start at the beginning, Lodie."

I did. Under ITs prompting I recalled details I would have forgotten. For a mansioner, this was fine memory training. Still, I didn't remember enough to satisfy IT. I had a sinking feeling of failure, just as I used to about the geese.

When I raved over how sweet the monkey was, IT held up a claw. "Emotion is of no consequence."

But it was! "Please, Masteress, listen. He is a kindly ogre under his gruffness."

"Inconsequential." IT asked a dozen more questions about the journey to the castle, then progressed to my meeting with the princess. IT *enh enh enh*ed endlessly over the monstrous shadow.

"If people in Two Castles know she is to marry His Lordship," I said, "they must be furious. No one in the town wants to be ruled by an ogre someday."

"I agree." IT went on to questions about what had taken place in the stable.

Finally, when I thought I might pass the rest of my life in the outer ward, IT asked, "Is there anything else?"

My mind squeezed itself until I had a headache. Oh! How could I have forgotten this? "Master Thiel was sleeping in the stables. He slept through Princess Renn's shrieking."

"Or seemed to."

I blurted, "Masteress, is he in need? Without a home?" Suffering? Could I help him?

"His father left him nothing and gave the mill and the mule to his brothers, but never fear. Thiel will make his fortune through marriage. Half the maidens in Two Castles are wild for him. If you have set your new cap for him"—*enh enh enh*—"you had best have more than three tins. Thiel's blood runs noble. His great-great-grandfather, a knight, was the first owner of Jonty Um's castle. Thiel's bride—"

"What happened?"

"Lodie, do not interrupt your masteress."

I apologized.

"Debts, extravagance. Jonty Um's grandfather bought the castle from Thiel's grandfather without regard for the opinion of the town."

Another reason for people to dislike the count.

"Thiel looks much as the old man once did. I do not fancy him for you, so it is just as well you are poor."

I didn't enjoy being teased. "The stall he'd been sleeping in was empty on my way out."

"Mmm. You peered into the same stall of a certainty?"

"I dropped a broom there."

"Think. He may have moved the broom to a different stall."

I blushed. I should have thought of that. "I picked this up in a wagon in the stable." I pulled the little pouch out of my purse and opened it. The contents were only a few half-dried leaves. When I brought them to my nose, I smelled peppermint.

Goodwife Celeste?

"What is it?"

"Peppermint." Had she been in the stables and then gone? I turned the pouch over in my hand, looking for some distinctive mark, but it was plain brown wool of ordinary quality. I thought back to the cog and was certain I hadn't seen a pouch. "Do the goodwives of Two Castles carry peppermint?"

IT held the pouch up against the sun. "A healer might. A traveler might. The animal physician may have dropped it. A goodwife of the town would keep her herbs at home."

"On the cog the goodwife Celeste gave me peppermint leaves. Do you remember I told you that I met her and her goodman when I was proclaiming?"

"Naturally I remember."

I took a deep breath. "I didn't mention that she warned me against you. She said you're moody and might do any-thing if . . ."

IT stretched ITs neck and aimed a puff of fire sky-ward. The flame guttered out before reaching the ground. "Because dragons have fire, we're believed to be hot-tempered."

IT did have a temper.

"Everyone has a temper, Lodie."

"Masteress, she wears a bracelet of twine. Master Thiel has a twine ring. Is there a league of wearers of twine jewelry?"

"Mmm."

Mmm again. I returned the pouch to my purse. "Masteress, I like her, and she may not have been in the stables."

"She warned you away from me!" IT stood on ITs back legs. "I will return at the nine-o'clock bells tonight. As soon as His Lordship's guests arrive, remain with him." IT flapped ITs wings. "Do not let him out of your sight. Trust no one. Keep him safe."

How could a girl keep an ogre safe?

IT circled above me. "You can shout. A person half your size can shout. Act!"

CHAPTER EIGHTEEN

In the kitchen, Master Jak, chief third assistant cook, whom I'd awakened the night before, swore at me for my late arrival, then grinned evilly. "Onions, *Eh*lodie. By thunder, onions." He led me to the long kitchen worktable.

I scanned the room for Master Thiel, but he wasn't there.

"Sit."

I climbed onto a stool next to a sack of onions that rose to my elbow. Master Jak supplied me with a chopping knife, a peelings pail, and a big bowl for the chopped onions. He said a scullery maid would take away the bowl when it was filled and bring it back empty.

"His Lordship likes onions in his soup and onions in his stew," Master Jak said, "and he is devoted to his onion pie.

Don't stop until they're all chopped. By thunder, no weeping into them, *Eh*lodie."

I began. Soon tears were falling into my lap, and yes, into the onions. Weeping made me think of mansioning. A true mansioner won't use an onion to make her cry. I wondered if a true mansioner could conjure happiness and not cry in spite of a mountain of onions. I couldn't.

Hoping the owner wouldn't mind, I took the peppermint out of its pouch and put a leaf on my tongue. The mint helped against the onions, but not much.

The onions and I were stationed at the menial end of the table, far from the actual cooking. At the important end, yards and yards away, a baker kneaded dough, her arms floury up to the elbows. Next to her, another baker rolled out pastry. A scullery maid complained that her mortar and pestle were missing, and how could she pound the garlic and thyme without them? Master Jak told her to find a bowl and a spoon and cease griping.

At his own table, the butcher cut apart a lamb. Blood ran down grooves in the table to a pail on the floor. A small spotted dog—not Nesspa—sat at the butcher's feet, staring ardently upward.

Master Jak and three others stood at the largest of three fireplaces, tending whatever was cooking. I wondered if Master Jak's companions were the chief second assistant cook and the chief first assistant cook and the exalted cook.

I considered whether Nesspa could be stowed here somewhere. The lower half of the enormous cupboard between the two lesser fireplaces was big enough to hold a sheep. As if a fairy was granting wishes, a kitchen boy opened the double doors to get a frying pan, and I glimpsed shelves crammed with pots and pans. I saw no other likely place to hide a dog.

Sharing my end of the table, a boy—my age more or less, cap strings untied, narrow face, small brown eyes—peeled cucumbers.

He winked at me. "I'm in your debt, young mistress, for taking the onions."

I was not partial to winkers, but I winked back. "I'm new, young master. I never saw the inside of a castle before today."

Another wink from him. "A castle's big so a count or a king can bring his friends in and keep his enemies' armies out."

"How clever." I nodded encouragingly. Tell me something that will lead me to Nesspa or that I can tell Masteress Meenore.

"Thick walls, soldiers within, enough food to last a month. If we die, the rats can eat us for another month."

Ugh!

He winked yet again. "If grand folk didn't have enemies, they could live in houses."

If poor folk had money, they could live in castles. "I

never saw an ogre or a dragon before I came to town."

"How do you like them?" He picked up another cucumber.

I'd minced three onions to his single cucumber. "They're both big. I saw the ogre turn himself into a monkey. What a sight that was!"

His smile reached his ears. "He's a fine monkey."

"Do you think him fine as an ogre, too?"

"His *Lordship*"—he stressed the title—"pays better wages than any other master, and never a beating or a harsh word." He winked. "Hardly a word at all. What does that matter?"

"The people of Two Castles seem not to care for him."

"That den of thieves! None of us comes from there. They won't work for him, and we wouldn't work for anyone else."

If all the servants came from elsewhere, then Master Thiel couldn't be a groom or any sort of servant. "They say His Lordship's dog was taken right here in the castle. Who would do such a thing?"

He thrust his head at me, then drew back because of the onions, no doubt. "We wouldn't!"

He had no more winks or words for me. I nicked my finger and sucked the drop of blood that beaded up. Master Jak would see red if the onions were pink.

The castle bells rang midmorning.

A hand gripped my shoulder. "By thunder, His Lordship

wants you to be cupbearer at the feast and pour for him, the king, and the princess." Master Jak turned me on my stool. "Have you poured before?"

The king! "At home, from pitcher to cup."

"At home." He sighed and let my shoulder go. "Pitcher. Cup. By thunder."

The boy laughed. Master Jak glared at him, and he lowered his head and peeled.

"I have a steady arm." But I didn't know how steady it would be, pouring for Greedy Grenny.

"Cellarer Bwat will show you. *Eh*lodie, those you serve should have what they want before they know they want it. Watch their hands, their shoulders, their faces. Even though you stand behind them, contrive to see."

How? I would lean over and spill wine on everyone.

"His Lordship requested you. The princess will be forbearing, but if you spill a drop, even a speck of a drop, on the king . . . By thunder, don't."

What if I did? A flogging? Prison?

A woman's voice called, "Master Jak, do you have the suet crock?"

He called back. "There's another in the cupboard." He put his hand under my chin and pulled my face toward his. I saw his pores, the veins in his eyes, a drop of sweat sliding down his nose. "If you spoil His Lordship's day—if you cause him a moment of grief—you will feel the wrath of a chief third assistant cook. Cellarer Bwat will come for you in a minute." He strode away.

I lifted the half-full bowl of onions onto my lap. With the side of my knife, I scraped chopped onions from the chopping board into the bowl.

Master Jak stood over me again. "I near forgot. After the second remove, before the mansioners perform, His Lordship would like you to recite for his guests."

"Recite?" I jumped up. "Something? Truly? Oh, Master Jak!" I wiped my tears with my fist. "What should I recite?"

"Whatever you . . ." He looked down.

I did, too. Unaware, I'd let my bowl slide to the floor, spilling the onions.

I was sorry, but I didn't care. I was going to mansion!

If I wasn't first sent to jail.

Cellarer Bwat's most prominent feature, his bushy, white eyebrows, stood out from his face. If my pouring went amiss, his watery blue eyes might spring open wide and pop his eyebrows off.

His lips were pinched, his nose a mere button. His head tilted permanently in a listening attitude. He led me out of the kitchen, walking bent from the waist, as if he spoke only to seated people. As I followed, I thought about what to recite.

I could tell the touching tale of Io, who was doomed

to roam the world as a heifer. No, not a good choice, to portray a shape-shifted cow in the presence of a shape-shifting ogre.

"Don't dawdle, girl."

"My name is Elodie, Cellarer Bwat."

The vast emptiness of the great hall had been filled. Boards mounted on trestles and placed end to end formed a table that stretched two-thirds the length of the chamber. A shorter trestle table had been erected on the dais, with the three chairs drawn up to it. Benches flanked the chairs. Neither table had yet been covered with cloth, and the bare, pocked wood looked shabby.

The walls were hung with linen panels, freshly dyed, colors bright. A scene of feasting spread across the outer wall. The diners could pretend the fabric an improving reflection, their persons made beautiful or handsome as they raised tumblers, fed one another, laughed, or sang.

On the opposite wall, the hangings depicted an animal parade led by a lion, ending with a mouse. In the middle I spied a large golden dog, a monkey, a beaver, a boar, and many more. Some of them I suspected of being fantastical: a creature with an endless neck, a striped horse, an awkward beast with a lump on its back as big as a wheelbarrow. I wondered if one was the high eena Masteress Meenore said I'd heard when I'd passed the menagerie.

Among all the animals there was not a single cat.

Servants were placing trestles for side tables. Cellarer Bwat took me to the end of the long table just below the dais, where a wine bottle, a pitcher of water, a goblet, and two tumblers had been placed. On the floor stood a beer barrel with a spigot screwed into its side.

In an urgent, loud whisper, Cellarer Bwat said, "You will uncork the wine with a sharp twist of the wrist." He demonstrated in the air, then gave me the bottle.

What tale should I perform?

I held the bottle in my left hand, the cork in my right, then twisted. Half the cork remained in the bottle.

Cellarer Bwat sighed and called in an even louder whisper for another bottle. "Pull while you twist."

Should I recite the speech of a young siren, newly arrived on her rock, before she has lured her first mariner to his death? It was moving and right for my years.

Cellarer Bwat said, "You will pass the open bottle below the noses, first of His Highness, then of His Lordship, an inch below their noses, no closer, no farther, so they may smell the wine. Do not pass the bottle under the princess's nose."

"Why not, Cellarer Bwat?"

"Her upper lip will grow. Wine has that effect on ladies."

The inner ward door opened. Cellarer Bwat fell to his knees with a crack that must have hurt. He tugged me into a curtsy.

"Stay down," he hissed.

I raised my head to see who'd entered. Cellarer Bwat pushed it down. I had only a moment to take in a tall, paunchy man with shoulders pulled back, wearing a bright red cloak.

The voice was familiar, in a lower register than the one I knew, but just as prone to soaring and plummeting. The speaker could only be the king. "I had hardly awakened when the loveliest breakfast arrived at my door. Scalded milk with honey, neither too hot nor too cold." His voice rose half an octave. "Perfect! Accompanied by two scones, and they were warm, too!"

A retelling of every morsel of his breakfast followed, while Cellarer Bwat and I knelt. From the corner of my eye, I saw the other servants kneeling, too. My neck cramped.

"Now I'm hoping it will be possible to secure a slice of ginger cake on this pretty dish." Porcelain rattled. He'd opened His Lordship's plate cabinet.

"Certainly, Your Highness." A servant must have taken the plate.

Feet and ankles in leather-soled hose entered the area of floor I could see. "What are you two doing?"

"Bowing to you, Your Highness," Cellarer Bwat whispered.

"Curtsying to you, Your Highness," I whispered.

"Before I came in, of course. You may stand."

We did. My eyes were drawn to the king's cap, which was set with rubies and emeralds. He wore no crown, but the rubies formed a band, like a crown, with the emeralds dotting the top of his skull.

"I am training her to be a cupbearer. She will serve you and His Lordship and your daughter this evening."

The king's face reminded me of a pigeon's: no chin, eyes as round as coins, and a down-turned mouth. He and his daughter both had long sloping noses and nothing else alike, lucky for her.

"I see. Excellent. A beginner." Royal sarcasm. He mounted the dais and sat in the golden chair.

I noticed that his tunic, wine red and embroidered with gold thread at the throat, had an oily stain on the belly and caked food on the sleeve.

"You may teach her now. She will pour, and I will drink."

Oh no! My fingers turned to ice.

Cellarer Bwat's face reddened. "But Your Highness, she isn't ready."

"No matter. As I am the king, it will be extraordinarily good practice for her. First I should like a tumbler of water. Water goes best with ginger cake, although our southern Lepai water tastes sweetest. Beer is preferable with plain. . . ."

A servant entered with his cake. The servants who had

remained kneeling rose gradually, as if prepared to lower themselves again instantly.

Cellarer Bwat and I carried the wine bottle and other preparations to the dais table. Then we circled around to stand beside the king. Two more servants struggled up with the beer barrel. Cellarer Bwat held my elbow and guided my hand as I poured water from pitcher into tumbler. Almost inaudibly, he whispered, "Pour slowly, gent—"

"I thought *I* was speaking. I thought I was king, and people were to listen when I spoke."

"Beg pardon, Your Majesty."

How could Cellarer Bwat tell me what to do without speaking?

"No harm done. White wine is best with aged rabbit, an infrequent treat. . . ."

With the king listing beverages and foods, and with Cellarer Bwat's hand under my forearm, I held the tumbler out to His Highness.

He took it carelessly and splashed the front of his cloak. I heard a sharp intake of breath from Cellarer Bwat.

"How clumsy," the king said.

A servant rushed to him with a cloth, but he waved her away.

"It will dry." He raised the tumbler, drank, then spit into my face.

CHAPTER NINETEEN

y mouth fell open, and water and spittle dripped into it. How dare he? "Your Highness—" My voice was indignant.

Cellarer Bwat's foot came down hard on mine.

The foot reminded me that I had rarely mansioned a humble role. I made my voice silken. "Beg pardon, Your Majesty. I regret your—my—clumsiness."

"I forgive you. There is a pink wine they make in . . ."

The king went on speaking and eating between sentences. I wiped my face on my sleeve. After he finished his cake, he called for a bowl of fruit.

Since Cellarer Bwat couldn't use words to instruct me, he held my hands and arms in a viselike grip that barred mistakes. With a mansioner's concentration, I noted every move: how high we filled a tumbler with beer, how high with water, how much wine went into a goblet after the wine had been pronounced drinkable.

His Highness didn't spit on me again, but he thrust out a leg and tripped one of the servants who was going off to fetch a fresh keg of beer. The servant apologized and was forgiven instantly.

I pondered whether the king liked the servant and me better for our humiliation, or liked us less, because he knew he had been at fault, really, each time.

The castle bells chimed noon. My mind drifted back to pieces I might perform. Perhaps a funny recitation would be best. I could tell an animal fable.

After the fruit had been devoured, the king raised the bowl, so a shaft of sunlight hit it. "Such excellent porcelain. See, girl, how the light glints through it?"

He was addressing me, and I didn't dare tell him to call me Elodie. "I see, Your Highness."

"I do not own such a fine piece. I wonder if his is all so good."

Then he sent for a bowl of chicken gizzards. If Greedy Grenny kept eating until the guests arrived, I wouldn't have a moment to rehearse. He licked his fingers after eating his gizzards. His fingers and lips shone with grease.

Suppose I recited the story of Princess Rosette, whose dog stole meat from the castle cook to prevent a wedding.

The tale had three aspects of His Lordship's danger: thievery, a dog, and a betrothal.

Greedy Grenny asked if the ogre kept any apple wine. A servant was dispatched. Meanwhile, the king began cracking walnuts, his latest craving. He had downed six tumblers of water, two of beer, and five half-filled goblets of wine. His insides must have been afloat, but he had given me a great deal of practice. Cellarer Bwat's guiding hand on my arm had gradually lightened. I had learned to pour.

The apple wine arrived. With a flourish and without assistance, I uncorked the bottle and passed it under the king's nose at precisely the correct distance. The king pronounced the wine excellent. "But it is not quite the flavor to accompany walnuts." He frowned. "I must have dried cherries."

I despaired of leaving the hall before the feast began. Humble, I told myself as an idea formed, feel humble. I curtsied so deeply that my trembling legs almost gave way. "Pardon me—"

Cellarer Bwat whispered a cry of dismay.

"How dare you address me? Insupportable!"

Prison for me. But I thought I knew him by now. I used my quaking legs and pitched over to the side and onto the floor, away from the table and his legs. "Oof!"

He laughed and went on laughing, while I tried to get up and made myself fall again.

"You may rise."

I scrambled up, awkward on purpose.

"You have leave to speak."

I told him I was to perform tonight and begged for time to practice. "I would hate to disgrace Lepai."

He gave me leave to leave. Cellarer Bwat's face was purple, I supposed because he would have to pour for the king now. I pitied him, but not enough to stay.

In the postern outer ward, a woman picked pears. I didn't want an audience, so I sped toward the south side of the castle, hoping it would be deserted. As I rounded the corner, three grooms on horseback trotted my way, exercising their mounts. Next to me, wooden stairs climbed to the battlements. I could practice on high, where the wind would carry my voice away.

Sixty-nine steps brought me to the wall walk. I called, "Halloo! Is anyone here?"

No answer but the breeze in my ears. The sun was long past noon. Soon the arriving guests would end my chance to prepare.

For those who've never visited a castle, the inner curtain wall walk is wide enough for two tall men to lie across it head to toe. During a battle, soldiers are stationed here to shoot arrows at an approaching army and to drop boiling water and rocks on an army that's arrived. The soldiers are protected from the enemy by the crenellated battlement, a wall that looks gap-toothed, like a jack-o'-lantern's smile. The tooth is called the *merlon*, the gum the *embrasure*.

But with no battle and no soldiers, I had room to rehearse.

Master Jak hadn't said how long my performance was to be. The tale of Princess Rosette could take half an hour. I couldn't ready myself for half an hour's performance in half an hour!

I strode down the western wall walk, skirting a chimney opening that belched gray smoke. Confine myself to five minutes. Start in the middle of the tale, since everyone knows the whole.

"The little dog"—I cleared my throat—"the little dog, pitying his . . ." No, I should begin at a more thrilling moment. I paced.

Yes! I had it. I climbed to the walk atop the northwest tower. From here I could see the harbor and imagine my voice crossing the strait to Albin and Mother and Father.

"At midnight"—deeper for a narrator's fullness—"while the princess dreamed of her peacocks, the nurse whispered in the ear of the riverboat master."

I paced, considering how to portray the moment when the princess would be thrown overboard.

Below, someone shouted. Hooves clattered on wood. I heard rumbling. The guest wagons must be approaching. I looked down and saw a horse-drawn cart rolling up the ramp to the drawbridge.

I had to protect His Lordship. But oh, I was going to make a fool of myself when I performed.

Six more carts wound up the road, followed by two oxen towing the purple mansion. I supposed the actors were within, the mansion needed only as a conveyance because the troupe would perform inside the castle. My heart rose at the gay sight of the pennants, rippling in the wind.

I started down the steps to the lower northern wall walk. What was that tawny heap on the walk below, snug against the inner gatehouse tower? A guard's woolly cloak?

Whatever it was, it was none of my concern with the count to watch over.

The cloak moved.

I raced down the steps. The cloak thumped its tail.

CHAPTER TWENTY

The dog's back legs were hobbled. The chain around his neck had been tied to a rope, which had then been looped over the finial, a spike atop the merlon. A bowl of water lay near his head. I crouched by him and held out my hand, which he licked. He struggled to stand but toppled, though his tail continued to wag, slapping the ground so enthusiastically it lifted his entire rear.

"Nesspa?" With my purse knife I cut the cloth that hobbled him and lifted the rope off the merlon.

His golden coat was knotted here and there. I had to brush away his eyebrow hair to see an eye, which turned reproachfully up at me. *Can't you tell I'm drinking?*

When he finished, he stood, legs trembling until he

found his balance. His back was almost as high as my waist.

"Come!" The dog trotted ahead of me without tugging. What a smart beast!

I shouted, "Your Lordship," although no one could hear me up here. We started down. Halfway, he must have sniffed his master, because he began to pull. I held on, barely succeeding in staying on my feet.

The gatehouse tower stairs took us down to the passage that led to the outer ward. This was the castle's main entrance, wide enough to admit four horsemen abreast. As I ran, I saw rose petals beneath my feet.

Ahead, their backs to me, a knot of people and the count blocked the passage.

Nesspa was pulling hard enough to yank my arm from my body. "Your Lordship!" I cried, and let the rope go.

The dog cleared a path through the crowd. I followed more slowly.

"Oh! La!"

"Nesspa!" The count let go the chain of his substitute dog—Sheeyen again—and crouched.

Nesspa leaped up, again and again, to lick the ogre's face.

"Nesspie, where were you? Are you hurt?" The count's big hands felt the dog all over.

Sheeyen sniffed Nesspa's rear quarter.

"Who found you?" He looked up, saw me, and beamed his rare, sweet smile.

A man took Sheeyen's chain and tugged her away.

Might the return of Nesspa, His Lordship's protector, thwart the plans of someone here or someone arriving?

Princess Renn leaned over to pat Nesspa's head and placed her free hand on the count's sleeve. For the feast she wore an orange cloak trimmed with royal ermine and an orange cap. "*Eh*lodie, where did you find him?"

Was she angry at me? She had wanted to find Nesspa and have His Lordship's gratitude.

To let her know I hadn't tried to outdo her, I said, "I wasn't searching. I was on the wall walk, practicing for the entertainment. He was tied there."

She didn't appear angry. "You are lucky. Jonty Um, isn't she lucky?"

"I'm lucky." He frowned, while continuing to pat Nesspa. "We searched the wall walk."

I wondered if he himself had searched or his servants had. I looked away from the reunion. My masteress would want me to see everything. Behind the princess, a woman hovered, a woman in middle age, tall but not so tall as Her Highness, the woman's cloak simple but falling in the loose folds of fine wool. The princess's maid, I decided.

A princess's maid could go unchallenged wherever she liked. She might have stolen Nesspa.

Count Jonty Um stood. "Misyur . . ." He beamed down

at the man holding Sheeyen. "He's unhurt."

"I'm glad, Your Lordship."

Was this a friend of the count's? I scrutinized the gentleman: wide forehead, uplifted eyebrows, soft chin, swarthy skin. Warm smile, but that might mean nothing. Prosperous in a blue silk cap.

"Sir Misyur," Princess Renn said, "might we add something to the feast to celebrate?"

Ah. Sir. This was His Lordship's steward. A count's steward would be noble, a knight or better.

His friendly smile widened. "What do you think, Your Highness?"

"A frumenty with flerr sauce. Jonty Um and I love it so. My father as well."

A frumenty was an ordinary custard, but flerr berries grew only on high mountain bushes that rarely flowered. Their taste was said to be sweeter than honey, more mellow than hazelnut, and more perfumed than muskmelon.

Sir Misyur's smile faltered. "The kitchen will do its best." He led Sheeyen across the inner ward in the direction of the stable.

I heard hoofbeats from the outer ward.

"La! Jonty Um, your guests have arrived."

"Nesspa, come."

I followed His Lordship and the princess through the passage. We broke back into sunlight as the first wagon driver reined in his horses. Grooms took the bridles, and servants helped the guests step down.

A few people held squirming cats. I counted ten guests and three cats. I observed His Lordship for a frown at the cats, but his face had lapsed into blankness.

A second cart drew in. First to jump down was Goodwife Celeste's husband, Goodman Twah. With his assistance, she descended.

I positioned myself behind a groom. I'd thought them too poor and not distinguished enough to be invited, but if they were indeed poor, today their cloaks were not—marten fur fringing the collars of both, and Goodwife Celeste's was embroidered with green thread in a pattern of leaping cats. What did she mean by wearing a cat design?

She raised an arm to adjust her cap. Her fashionably long kirtle sleeve fell away, revealing a silver armband, and with it, her bracelet of twine.

A third cart rumbled across the drawbridge.

"La! Here's Thiel!" The princess left Count Jonty Um's side.

How could he be arriving, when he'd spent the night here? And how could he be a guest? Yet there he was, holding his cat Pardine as one might cradle a baby. The cat was decked out in a twine collar.

As usual, I blushed at the sight of him.

Gallantly, he let everyone descend ahead of him, seven

men and women, three young children, and four cats. Two of the men stood as tall as he. Both were fleshier and older, but their eyes were gray, too, and their jaws strong despite plump jowls. Cousins? Brothers? Neither appeared wealthy, but their cloaks were respectable. By contrast, Master Thiel wore his usual threadbare tunic and no cloak. When he jumped from the cart, I saw he wore shoes today, poverty shoes, with a drawstring at the top, like mine.

Blushing, too, Princess Renn pranced to him. "Thiel! Such news we have! Jonty Um's dog has been found. Joy!"

"Great tidings indeed," he said, smiling and moving Pardine to his shoulder.

"Come! You must congratulate him. He will want to hear from *you*." She took the sleeve of his tunic and, like an excited child, tugged him toward His Lordship.

Why would a count care what a miller's son, a mere cat teacher, said? Why had Master Thiel been invited to the feast? Because of his noble blood?

Why had any particular one of them been invited? Had Count Jonty Um invited many more, and these were the only people who had accepted? Had they come as a confederacy against him?

"Your Lordship, I hope your companion has been restored to you in good health."

"Welcome, Master Thiel. Yes, in good health."

"Now Jonty Um is happy," Princess Renn said, "and we all can be happy, too."

Happy, I thought, except for the poaching, the thievery, and the hatred of the people of Two Castles. Happy, except for every cat wanting him to turn into a mouse. Strange happiness.

CHAPTER TWENTY-ONE

I hovered on the fringe of the crowd as five more carts arrived, each one met by the count with a single nod and a stiff smile. He would never win them over with those. The monkey would have done better.

The mansioners rolled in after the last load of guests descended. His Lordship didn't remain to greet Master Sulow, so I couldn't see what interested me most, the mansioners and the lucky apprentices.

In the great hall, King Grenville sat again at the dais. I knew he had left and returned, because his tunic was now blue. From here I couldn't see if this tunic was also soiled.

Once inside, we all bowed or curtsied.

"Rise. Rise. No need for ceremony with me."

I rose and looked around. White linen tablecloths, candelabra on every table, each candle already lit—during daylight! Oil lamps glowed along the walls and marched atop a line of stanchions between the serving tables and the long guest table. Roaring fires blazed in all three fireplaces. Only the sun itself could have cast more light.

A dog and a guard were stationed at each fireplace. The guests spread out, forming loose groups in the open area between the end of the long table and the door. I stood alone, wishing I could eavesdrop, but people were speaking too softly.

Nesspa barked as loud as a box of breaking pottery.

Master Thiel shouted, "Pardine!"

The cat dashed my way, then swerved to avoid me, but I grabbed him by the nape of his neck, and he hung from my hand, peaceable as a fur sack—peaceable, but with a leather purse in his mouth.

King Grenville cried, "What's afoot?"

Princess Renn answered, "Just a cat, Father."

I pried the purse from his teeth. Had Master Thiel taught him this trick? Was Pardine the only cat that knew it? Did Master Thiel indeed have my copper?

A red-faced Master Thiel hurried to me. He took Pardine, whispered in the cat's ear, and set him down. The cat walked away from us in a snaking line across the hall. Master Thiel stayed at my side.

"That's mine." A man stood over me and held out his hand.

I gave him the purse.

The man was one of the two who resembled Master Thiel. He held the purse in a tight fist, and his voice was tight, too. "Father knew what he was about, Thiel."

"Our honored father had the right to judge me, Frair, but . . ."

So this truly was one of Master Thiel's brothers who'd inherited the mill and the mule.

". . . Pardine is just a cat and—"

"*Your* cat." Master Frair's voice was harsh, a judge pronouncing judgment.

"My cat." Master Thiel's voice was velvet over a knife.

I felt afraid until Master Frair strode off to his goodwife.

And Master Thiel smiled down at me.

I smiled down at my shoes.

"Thank you for the rescue. Pardine has been carrying off this and that from my brothers since he was a kitten."

From his brothers and no one else?

"Why, you're the girl at Sulow's mansion, the girl who portrayed Thisbe. Have you found a situation here?"

I nodded, a half-truth. "My name is Elodie," I said, since he seemed to have forgotten.

"Too bad, Mistress Elodie. You should be a mansioner. Sulow never has anyone good in the child roles."

Lambs and calves! If only I were five years older. "Did Master Sulow decide to take you and Pardine?"

"He refused, and so I have no master."

"Thiel!" Princess Renn cried. "Come see the monkey on the wall. It is Jonty Um as a monkey. What a pretty monkey he makes."

I had forgotten to keep my eyes on His Lordship! The count stood safely with Princess Renn, Sir Misyur, and Nesspa, who'd curled up at his master's feet.

"Pardon me, Mistress Elodie," Master Thiel said, bowing and leaving me.

When would he and I ever again converse?

As I watched the count and his companions, the princess ran her hand around the outline of the monkey and chattered and gestured energetically. Sir Misyur nodded along with her words. His Lordship stood erect, treelike, his expression unreadable. If he loved Princess Renn, I couldn't tell.

If he was enjoying having visitors, I couldn't tell that, either.

Master Thiel rocked back on his heels, hands behind his back, speaking, admiring the monkey, I supposed. Pardine padded to him and rubbed against his leg. He picked the cat up. Pardine and the ogre seemed not to notice each other, but Nesspa stood and shook himself.

I looked around at the other guests. What were the

telltale signs of a poacher, a dog thief, a thief of castle sundries? I couldn't guess.

Serving maids entered with trays of tiny meat turnovers. I wondered if I should begin my cupbearing, but no one told me to, so I remained where I thought I should be, closer to His Lordship than to my post on the dais.

Goodman Twah and Goodwife Celeste moved between me and His Lordship. I went to her side. Why? Because I liked her, because I felt safe in her presence, because I could see the count from here, because I distrusted her. I distrusted them all, but she was the only one I could approach.

She must have sensed me, for she put her arm around my shoulder without looking down. Her hand tapped out a light rhythm. Mother used to mark nursery rhymes for me just this way, with a soft hand on my head or my belly.

Sir Misyur spoke into His Lordship's ear.

"Thank you all for coming," Count Jonty Um boomed. He made an awkward try at a joke. "I cannot gather myself, so there could have been no gathering without you."

"La! You are witty."

A few people laughed politely.

"Where is the humor?" King Grenville said from the dais. "Renn and I were already here. He could have gathered us."

Goodwife Celeste's hand stilled on my shoulder.

Sir Misyur cleared his throat, and a dozen men and

women ran into the hall from the inner ward and began to juggle oranges. I had seen juggling with wooden balls, never with oranges. Would they be eaten later or discarded?

"Elodie, how nice to see you," Goodwife Celeste said. "Have you become ennobled since yesterday? Are you Duchess Elodie now?"

I shook my head, embarrassed. "I am to be cupbearer to Count Jonty Um, Princess Renn, and the king."

"Cupbearer? Almost as much an advance as ennoblement. Congratulations! And you have changed masters from a dragon to . . ." I watched her swallow *an ogre* and replace it with "His Lordship."

"You are resplendent, mistress. Have *you* been ennobled?"

She looked down at her cloak. "Borrowed finery. My daughter married well." She indicated a youngish woman a little distance away, a woman of Goodwife Celeste's height and girth.

The daughter's cloak was faded and without fur. She must have lent the best to her mother. The daughter might have married well, but not well enough for two splendid cloaks.

The midafternoon castle bell tolled. The jugglers bowed or curtsied and ran out, leaving behind a faint smell of oranges. A servant, the ewerer, stood with a pitcher in front of the carved wooden screen that shielded the door to the kitchen. Another servant held a basin.

Princess Renn took His Lordship's hand, having to reach up, as a child must to hold the hand of its father. He smiled at her, a smile that seemed dutiful. They made their way to the ewerer, he shortening his stride, she lengthening hers. When they reached him, she held out her hands and scrubbed them as the ewerer poured. The water flowed over her hands and into the waiting basin.

His Lordship washed next and playfully sprinkled water on Nesspa's snout. Princess Renn sprinkled water on the count. His face reddened.

"La! You are so serious!"

The guests formed a line to wash their hands. I tagged along uncertainly and stood at the end. A cupbearer should have clean hands, no?

His Lordship proceeded to the dais with the princess and Nesspa. Each guest washed in turn, many setting down a cat to do so. When the basin filled, a servant emerged from behind the screen to replace it. Likewise, when the ewer spilled its last drops, a servant arrived with a full one.

Would the king be the only diner with dirty hands? Was he permitted, because he was king?

No. Another ewerer and another basin carrier went to him.

"Ah," he said, sounding pleased. "I regret putting you to extra trouble."

After washing, the guests took their seats. Each seemed

to know his or her place. Master Thiel, holding Pardine, sat a few guests away from his brothers and their wives, all of them near the lowly end of the table, far below the salt. He began instantly to converse with the young woman on his right.

Goodwife Celeste, her goodman, and their daughter and son-in-law were situated in the middle of the table, even with the salt.

Fourteen people filled the high table benches: Sir Misyur, the princess's maid, and the most richly dressed and bejeweled of the guests. I identified the lord mayor of Two Castles by the brass chain of office slung across his chest. The mayor and one of the women each held a cat.

Was I supposed to begin cupbearing now or wait for some signal? The ewerer and basin holder left, and I felt alone and exposed. Several yards away, Cellarer Bwat hovered over a table laden with bottles and jugs. I wished he would say what to do, but he just stared pointedly at me, his face purple again.

He must mean I should go. I ran to stand between the king and Princess Renn.

Servants rushed in bearing steaming platters. Some deposited the platters on the tables and hurried back to the kitchen. Others positioned themselves behind the guests' benches at the lower table. Three stood to my right and three to my left behind the benches on the dais, my fellow cupbearers, I supposed.

None of them did anything except join Cellarer Bwat in staring at me. I looked down to see if I'd torn my apron.

Princess Renn said, "La! *Eh*lodie, now you must pour the wine."

"Jonty Um," King Grenville said, "you chose an idiot to pour for us. Though I taught her myself this morning, she learned nothing."

"She will do, Your Majesty," the count said.

"She is not from Two Castles," Princess Renn said by way of excusing me.

My face burning, I reached between her and His Lordship for the wine bottle, which I uncorked in the fashion I'd learned. I passed the bottle under the king's long nose and the ogre's big freckled one, and poured.

CHAPTER TWENTY-TWO

nce begun, I poured well enough. Better than well enough, since the king paid no attention to me. While pouring, I observed for my masteress—and fretted for myself about my coming mansioning.

The guests and their children numbered sixty-eight, and I saw twine jewelry on twenty-four of the adults. I counted eighteen cats, but more may have been out of sight under the table.

The princess alone seemed in a festive mood. The hall was chilly, too vast to be warmed even by the three roaring fires, yet she threw off her cloak, revealing a scarlet kirtle. She talked ceaselessly, emphasizing ideas with grand gestures. Little food passed between her lips, but she shared tidbits from her bowl with everyone on the dais, sending her jeweled knife from hand to hand to the ends of the table.

Her father proffered treats to his neighbors, but he scowled when his morsels were accepted, and everyone soon learned to decline his offerings.

The count's manners seemed perfect to this farm bumpkin. He shared generously and accepted tidbits with good grace. I observed that he and Sir Misyur curled their fingers around their spoons in exactly the same fashion. The steward had taught his master well.

Except for Her Highness, such a quiet feast this was! Even the children behaved with decorum.

Courses surged out of the kitchen. I had eaten nothing since dawn and was hungry when the meal began, but the glut of food exhausted my stomach through my eyes.

Or worry replaced appetite: worry for His Lordship, worry over my approaching performance.

According to Albin, at a banquet every round of three courses, called a *remove*, was followed by an entertainment. According to Master Jak, my turn would come at the end of the second remove. After the first a minstrel sang, accompanying herself on the lute. I guessed her to be one of Master Sulow's mansioners. She warbled in a voice as soft as chamois, and even the princess quieted to hear.

The song began with a knight setting forth,

> *To fight the giant whose shadow*
> *Blotted out the shining sun.*

Giant, she sang, but I suspected she meant *ogre*. From my vantage point behind and to the side, I saw His Lordship's cheeks become mottled red and white. Princess Renn's hand patted his shoulder, but I doubted he was aware of her.

The knight killed seven giants in as many verses. This was the refrain:

> *Be the giant tall as the sky*
> *With teeth sharp as spikes,*
> *Eyes piercing as pikes,*
> *And fists like hammers.*
> *May he roar and thunder,*
> *Yet he will die.*

When she finished, the applause, muted at first, gained strength. The guests at the lower table rose to show their appreciation—and their dislike, perhaps hatred, of their host. I was astonished at their boldness.

Goodman Twah and Goodwife Celeste both clapped enthusiastically, although they lived elsewhere. What reason did they have to despise His Lordship?

He clapped without enthusiasm, ignoring the insult.

The minstrel curtsied and ran into the inner ward.

Princess Renn raised a bit of bread to Count Jonty Um's lips. "I like songs better when no one is slain."

He chewed, his face still blotchy red.

Master Sulow had certainly chosen the ballad. Why?

Three menservants emerged from behind the kitchen screen carrying the feast masterpiece: a roasted peacock. I had heard of this delicacy but never seen it, and wished I weren't seeing it now. It would have looked like any other cooked bird—if it hadn't still had its beak, and if its beautiful plumage hadn't been stabbed, feather by feather, into its crispy back.

"Jonty Um," Greedy Grenny said, "twenty-five dishes thus far, four with saffron."

"I hope Your Majesty enjoyed them," His Lordship said.

"Yes, certainly. The point is, I served only three saffron dishes when the king of Belj visited."

"Fie, Father!" The princess laughed. "Mayn't Jonty Um be more generous than you are?"

Greedy Grenny laughed, too. "He may. I prefer saffron in my belly to saffron in the belly of the king of Belj." He wiped his hands and his face on the tablecloth and stood.

The guests quieted. Servants paused in their serving.

"Loyal subjects, tonight is more than a feast of friends. Tonight will be remembered forever in the history of Lepai. My daughter—"

"La!" The princess tossed her head. Below her cap, her yellow hair flew about.

"Princess Renn has confessed to me her affection for my subject Jonty Um, the wealthiest man, er, the wealthiest *being* in Lepai, after the crown."

If silence could hush, this silence did, as though the world's winds had stilled and all creatures ceased moving.

"Even a king cannot ignore the feelings of his only child."

But she'd told me he arranged the betrothal. What a liar he was!

"I have approved their union. Dear subjects, think how safe Lepai will be with His Lordship defending us. Think how strong we will be with His Lordship leading our attacks. My daughter and His Lordship will wed, and, in due time"—he chuckled—"but not very soon, I hope, Count Jonty Um will succeed to the throne."

Princess Renn threw her arms around the king's neck and kissed his cheek. He looked pleased with himself. Why not? A happy daughter and greater riches.

I discovered I was happy, too. This ogre would be a better ruler than either the king or his daughter. King Grenville had no kindness and the princess was too flighty. Count Jonty Um's character combined steadiness and compassion.

She spun in her chair to her betrothed. Rising halfway, she kissed him on his cheek. "La! It is lucky you are tall."

His arm went around her. It was an awkward gesture, but his smile was certainly glad.

Mmm . . . I thought, wishing I could tell if he loved her. I liked the princess and didn't want her in a marriage without affection. Whatever he felt, however, he would be good to her. Perhaps that was enough.

Sir Misyur cried, "Hurrah!"

The cheer was taken up with gusto by the servants, listlessly by the guests. When the voices died away, Sir Misyur said, "My lord, tell them the sort of king you'll be!"

Count Jonty Um stood.

He should have remained seated, I thought. His shadow crossed the dais and darkened a few feet of the lower guest table.

"My friends . . ." He sounded husky. "My friends . . ."

I looked around the hall. Master Thiel and his brothers raised their knives and ate again. The brothers' wives did the same. Goodwife Celeste turned the twine around her wrist and whispered into her goodman's ear.

"Your Highness . . ." His Lordship paused, consulting the ceiling not far above him, as if words might be written there. He swayed, but steadied himself with his hands flat on the table. "Thank you. My friends . . ."

Princess Renn said, "Jonty Um, tell them not to worry." She faced the guests below her. "He'll be a good king. La!

When he's been king a week, you'll forget he's an ogre."

His flushed face deepened to scarlet. People stopped chewing. Knives and spoons halted in the air.

Let them think about something besides the princess's foolish words. I threw my wine bottle to the floor, hard, so it would certainly break. Purple sloshed on my kirtle.

The crash broke the spell. After a moment of surprise, conversation resumed. His Lordship sat without delivering a speech.

Cellarer Bwat rushed to me with a length of linen and began to mop up the wine and broken glass. I bent to help.

The king twisted in his golden chair. "Did the girl splash me?"

Cellarer Bwat examined King Grenville's cloak hem, where I saw stains as big as my hand. "Not a drop, Your Highness."

Greedy Grenny returned to his gluttony. "Of course I wouldn't have minded being splashed. I never object to anything."

Cellarer Bwat whispered, "Excellent, Elodie. Well done."

I thought this was sarcasm until he patted my hand.

A servant carved the peacock while the second wave of courses issued from the kitchen. Soon I would be called upon to perform. The tale of Princess Rosette seemed too complicated now. But what to do instead? Possibilities ran through my mind, none of them right: too long, too sad, tedious.

As I poured water for the princess, Master Thiel's brother Frair choked. His wife slapped him roundly on the back. He spit out a morsel of food.

And I knew what to mansion: a scene from *Toads and Diamonds*. The tale had no dogs or thieves and not much of a betrothal, so it was little like the present circumstance, but I knew it well enough to perform unrehearsed.

I was still frightened. How mad to debut before a king! And Master Sulow would probably be watching, too. My hands were so slick with sweat, I feared I would drop a pitcher or wine bottle. Yet my feet were numb with cold.

Two boys and a girl of my approximate age began to set up scenery against the wall beyond the end of the long table. They put out a tidy lady's chair, an enormous chair, four pillows.

I deduced the three were Master Sulow's new apprentices. They seemed unremarkable—no flourishes as they set the pillows on the chairs and brought in three large wooden pots planted with rosebushes. Not so much as a glance at the audience. If they were portraying Little Masters Humdrum and Little Mistress Humdrum, they could hardly have done better.

But maybe Master Sulow had instructed them to mansion these vacant characters. The true selves of the apprentices might be much different; they could be mansioning prodigies.

Perhaps they would gladly change places with me if they knew—charged with protecting an ogre, deducing and inducing for a dragon, soon to mansion for an entire court.

The roses they'd brought out could mean only *Beauty and the Beast*. The minstrel had sung about a giant; the mansioners were going to enact the story of a monstrous beast.

What would happen if Count Jonty Um's forbearance snapped?

Nesspa lifted a paw onto his master's knee. I knew what the gesture meant, and so did His Lordship, who stood. If he left, I would have to accompany him.

"Jonty Um, don't go. Can't you send someone? *Eh*lodie?" The princess turned my way. "You don't mind?"

His Lordship looked at me uncertainly.

I couldn't go. My masteress said I mustn't let him out of my sight. Yet how could I refuse?

"La! I forgot! *Eh*lodie is going to entertain us, but you mustn't leave either, Jonty Um. Your guests will be offended, and you want to see *Eh*lodie."

Sir Misyur beckoned a manservant, who hurried to the dais. Thank you, Princess!

Count Jonty Um mussed the fur on Nesspa's head and told the servant, "Don't let his chain go." He bent over and put his face close to Nesspa's. "Come back to me."

Tail wagging, Nesspa accompanied the servant out of the hall. Other servants took away empty dishes and platters.

Sir Misyur nodded to me.

I am a mansioner, I thought. *Toads and Diamonds*. Two sisters, one cruel and ugly, one kind and pretty. I am one. I am the other.

I left the dais and stood in front of Master Sulow's scenery. Be with me, Albin, I prayed. Let His Lordship not regret his kindness.

On shaky legs I curtsied first to the king and then to everyone else. Forgetting to keep the count in sight, I turned my back. Ah. A rose would help me begin. I placed myself so everyone could see me snap one off and pop it in my mouth. Pui! It tasted bitter. I faced forward.

Princess Renn understood instantly and ruined the surprise for everyone else. "Look, Jonty Um! The flower will fall out when she speaks."

But His Lordship's eyes were on the door Nesspa had left by.

Portraying the kind, pretty sister, I fluttered my eyelashes. In a honeyed voice I said, "Dear . . ." I made an O with my mouth, revealing the rose on my tongue.

Light laughter rippled through the hall. I removed the rose, dug a shallow hole in the floor, and planted it, as if the flower, though lacking roots and most of its stem, might grow again.

The laughter deepened. As I stood, I checked His Lordship, who still gazed at the door. Master Thiel laughed. Goodwife Celeste nodded and laughed.

I leaped sideways, turned my cap backward, and screwed my face into a grimace, transforming myself into the selfish sister. My mouth opened as wide as it could. I imagined a Lahnt moonsnake slithering out. Although I tried to say *sister*, my mouth couldn't close for the *s* or *t*. "Ih—" I placed my hands to catch the snake.

The king shouted, "Ha! She's funny."

The laughter rose again. Then it trailed off, and the room fell silent.

A cat hissed. A dog barked. My eyes followed the bark to one of the fireplace dogs, who barked again, without rising from where it sat. I turned to the dais. Nesspa had not returned, and led by Pardine, every cat in the hall was stalking the ogre.

CHAPTER TWENTY-THREE

"Shoo, cats!" Princess Renn cried.

Master Thiel shouted, "Pardine! Come to me!"

Yelling and waving my arms, I ran at the cats, but they ignored me. I scooped up two. One squirmed free. The one I still held spit and tried to scratch.

His Lordship hugged himself, as if he were cold, or for protection. His face looked mottled again. His nostrils flared, and his eyes widened pleadingly.

The guests and servants were motionless, too shocked or fascinated to move.

The count's arms went up. I'd seen this before. His mouth opened wide, and he began to tremble.

Princess Renn shrieked. Pardine leaped onto the table

and crouched, poised to pounce.

I rushed to the dais, tripping over a table leg and hurtling on. When I reached the ogre, I threw the cat I held to Sir Misyur. My arms grasped the ogre's quaking body but couldn't hang on. He was too big and shaking too hard.

"Stop, cats!" I shouted. "Stop, Your Lordship! Stop! Stop!"

The count's features coarsened. His hair grew and thickened. He bent over at the waist as his torso lengthened.

I backed away. Everyone did. I heard screams.

His shoulders broadened, first straining his tunic, then bursting it. I smelled musk. His gold chain snapped with a *ping*. The pendant thudded onto the floor.

The cats froze. Pardine yowled from his place on the table.

His Lordship's front legs—no longer arms!—overturned the tabletop. Bowls and glasses slid off and smashed when the wood came down on them. Guests on the dais jumped off. I jumped, too. The princess held her father's hand and pulled him away.

He shouted, "There's peacock left. Ogre, eat peacock!"

We all scattered to the walls, leaving a throng of cats motionless on the floor or on the tables below the dais. The dogs at the fireplaces kept their places, appearing unworried.

The lion snarled.

Nothing remained of His Lordship but the flush—the lion's cheek fur blushed a faint pink.

No one stirred, every one of us likely thinking the same question: If I run, will he chase?

I watched his eyes—polished black stones with nothing of the count in their gaze. He padded gracefully to the dais's edge and roared.

The sound echoed off the walls, grew, echoed, reverberated, until I thought the castle would tumble down. My eyes dropped from the lion's eyes to his fangs and back up to the eyes. The fangs were not to be looked at!

He blinked, and when he opened his eyes again, I saw awareness in them. He choked off the roar, shook his head as if to clear it, and vibrated again.

But he didn't return to himself. He shrank.

I ran to him again and grabbed the loose skin on his back, but it melted away in my hands.

Pardine took both of us into his gaze. I felt the cat's longing: *Become a mouse. Become a mouse.*

"Don't become a mouse!" I yelled as he continued to diminish. "Not a mouse! Bigger!"

Moments passed. He shrank more. And more.

On the floor, a brown mouse trembled next to the pendant. His whiskers twitched once. Then he streaked toward the kitchen, pursued by cats. People followed, Princess Renn and I in the lead.

I ran faster than she did, but the cats outstripped me. Crashes came from the kitchen. I entered in time to see Master Jak snatch a cat while the tail of the last chasing cat exited to the inner ward.

Count Jonty Um, let me reach you! I bounded across the kitchen. Don't be eaten!

"Wait for me!" Princess Renn cried.

I burst outside. In the inner ward, all was serene under the night sky.

"La! Alack! Oh, la!" the princess wailed. "He's gone!" She sank to the ground.

I crouched, facing her in the dim light, and blinked back tears.

"They'll eat him, my tall Jonty Um."

"No. We'll find him." But I imagined a cat's bloody teeth, His Lordship's anguish, the mouse's little kicking legs. I shuddered and repeated, "We'll find him."

"Alack! Alack!" She wrapped her arms around her knees and rocked.

Master Thiel dashed out of the kitchen. He rushed to us and pulled me up. "It may not be too late."

The princess stood, too. "Go to the barracks, *Eh*lodie. I'll try the gatehouse."

Why the barracks? But I ran there anyway.

In the dark I saw the shapes of trestle beds mounded with their occupants' belongings. No movement. I left quickly and descended the stairs to the stables, a better destination. If the mouse led the cats here, they might startle a dozen ordinary mice and satisfy themselves.

A groom approached me. "What is it, young mistress?"

"Did His Lordship as a mouse . . . Did a multitude of cats . . ." They couldn't have. The scene was too peaceful. A stableboy with a mucking shovel entered a nearby stall. Another carrying a pail moved away from me down the line of stalls.

"No one's come in." The groom's voice tightened. "He became a mouse?"

Master Dess stepped out of a horse stall.

"Master Dess!" He could do anything with animals. I blurted out what had happened.

He hunched down. "Honey, honey," he sang close to the floor. "Come to Dess, honey." Still bent over, he hurried toward the doors to the outer ward.

I returned to the inner ward, now crowded with guests and servants. Sir Misyur, holding Nesspa, was dividing the servants into groups to search the castle. Master Thiel joined the group on its way to the cellar under the kitchen. Other guests called their cats, but he didn't call Pardine.

Two cats came, both ambling out of the kitchen with a well-fed air. My stomach churned.

The princess descended the steps from the battlements. Maybe she thought His Lordship would go where Nesspa had been found, but I doubted a mouse could manage the stairs on its short legs.

Silly as she often was, she seemed a tragic figure now, taking each step slowly, dejectedly, one hand on the curtain stones to balance herself.

Sir Misyur patted Nesspa's head and let go of his chain. "Perhaps the dog will lead us to his master."

But Nesspa just curled up at the steward's feet.

Some thought dogs clairvoyant. If his master were no more, mightn't he be howling?

An early star flickered in the eastern sky. Soon I would have to meet my masteress and confess my failure. Sir Misyur told me and two servants with oil lamps to search the barracks, so I returned there. We peered under every bed and poked every pile of belongings while my ears strained for a cry of discovery outside.

We left the barracks as the castle bells rang nine. A black shape winged ITs way toward the castle.

CHAPTER TWENTY-FOUR

O h, how I wished I didn't have to meet my masteress. I started through the postern passage to
the outer ward but had to stop in the middle,
overwhelmed by a flood of tears. His Lordship had shown
himself to be good, only good. If alive, he was suffering.
If dead . . . I didn't want to think about it. And if he was
gone forever, so was the monkey. That merriment, gone.

I should never have let Count Jonty Um and his dog be
separated. Nesspa would have stopped the cats. I continued
through the tunnel, sniffling as I went. Outside, I hurried
to the back of the castle where Masteress Meenore and I
had met before, but IT wasn't there.

I heard shouts. A plume of purple smoke rose above
the battlements. I ran.

There was my masteress, ITs legs set squarely, ITs wings spread on the ground, blocking the passage that led between the outer gatehouses to the drawbridge. I wound my way among guests waiting to climb into carts.

Flames played around ITs lips. "Someone will answer for His Lordship's misfortune."

How did IT know?

"You will all oblige me by remaining to answer my questions."

Sounding not at all frightened, a man said, "Ask us in Two Castles tomorrow, Meenore. I want my bed."

IT didn't budge.

"I will not buy a skewer ever again if you don't let me go." The voice belonged to one of the men on line on my first day.

IT swallowed ITs flame.

A chorus of protests ensued. My masteress would lose the custom of all of Two Castles if IT didn't let people leave.

ITs smoke blued. IT gave in and rose into the air.

I raced back to where I'd expected IT to land.

Behind me, IT trumpeted, "Tomorrow I will come to each of you. You will not escape me."

Circle overhead, I thought. Give me a few minutes. I didn't want IT to know I'd witnessed ITs humiliation.

I wondered why anyone would tell IT the truth now or tomorrow. The guests were probably hoping for an end to

His Lordship, even if they'd played no part in bringing his end about.

But any of them might have done it. A simple gesture would have been enough. Goodwife Celeste had shown me on the cog how to start a cat stalking. She herself might have given the signal.

I reached the back of the castle and stood panting.

My masteress landed in a cloud of blue smoke. "We are both disgraced, Lodie. I saw you at the drawbridge."

"Masteress, how did you know His Lordship is gone?"

"You just said so." *Enh enh enh.* "Tell me all."

Standing close to ITs warmth, I related everything I could remember. IT questioned me again and again about who said what and where and when and with what expression, what tone of voice, what gestures. Such a misery it was to recite the tale over and over and never be able to change the ending.

As I spoke, weariness struck. I sat on the grass, certain that if I kept standing, my knees would buckle.

"Stand, Lodie. I need you alert."

I struggled up.

"Hold my wing."

I reached out gingerly, afraid of being burned, but the wing was no hotter than cozy, and it was bracing. My tiredness fell away.

"How many guests brought cats?"

"At least eighteen."

"At least?"

"Definitely eighteen." Or more.

"What were their names?"

"The cats?"

"Don't be foolish. The guests' names, the ones with the cats."

IT was being horrible. "Master Thiel brought Pardine. The mayor's wife had a cat. Goodwife Celeste's son-in-law had one. The man whose water you heat." I squeezed my eyes shut in hopes of extracting more from my memory. "I don't know who else."

"I see," IT said coldly.

This wasn't fair! IT should have hired an assistant who knew Two Castles—and left me to starve. "I'm sorry."

"No doubt."

Goodwife Celeste was right about the moodiness.

"Masteress . . . why did Master Thiel arrive with the other guests when he'd been here last night?"

"The correct question is, Why was he here last night?"

I could say nothing to please IT. "Yes, why?"

"We will ask him, now that we know the proper question. Tell me again: You saw no one signal the cats?"

I shook my head. "My eyes were on His Lordship, except when I looked down, where the snake was coming out of my mouth."

The skin above ITs snout crinkled, which I deduced or induced meant confusion.

"The imaginary moonsnake."

"Ah. Go to bed, Lodie. Perhaps you will dream something useful." IT lifted into the sky.

When would I see IT again?

I started toward the gatehouse, although, with His Lordship gone, I no longer had a right to sleep in the castle.

No one stopped me. The guards didn't even look my way. In the great hall, the tables had been taken down. Only one lamp was still lit. By its glow I saw that several servants were already asleep. Others sat up, their pallets pulled close together in clusters.

I wanted to hear the conversation.

My pallet, bulging with my satchel, was an island yards from the others. I carried it to the nearest cluster.

But as soon as I set it down, a woman servant turned around. "Sleep elsewhere."

I chose better this time, placing myself behind Master Jak's broad back, where no one seemed to notice me. Now, if only I had the cupped ears of a donkey for better hearing.

". . . beeswax candles . . . niece . . . Beeswax! Worth . . ." I heard a sniffle, something mumbled.

". . . kind . . ."

". . . Two Castles . . ."

I leaned over the edge of the pallet, set my forearms

down, and pulled myself nearer to the voices. The pallet's wooden frame slid silently on the dirt floor.

Ah. Now I could hear.

"What was the longest he ever stayed a monkey?"

"Two weeks, by thunder." The speaker was Master Jak. "When he grew big again, he half ate the castle out of food. Never lost his ogre appetite."

"Might he . . ."

"Perhaps."

"In a hidey-hole."

"Growing hungry."

"Frightened, by thunder."

Silence fell. These people loved him. I wondered if I'd hear like talk from each cluster and from the sleeping servants if they were awake.

Someone snuffed out the lamp. People became shapes. The murmuring continued. I wished they would talk about the moment before the transformation. Master Jak had been in the kitchen, but some of the others might have served the guests. One might have seen or heard something: a nod, a word, a guest's hand flash in a cat signal.

The whispering began again.

"Misyur will read the will."

"Tomorrow?"

"Not tomorrow, by thunder. We'll keep searching tomorrow. But soon."

"What will become of us?"

Whispering voices sounded much alike. I had recognized Master Jak's only because of his *by thunder* and the masculine rumble under his whisper.

My heart skipped. Could I ask a question and have each think another had spoken?

The conversation moved along. "Will the king let His Lordship's will stand? His Highness wants this castle."

"Two castles in Two Castles, and both his."

"We'll lose our places, very likely."

"I wouldn't serve Greedy Grenny if he got down on his royal knees and begged me."

"He went back to eating after His Lordship turned into a mouse. I won't serve him either."

The murmurs turned to where servants might be needed. Slowly, slowly, I crawled off my pallet, holding my breath, hoping the whispers would cover my tiny sounds.

I wanted my voice to come from within the circle, and at last I knelt between two people. The servants discussed the merits of serving nobility or burghers. I rehearsed what to say and how to say it, while waiting for a pause. If they had gone over my question already, they'd catch me.

My knees grew numb. They spoke of monthly half holidays and wages.

Finally, silence fell.

My heart raced. I counted three beats, then whispered, "Did . . ." Mansion the accent! Draw out the vowels. Pound the consonants. "Did anyone see a signal along the table? A . . . a signal to the cats?"

I drew back.

Pause . . . Pause . . .

They were going to find me!

Pause . . .

"Or a signal from the dais, by thunder. Any of them up there could have done it."

"It happened so quick."

I inched back to my pallet.

"They were lifting tumblers, their knives . . ."

"Feeding each other."

"The princess gave away more than she ate. Not like her father."

"Everyone was laughing at the snake coming out of the girl's mouth. I laughed, too."

"Egad, Master Thiel could have done it. Hates His Lordship."

A female whisper said, "They all hate His Lordship."

"Not so much as Thiel."

"Nesspa would have protected his master."

"Thiel didn't have to signal. Likely he gave the cat instructions. That Pardine is as smart as—"

"We mustn't name folks. We don't know."

"If it was a signal, who could see a wrist flick in all those people?"

"By thunder, I would have seen."

"By thunder, you mightn't have. Somebody could have signaled under the table."

"If one cat saw the signal, all would join the chase."

"Perhaps no one signaled. A cat might just go."

"The dogs at the hearths should have protected him."

"They had bones to chew. He didn't make a pet of any of them."

The voices quieted again, and soon the broad back in front of me stretched out flat. The others settled, too.

I reviewed every remark, my thoughts snagging on Master Thiel. Could he show such courtesy and good humor and still try to murder a person—an ogre?

I hadn't thought the word *murder* before, but if His Lordship had been eaten, then murder it was, and no cat the true killer.

CHAPTER TWENTY-FIVE

 woke suspecting Master Dess, who knew all animals, not merely cats. He could understand the animals that lived inside His Lordship better than the count did himself. Master Dess might share Two Castles's hatred of an ogre, or he might have been paid, and he might have known exactly what the ogre would do in the face of stalking cats.

But he hadn't been in the hall.

He might have been in league with someone who was.

Master Dess, who seemed so kind, might be a whited sepulcher, the worst villain of all, according to Mother.

Or Goodwife Celeste might be the villain. She certainly had secrets, and she'd worn a cloak embroidered with cats.

Oh, not the goodwife. She wouldn't kill. My masteress

told me to doubt everyone, but he also said to use common sense. Common sense ruled out Goodwife Celeste.

But it didn't rule out Master Thiel or Master Dess.

When I entered the kitchen, no one sent me away. The search for the mouse continued, although I wasn't able to take part because King Grenville had requested that I wait on him. I almost wept.

Master Jak let me eat a thick slice of bread and then told me that the king was in his chambers in the northwest tower. "Take this to him." He held out a tray loaded with more food than I would eat in three days. "Egad, I'm pleased His Lordship thought we needed you."

A minute later I rapped on the tower door. A guard admitted me to the first story, which held the castle armory. I knocked again on the second level, and His Majesty bellowed for me to enter.

I never thought I would see a king's hairy legs. He stood at his window embrasure in a silk undershirt that hung to just below his knees.

No guards, only His Highness and I. My heart thumped.

Holding the tray in an iron grip, I curtsied. The dishes rattled, but nothing spilled.

The room was a parlor, not a bedchamber, which must be upstairs. The biggest area was occupied by two benches that faced each other, both piled with pillows, with a low, rectangular table between. A chest butted against one wall and a small cabinet against another. A round cloth-covered table and two chairs kept company by the fireplace, where a fire blazed. I placed the tray on the round table and hoped that was right.

His Majesty stumped to the chair nearest the fire and sat. "Girl, make the snake come out of your mouth again."

I didn't understand. "Your Majesty?"

"When you crossed your eyes and pretended a snake was coming out." He bit into a slice of bread and spoke with his mouth full, white bread and yellow teeth. "That was comical. Do it again."

I stared. He began to frown. I crossed my eyes and held out my arms for the imaginary snake.

He laughed. "A pity you were interrupted. What comes next?"

For once I didn't want to mansion, but I enacted the rest of the tale. When the prince rode in to see the pretty sister, I straddled the spare chair and made it clatter back and forth on its wooden legs. I snapped at the chair's imaginary withers with an imaginary whip.

The king even stopped eating to laugh. When I finished, he said, "To think of you here, performing for me alone! How lucky I am. Again, girl. No, wait. Take my tray and find my daughter. She must see it, too. Bring her a breakfast as well, and I should feel so very fortunate for a leek pie in brown sauce."

The kitchen was half empty. At the long table Master Jak cut butter into flour.

He nodded when I told him what the king wanted. "My pies are half ready. Come back in twenty minutes, and you shall have it. The princess is in the great hall. By thunder, Her Highness has a new idea every moment, and Sir Misyur must listen."

But instead of entering the hall, I cut through the inner ward to the count's apartment, where the door stood open. Inside, a guard sat on a stool along the inner wall with a tureen lid in his lap. Between his feet lay a wedge of cheese.

His chin came up when I entered, and he blinked sleepily at me. Then his hand flew to the hilt of his sword. "What is it, girl?"

I went to him. "I was sent to find Her Highness."

Nesspa lay by the fireplace hearth. His tail thumped the hearthstones. I went to him and patted his head.

What if the mouse was in the walls in this room, comforted by Nesspa's presence?

What if this guard was the cat signaler?

"Not here."

I could see that. "What will you do if a mouse comes out?"

"Clap this over it." He raised the lid.

"Then what?"

"Bring it to Master Dess in the stables."

"What will Master Dess do?"

"He's magic with animals, says he'll know a mouse that isn't a mouse."

"Can he turn the mouse back into His Lordship?"

"Dunno. Maybe he'll cast a spell."

"What is he doing with the real mice?"

"What one does with mice."

Feeds them poison. That's what we did at home, and I'd hated it. But Master Dess might make a mistake! He might even make a mistake on purpose!

I hurried to the stables, guessing that I had ten more minutes at least before Master Jak would be ready.

Master Dess stood crooning in a horse stall just beyond the big aisle. I approached, and he beckoned me in with him. Master Gise, the head groom, entered behind me with a bucket.

"Another mouse." He handed the bucket to Master Dess. "Who is she?" Meaning me.

"A lass from Lahnt. His Lordship took her in."

As the bucket passed between them, I saw a frantic mouse scrambling at the bottom, trying to climb out.

Master Dess reached for it.

He would have his pick of common poisons. Farm folk knew them all: frogbane, tasty false cinnamon, ground boar tusk, apple-pit powder, and the many poisonous mushrooms.

Albin had schooled me in the more exotic poisons that appeared in mansioners' tales, such as murder milk. I knew the poisons that killed quick and the ones that killed slow, those that caused fever or stomach pain or sleep. It had amused Albin to school a child in such gruesome arts.

The mouse stilled in Master Dess's hand.

Let it be His Lordship, I prayed.

Master Dess looked into the mouse's eyes, then shook his head.

Now he would kill it. I snatched it from him and began to run out of the stable with the squirming creature. I'd saved this one, but how many had already died? Had Count Jonty Um been among them?

I was halfway to the door. What would I do with the mouse?

It answered by wriggling out of my hand. I lunged, but it raced into a stall. I gazed after it and fought back tears.

"Honey . . . Girl . . ." Master Dess came to me. "I wasn't going to kill the poor mouse."

"You weren't?" I felt shaky with relief.

Master Gise walked toward us. "His Lordship doesn't let us kill mice."

I should have guessed.

Master Dess touched my shoulder. "Someone will find

the mouse again, or not. It wasn't the count."

"Have you examined the other animals, Master Dess, not just the mice?"

He nodded. "All the beasts."

"I'll see if more mice have been found." Master Gise started out of the stables.

I guessed I still had a few minutes. "Er . . ."

"Yes, honey?"

"The night we arrived in Two Castles . . . you heard someone outside the king's castle, do you remember?"

"That was you, girl? Why didn't you speak out?"

"Um . . . you sounded angry. I—"

"I was angry, honey! After your coin was stolen, a thief took one of my cows, a good cow I had for five years."

"Have you gotten her back?"

"Not yet." His voice was as grim as it had been then.

"I'm sorry." A mystery solved. But the stolen cow was unsolved for Master Dess.

I left the stables.

In the kitchen Master Jak was spooning sauce over the leek pie. He made room for it on a tray that was as heaped with food as the king's breakfast tray had been. "You are prompt to the minute, *Eh*lodie. Hurry. No doubt his royal gluttony is impatient."

As I passed behind the screen to the great hall, my nose caught a faint but biting odor.

Master Thiel sat cross-legged on the floor before one of the fireplaces. The source of the stink, a glue pot, rested on the hearth, and he held together two pieces of a broken bowl.

Master Thiel. Always where least expected.

A glue jar and his satchel lay at his elbow, the satchel bulging with the tools of a plate mender's trade. He was a plate mender?

I surveyed the great hall. The sleeping pallets had been stacked, and the dinner tables were not yet set up. A manservant crisscrossed the hall, strewing rushes from a burlap sack. Seated on a low stool on the dais, Sir Misyur hunched over a writing board on his lap. He dipped his quill pen in ink and scribbled something on a sheet of parchment.

Looming above him, the princess balled the cloth of her skirt with both hands. "Have they checked the wall walk again, Misyur?" Her voice careened up and down the scale. "Have they combed the cellars?"

I should have gone straight to her, but instead I went to Master Thiel. When I reached his side, I crouched and whispered, "Where is your cat, Pardine?"

He smiled, and I almost lost my balance. "Pardine is rented today to a burgher's wife whose own cat recently died." His expression became serious. "Did you think I'd bring Pardine here after yesterday's calamity?"

I blushed. "No, of course not."

"I came to help, but Sir Misyur said all is well in hand, so I decided to mend a dish or two. Even lords need their plates mended from time to time."

I nodded and backed away to the middle of the room, not tripping over my feet purely by accident.

"Misyur," the princess said, "why are you writing when—"

Sir Misyur craned his head up toward her, a tic pulsing at the corner of his eye. "I am recording where the search has been made, what has been found, where—"

"If not the wall walk or the cellars, he would hide in a donjon, where food is plentiful."

"Your Highness," Sir Misyur said, "two maids are circling the wall walk this very moment. Four menservants—"

I coughed. Both of them turned.

"His Majesty requests you." I curtsied.

She let her skirt go and waved her hand. "Requests which of us? No need to bow, *Eh*lodie."

I straightened. "You, Your Highness. He instructed me to bring a breakfast for you." I held out the tray.

"But I'm not hungry, and I'm helping! We're finding Jonty Um." Her huge eyes filled, reminding me of blue-yolked poached eggs.

How wicked I was to have such a thought!

"I'm coming." Her hair bounced below her cap as she leaped off the dais. "My father would not like to know I jumped."

I smiled. "I won't tell."

The king's first words were addressed to me. "Half an hour is not long for a king to wait for his command to be obeyed. How lucky I am to be a king."

Instantly Princess Renn said, "La! I came as soon as I was told."

I flushed. She turned to face me. Under pretense of taking the tray, she mouthed, *I'm sorry.*

Perhaps he did worse to her than he did to servants.

She placed the tray on the table. "I'm sure the cook was slow, Father, not *Eh*lodie."

"The girl has a name? A name in three syllables?"

This made me as angry as anything else he'd done.

"Yes, Father. *Eh*lodie."

"How grand of her. Come here, girl."

I moved a little closer.

He frowned. "Has she come near, Renn? Do you believe she has approached me?"

"No, Father." She murmured. "Perhaps she is afraid."

"Of me? Come, girl. I won't spit at you again."

Not comforting, but I advanced and stopped a few inches from him.

"Most mansioners paint their faces, if I am not mistaken. Extend your face, girl."

I put my face forward and dug my nails into my palms.

"You don't mind my finger in your jam, do you, dear?"

"No, Father."

He dipped his forefinger in. I closed my eyes. He might accidentally or purposely poke one of them out.

"One sister is pretty. . . ." His finger rubbed jam into my left cheek and stroked it across the left half of my lips. "And the other is not." After a moment he smeared something warm on my right cheek and across the right half of my lips.

I licked my upper lip on the right. The brown sauce.

"Mustn't." He applied the sauce again. "Ah. Stand away so my daughter may see."

I opened my eyes.

"Is she not improved?" He didn't pause for an answer. "You would have benefitted from my assistance yesterday, girl. Now perform the piece again."

Shamed tears flooded my eyes. Do not cry, I thought, or he will be glad. I blinked them away and reenacted the scene. I did it well, too, to spite the king and please his daughter.

She didn't laugh until I had the prince search the floor for jewels, my nose just above the wooden planks. But then she did and kept laughing until I finished.

"I am delighted to hear your laughter." His Highness speared a chunk of his leek pie and put it in his mouth. "All but the pie is for you. You are too thin, my love."

She took a hard-boiled egg and picked at it with her fingers.

I backed away. If they ignored me for a few minutes, I would slip out.

"I want you at your prettiest. With the ogre vanished, you still need a husband."

I froze.

"I have chosen a better one."

She swallowed and blinked. "So soon?"

"The night of grieving is over. Now is the day of joy, my dear."

"La! Only it is so soon."

He frowned.

"Is he tall and rich, Father?"

"He is rich. He will be tall. His father, the earl of Profond, is tall."

She swallowed again. "How old is the son?"

"He was born six months ago. Love is deep when it starts early."

"Cruel!" The word exploded out of me. My hand flew to my mouth to snatch it back, but it seemed to fill the entire tower.

CHAPTER TWENTY-SIX

"I—cruel?" the king said mildly.

I looked down at my shoes peeking out from my hem. How worn they were, water stained and grimy. What would His Highness do to me?

"Am I cruel, daughter?"

"You are never cruel. Does the son have ringlets in his hair?" Her voice lightened. "Ringlets are charming."

"I am told he has golden ringlets."

"Will he be handsome, do you think?"

I looked up.

She threw her arms around the king's neck. "You are goodness itself." She raised her head. "*Eh*lodie, my husband will be tall and rich, and he will never turn into a mouse. How happy I am."

King Grenville patted her back. "I'm glad, child."

"And how sad I was a moment ago."

"Eat, my love. The sausages are very fine."

She returned to her seat. "If they are fine, we must share them." She cut off a chunk and fed it to him.

While chewing, he continued. "The count would have been a great help against Tair, but the earl is eager to put money into the undertaking." He seemed to remember my presence. "Girl, you may leave. You will do well to stay out of my sight unless a real snake is exiting from your mouth. That I would like to see."

His laughter followed me out the door.

In the inner ward, I went straight to the well. The jam came off easily, but the sauce had hardened. On my chin I needed to chip away a congealed bit with my fingernail. When I thought I had rinsed the food away, I scrubbed again. I felt dirty under the skin.

From the well I returned to the great hall to ask Sir Misyur how I might help in the search—not to see if Master Thiel was still there, which he wasn't.

Several servants carried trestles to the middle of the hall, in readiness for a meal, I supposed.

"Elodie," Sir Misyur said, looking up. "Nesspa must want a walk. Will you be so kind as to take him to the outer ward."

I got him from the count's apartment, and he pulled me into the postern passage, which was long enough to be dark even in midday.

"Young Mistress Elodie?"

My heart lurched with fright until I recognized the voice. Then it simply lurched. In the gloom, I saw Nesspa leap up to lick Master Thiel's face.

"May I walk with you?"

I nodded, although he couldn't have seen my head bob.

Outside, Nesspa ran here and there, sniffing as I let out his chain.

Master Thiel slung his sack over his shoulder. The coins in his purse jingled. "There is a question I would like to ask you."

The start of a Lahnt love song ran through my mind: *A secret meeting and a secret, a sweet greeting . . .*

"You may ask." How grown-up I sounded!

"In Master Sulow's mansion, what were your thoughts when you pretended to be Thisbe?"

This was his question?

I sighed. "I was very hungry. Remember the bowl of apples? I pretended an apple was Pyramus. I adored that apple."

Nesspa sniffed a patch of grass, then barked and scuffed up clods of dirt with his back legs, after which he tugged me away, following a new scent.

"And last night, when you mansioned the princesses?"

"I simply thought about the fairy tale. When I was the princesses, I imagined myself in their stead." The words repeated in my mind: *I imagined myself in their stead*. The words were important, but I didn't see how. *I imagined myself in their stead*. "Why do you ask?"

"I hope to be . . ."

I looked up.

He was blushing. ". . . something more than a plate mender or cat teacher. Despite Sulow's first no, becoming a mansioner may be within my grasp, and it would be"— he paused—"an exciting life."

No one could be a true mansioner who wanted the life, not the mansioning.

Nesspa raised his head. He sniffed the air, then howled deep in his throat and ran, pulling me helplessly along.

Master Thiel grabbed the chain just above my hand. Between the two of us, we controlled the dog, who continued to strain toward the south ward, keening eerily. We followed, Master Thiel so close to me that my shoulder jogged his side. He smelled of hay—another night in the stable, perhaps.

Was Nesspa taking us to the ogre, safe out here by some miracle?

When we neared the southwest tower, I heard groans above Nesspa's whines. Master Thiel and I stopped restraining the dog and raced behind him.

We rounded the tower. Not many yards away, an ox lay on the ground, bleeding into the grass.

"Get Master Dess from the stable," I yelled. Master Thiel could run faster than I could.

His face was pale, as mine must have been. "Can—"

"Go!" I cried.

He left me at a run.

The blood was seeping from gashes that striped the beast's neck and shoulder. He struggled to his knees, then collapsed on his side, panting heavily. Nesspa wagged his tail and licked the wound.

"Poor thing." I stroked the ox's face. Lepai oxen are mild-tempered. "What happened to you?"

Masteress Meenore could have done this.

A lion could have done it. My hand stopped in the air above the beast's cheek. Had the count turned back into a lion?

Or might this ox be His Lordship?

Master Dess arrived soon, carrying a sack, but Master Thiel didn't come with him.

"Honey, honey. Dess is here." He pressed linen from his sack into the cuts, layer upon layer of cloth until the blood stopped showing through.

"Master Dess . . . is the ox—"

"Just an ox. Girl, put your hands here. I need to move

him." He had me take his place pushing down on the bandages.

"Like this?" I wished my hands were bigger.

"Yes, and don't stop pressing."

No one could move an ox if the ox didn't help, but Master Dess got his hands under the beast and murmured in his ear. The ox groaned and rolled backward a few inches.

"Now your mouth, honey, honey." He eased it open. "Keep holding, girl, girl." He placed a large leaf on the beast's tongue. Then he gently closed the mouth and released me from my task. "If you and Master Thiel hadn't found him, the beast would soon have been beyond my help."

"He'll live?"

"Likely he will." The ox squirmed. "There, honey. I'm here. I'll stay with him now."

I had been dismissed, but I hovered. "Did a lion attack him? Did—"

"I don't know." His voice was harsh again.

I brought Nesspa back to His Lordship's apartment. Afterward I paused in the inner ward, uncertain what to do next.

Voices came from the kitchen. I heard "lion" and stood in the doorway. News of the ox couldn't have reached anyone yet except by way of Master Thiel's tongue.

Master Jak set me to peeling and slicing turnips. The kitchen servants were jubilant, despite the ox. All were certain that His Lordship had been the lion. He lived and would return soon in his usual form. I wished I shared their certainty, but I kept thinking of my masteress killing the hare in almost the same spot as the ox had fallen.

A maid said, "What if he remains a lion? What if he cannot change back?"

"He stopped being a mouse, didn't he?" Master Jak said. "And he never harmed a hair on a human being before, though he was big enough as his ordinary self."

"But," the butcher said darkly, "they'll think the worst in Two Castles. When he's an ogre again, someone will try to kill him." He whacked his chopper down on the neck of a struggling chicken. "By cat or arrow or ax, eventually someone will succeed."

CHAPTER TWENTY-SEVEN

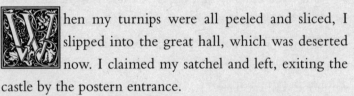hen my turnips were all peeled and sliced, I slipped into the great hall, which was deserted now. I claimed my satchel and left, exiting the castle by the postern entrance.

I started down the track that would take me to the road to town. But after a few steps, I stopped. I couldn't go to IT if I believed IT could have mauled the ox.

Did I?

I stared up at the sky, which was milky with haze across the sun. Not far from here, IT had dropped out of the air to shelter me from the rain.

IT wouldn't hurt an ox. I didn't deduce or induce or even use common sense to decide. Lambs and calves, I trusted IT.

At the menagerie the gate was open again or still open,

but this time two guards flanked it, facing inward.

Although I had planned to go directly to my masteress, I went in under the noses of the guards, who seemed not to notice me. Beyond the ornamental shrubbery, a peacock strutted, its feathers fanned open. I recalled the roasted peacock at the feast.

"One tin for entry!"

To my right a plump man sat on a high stool with a basket in his lap—the menagerie keeper, no doubt. I dug in my purse.

"Everyone must pay. Except the king and the princess and anyone they say doesn't have to pay. Did one of them say that to you?"

I was tempted to lie, but I shook my head.

"An honest girl needn't pay. Honesty is worth a tin. Parade of people today."

Who?

"The princess didn't pay," he said. "And she told me to let that pleasant young man, the miller's son, in for free. They arrived early." He slid down from his stool and turned out to be no taller than I. "Come." He headed toward an avenue of cages and pens. "You want to see the monkeys. Everyone did. No one lingered. They've all gone. I'll go with you myself. Perhaps the creatures are shedding golden hairs."

"Who else visited?"

"His Lordship's steward and the animal physician. Master Dess visited all the animals, stayed awhile at each cage. And half the town came—the tailor, Master Corm, the baker, Master Gatow, and . . ."

Naturally they'd come. As the menagerie keeper listed the townspeople who'd stopped by, I clenched my jaw with impatience. He walked so slowly, and I, too, wanted only to see the monkeys. If His Lordship were anything else, I wouldn't be able to tell, but I might recognize him as a monkey.

Still, I looked around. I had never visited a menagerie before. Some animals were shackled as well as caged, and both the cages and the pens needed cleaning.

I asked the menagerie keeper to point out the high eena, which turned out to be a striped beast, the size of a wolf, who stood motionless in a corner of its cage.

Before reaching the monkeys, we passed an assortment of other beasts: a huge creature with a murderous-looking horn, a yellow-and-blue snake, a dozen ratlike animals with long snouts, and more.

The monkeys' cage was at the end, holding three adult monkeys and a lively monkey child, who climbed the bars of the cage. Two adults sat together, one of them picking through the fur of the other. Across the cage, the third adult lay on its side and seemed to be asleep.

"You've always had three?"

"The third came last year, and the little one was born here."

The monkeys ignored us. Not one smiled at me. I felt a pang in my chest.

"Master, is there more than this?" I gestured at the line of cages and pens.

"No more animals, except the fleas."

We started back to the gate. When we reached it, I bade him farewell and thanked him for his kindness.

"No trouble. Had to get down from my stool anyway. End of day. Feeding time."

"Master? Do you lock the gate at night?"

"Not I. No key. His Majesty's guards do it after I've gone."

The guards might forget sometimes, I supposed. I curtsied and left him. When I reached the lair, I found it empty, so I hurried to the market square, where the marchpane vendor said IT hadn't sold skewers today.

"IT came earlier," she said, "and bothered people with questions about the ogre's feast."

I decided to wait in the lair, but on Sabow Street I saw a column of black smoke ahead and remembered that IT sometimes made the fire hotter for Master Bonay, the blacksmith. I followed the smoke.

ITs shoulders and trunk filled the doorway of the smithy. ITs head was inside.

The shop abutted the town wall, set apart from the line

of houses across the way. And no wonder it was alone: The entire building glowed fiery gold.

Master Bonay stood nearby, holding his poker in his right hand. He turned as I approached, although I don't know how he heard me over the rush of fire. "Ah, the dragon's apprentice."

"Assistant, master."

Ash drifted down on us.

He grinned. One of his front teeth was gone, but the others shone white against his sooty face. "A great day. Meenore the Unfathomable, the Stingy, lights my furnace for free."

Smoke eddied from the side of the shed as well as from the chimney. Curious, I went there and discovered a window. I waved to clear the smoke, peered in, and gasped.

A thick jet of white fire shot from ITs mouth into the forge, the flame roaring as it spewed forth.

How could IT create such an inferno?

Nearby, a man worked a bellows. I marveled that he didn't melt.

Master Bonay spoke into my ear. "I used to pump the bellows." He chuckled. "Better to be a master than an apprentice."

Undoubtedly. I crossed the street to where the heat was less fierce. Master Bonay joined me there, and we waited several minutes while, gradually, the noise dwindled. The shed's incandescence dimmed. A few minutes more and my masteress backed away from the doorway.

"Bonay?"

"Behind you."

IT turned. ITs eyes were paler than I'd ever seen them.

"Bonay?" A set of almost transparent eyelids lifted. IT had two pairs of eyelids. "There you are. Lodie, you are in time to hear Bonay answer my inquiries."

How did IT know I hadn't come on some urgent matter?

"Fire away, Meenore." Bonay laughed at his own joke. *Enh enh enh.*

The smith hadn't been a guest at the castle. Why was IT questioning him?

"Do you believe the ogre is now a lion, Bonay, a lion who mauled his own ox?"

"I believe it. I heard a lion's roar a few nights ago—"

As I had.

"His guests saw him turn into a lion. Only a fool would *dis*believe." He shrugged. "Makes no difference to me if His Lordship the lion is still prowling." He raised his poker. "I have this and my cat."

"Tell me, Bonay, if you have your cat and your poker, why wear an aegis?"

What was an eejis?

Bonay looked down at the bracelet of twine on his left wrist.

"Lodie," IT said, "you've wondered about the twine. We have a saying in Two Castles: *Innocence bares its wrist and trusts its luck. Guilt wraps its wrist and trusts no one.*"

I understood. The twine bracelets were a protection from harm—for people who had done harm.

Goodwife Celeste wore twine, and so did Master Thiel!

"Guilt isn't the only reason to wear a bracelet, Meenore. I need protection from fire, a roof beam collapsing."

"I fly over town at night when the mood strikes me. Most houses are asleep, but your shed is awake. Who is giving you silver and gold, Bonay?"

The apprentice emerged from the shed. "The fire is hot enough, Master."

"You may use the tongs, Gar. You're ready. I'll come in to see what you've done."

The apprentice disappeared back into the shed.

"This is none of your affair, Meenore."

"We have a bargain."

He relented. "Burghers in debt bring me silver some-times. Occasionally gold."

Violet smoke rose from ITs nostrils. "Burghers in debt take their precious metals to a jewelry smith. Who really brings you silver and gold? Do not lie to me."

"I didn't agree to be insulted. I answered your question. My obligation is discharged." He shifted the poker from his left hand to his right. "You are all smoke and no fire, Meenore."

234

IT grinned. "Two Castles boasts three blacksmiths, but the king sends all his sword work to you. Why is that, Lodie?"

Bonay's face was still sooty, so I felt rather than saw him pale. I cast about for an answer.

"I pay for your services!"

"And the others would as well. Lodie, Bonay has the king's custom because Bonay's fire is hottest."

And the fire was hottest because Masteress Meenore heated it.

"I will ask once more: Who brings you silver and gold?"

"Do not say I told you."

"I make no promises."

Bonay dug his poker into the dirt and rocked it back and forth. "Thiel brings me silver."

I swallowed a gasp.

"And when they come to Two Castles, a Goodman Twah and his Goodwife Celeste bring both gold and silver. They come infrequently, but they bring a great deal. I don't have to pay them as much as I pay Thiel, who bargains hard."

"Anyone else?"

Anyone else I admired? The princess? Sir Misyur? Master Dess?

"Just those three—Thiel and the old couple."

My masteress wouldn't let me into the lair or listen to any of what I had to tell until I had washed myself and laundered my clothes. The sky had darkened to night by then, and I was damp and cold, but the lair warmed me.

An area between the cupboard and the door had been curtained off. Curious, I approached the curtain.

"Leave it be, Lodie."

I backed away.

The cheese and bread were in bowls on the fireplace bench.

"I have new cheese. Tell me how you like it." IT threaded skewers and toasted them in the fireplace, one for IT, two for me. "And we still have a few figs and dates from His Lordship's visit. They are in a bowl in the cupboard. Fetch it."

I wondered if IT had saved the delicacies for me.

When the skewers were toasted, I sampled the new cheese, which was sharper than any I'd ever tasted. "Mmm. Delicious."

"Make more skewers if you like." IT settled on ITs belly, ITs head and neck along the floor between me on the bench and the hearth, ITs eyes on me. "And tell me everything."

I did so, ending with my visit to the menagerie.

IT raised ITs head. "When you found the ox, you saw nothing of a lion?"

"Nothing."

"The grass around the ox had not been disturbed? You saw no tracks?"

"The grass was bloody, but not torn up."

"Why is this detail important, Lodie?"

I imagined a lion, stalking a grazing ox. The ox smells something amiss, lifts his head, turns. Sees the lion. The ox gallops. The lion is faster and springs. The ox swings his horns, misses the lion. The lion's teeth rake the ox's shoulder. The lion's claws scratch.

I closed my eyes tight and screwed my face into a grimace, feeling the pain of the ox.

The ox whirls, trying to get free, sending up great clods of dirt and grass.

"Oh!" I opened my eyes.

"Yes, Elodie?"

"There was no lion."

CHAPTER TWENTY-EIGHT

"Was there a dragon? Did I do it?"

I didn't have to think. "There would have been a struggle as well. You didn't do it. But I knew that already."

The ridges above ITs eyes rose. "Ah. You have already exonerated me." IT sat up and picked ITs teeth with a skewer. "Undoubtedly the attacker planned to create signs of a struggle. If Nesspa had not barked and given warning—unintentionally, certainly—you might have caught him or her at it. Someone wants the folk of Two Castles to believe in the lion, and most do believe, save us deep thinkers."

"Then who or what attacked the ox?"

"Yes, who? Who indeed?"

I considered. "A person with a rake. Someone the ox

trusted. Someone he wouldn't run from."

"But who? You stayed in the castle. You may know better than I."

"The stable master Gise . . . The grooms and stable hands. Master Dess, the animal physician . . . no animal fears him. And the beasts may be used to Master Thiel if he often sleeps in the stable."

"You are ready to accuse handsome Thiel?"

To cover my discomfort, I helped myself to a handful of cheese squares. I no longer knew what Master Thiel might do.

IT said, "He was with you. He couldn't have interrupted himself. May he be exonerated too?"

I hoped he might be, but I wasn't sure. "Perhaps he was frightened off before I came."

"Then someone else would have discovered the ox."

"Anything might have startled him." I frowned, searching for ideas. "The grooms exercise His Lordship's steeds in the outer ward. At the sound of hooves Master Thiel—or anyone else—would have run without looking back, but the grooms might not have rounded the tower. Then he might have gone with me to discover the ox, which he knew was there."

"That is cold-hearted enough for Thiel. Anyone else?"

I hesitated, hating to say the words. "His Lordship as himself, not as a lion. But why would he maul his own ox?"

"I doubt he did. Common sense deems it unlikely."

I felt tears coming. "He is likely dead, isn't he, Masteress?"

"Common sense says yes, but induction and deduction have not yet proved the result."

I swallowed the tears. "He may be alive?"

"Or dead. We may never know."

I felt like a bird that kept rising and then being thrown to earth.

"I will hate not to know. Not knowing will gnaw at my liver. Dragons have livers, too, Lodie."

"Masteress, whoever mauled the ox wanted to endanger His Lordship, right?"

"I can think of no other reason."

"Does that person know for certain that His Lordship lives?"

"It would seem so, but that conclusion is not proven either."

I sighed, then yawned in spite of myself.

"Lodie . . . when Thiel was mending His Lordship's plates, did you notice his satchel?"

I missed nothing when it came to Master Thiel. "It was at his elbow."

"Did it lie flat?"

"No. I saw the angles of his tools through the cloth."

"Think, Lodie."

I was too tired to think.

IT waited.

The plate mender rarely came to our cottage on Lahnt. Poor people learned not to be fumble-fingered.

What were a mender's tools? A glue pot. Thiel's had been on the hearth. A glue jar. Next to the sack. Two or three clamps, which would occupy little space. I could think of nothing more.

No!

Yes. "Some of His Lordship's goblets and bowls and such were in the sack." I marveled. "With Sir Misyur in the hall, too."

"Thiel is a master thief, light-fingered enough to steal a man's beard."

I smiled at the idea.

Enh enh enh.

"And Pardine is a master thief among cats," I said. "He must have taken my copper."

"Very likely."

"Do you think Master Thiel is the thief His Lordship told us of, who made off with the linens, the wall hanging . . ." I'd forgotten what else.

"Also very likely."

He had probably taken Master Dess's cow, too. But we still didn't know who the poacher was. Or, most of all, who had signaled the cats.

"How can Master Thiel make people like him and then rob them?"

"Speculation exhausts the mind, Lodie."

"Do you think His Lordship discovered Master Thiel's thievery?"

"Possibly."

"And so Master Thiel set the cats on His Lordship and mauled the ox?"

"Perhaps, Elodie."

"Elodie? But I'm speculating!"

"You are deducing."

Deducing when IT called it so, speculating when IT called it so. How happy I was to be back in ITs company!

"Be wary of Thiel."

I imagined him, not only his form but also his friendliness, his way of setting everyone at ease. "Is he the one you think the most likely?"

"There is an entire town and a castle to choose among."

I couldn't help yawning again.

"You would like to sleep?"

ITs voice had a lilt I hadn't heard before. IT plodded to the new curtain and drew it back.

"Lambs and calves!" Three big pillows mounded under a linen sheet (no blanket needed in the lair). A small pillow lay at one end of the bed—a pillow for my head, such as rich folk had. I ran my palm across the linen, which was smooth as butter. The pillows were soft as white bread.

"I layered straw under the pillows."

I sat. "I'll float!" I had never slept in such a fine bed.

"The straw is fresh. The pillows are stuffed with down, and the linen is scrupulously clean, as are the pillow covers. Good night, Lodie." IT pulled the curtain closed.

"Good night, Masteress Meenore." I shed my kirtle and slid under the sheet in my chemise. My last memory before sleep is of pushing the little pillow aside.

I woke up remembering what I'd failed to report last night.

IT had cooked pottage for breakfast, and IT watched me closely as I put the first spoonful into my mouth. "Do you like it?"

I nodded and managed not to spit out the mouthful, but there were limits to my mansioning.

IT took my bowl away. "I will prepare skewers. What did I do wrong?"

"The beans have to be cooked first."

"Ah. I enjoy them raw."

Certainly, if you can cook them in your stomach.

"You may cube the cheese."

I began to cut. "The princess is betrothed again." I explained.

"Mmm."

I hated *Mmm*! "What do you conclude, Masteress?"

ITs voice tightened, became *mistressish*, as Father would say. "It is not for an assistant to question her masteress."

Mmm, I supposed, was sacred, so I asked something else. "Did you discover anything yesterday before I came?"

"I passed the morning," IT said, not minding this question, "circling the castle, flying low, scanning for a fleeing mouse or any creature behaving in an untoward manner. But if His Lordship in any shape had been north of the castle while I was south or vice versa, I would have missed him. I cannot deduce that he was not there."

"In the fields a hawk or an eagle might have caught him."

"In the afternoon I visited Thiel's brothers. After I threatened to boil away the water in their millstream, they were happy to answer my questions." *Enh enh enh.*

I smiled. "What did they tell you?"

"That Thiel does not live with them, that they know not where he lives, that they saw no one signal the cats, and that they gave no signal themselves. They were abundantly supplied with *no*s, both of them. I peered in a window of the mill house. Every comfort in full measure. Whatever one thinks of Thiel, the old miller was unkind to him."

"If his father had left him anything, he might not have become a thief."

"He stole before his father died, Lodie."

Oh.

The nine-o'clock bells rang.

"Then, in the square, I interrogated this one and that. The townsfolk expect a lion to run up and down the way, dining on people as he goes. They are worth nothing, the lot of them. If His Lordship becomes His Lordship again, he will not last long. He would do better to come back as a lion and really eat them."

CHAPTER TWENTY-NINE

hen we had finished our breakfast, IT announced that we would visit Master Sulow and his troupe. "You say mansioners are observant. We shall find out."

Master Sulow had seen my performance at the banquet. Had he liked it? Had he hated it?

As I walked to the mansions, missing ITs warmth, IT flew to and fro, ITs shadow scribbling across the landscape. Both of us looked for any animal not acting as it should. Most likely we were too late, but we looked.

Finally the meadow ended. I was close enough to see the cats lolling under the mansions.

My masteress landed and lumbered along at my side. "The villain, whoever he or she is, must object to my questions. You may be in danger. I am near invulnerable, but he or she may attack me through you."

I shivered, then felt surprise. IT would be injured if I were hurt?

"My wing is an impervious shield. Seek its shelter if need be. Do not stray far from my side until the danger is over."

I swallowed over a lump in my throat. IT wasn't using common sense. No one would think of harming me to stop IT.

As before, we reached the mansions from the rear. I heard voices calling to one another, the beat of a hammer, the thud of a mallet. Someone laughed. Then came a cry like none I'd ever heard—a bleat, a bray, a deep wail—all three at once.

"That, no doubt, is Master Sulow, portraying himself as a donkey." *Enh enh enh.*

We rounded the side of the purple wagon.

Master Sulow, wearing a bull's mask, strode back and forth before the black mansion. He sounded like nothing human even as he began to blare words: "Whoever imprisons me will die. I am the whelp of a woman, son of a god."

I had it. This was *Theseus and the Minotaur.* Just as at the count's feast, the next entertainment would be about a beast, this time the bullheaded minotaur, portrayed by Master Sulow.

The front walls had been removed from three mansions.

Within the green (for love), trees had been painted on the side walls, and cutouts of trees stood before the back curtain. In the purple (for pomp), a cutout of a castle blocked most of the curtain, and the stage was bare. In the black (for tragedy), the prow of a ship with a single black sail projected from the left-hand wall. Wooden ocean waves, painted blue-green, scalloped the floor.

In front of the mansions a low wooden fence, unfinished, zigged and zagged and was the source of the hammering and pounding. The apprentices I'd seen at the castle were busy building it, one of the boys steadying the fence while the girl hammered and the other boy held a pail, probably containing nails.

Beyond the fence, four rows of benches had been set facing each open mansion. These seats would accommodate those willing to pay extra for comfort. The rest—called the *tin audience*, because they paid only a tin or two—would stand.

A group of journeyman mansioners and older apprentices stood by the closed yellow mansion, closed because there was no comedy in *Theseus and the Minotaur*. I recognized the minstrel from the ogre's feast. The journeymen spoke lines to one another, softly enough that they didn't compete with their master, who was trying his lines one way after another. Now he alternated an animal and a human voice. The first made me fear the beast; the second made me pity him.

Experimenting further, he began softly and rose to a

rage, animal the whole while. Next he gave an all–human reading drenched in bitterness.

He surpassed Albin and all the mansioners I'd admired in Lahnt. Not merely surpassed. The gulf that separated genius from talent stretched between. If he'd accepted me as an apprentice, how much I could have learned!

And if I'd stayed with Master Sulow, I wouldn't have grown to love His Lordship. I'd be free of the grief that traveled everywhere with me.

But I wouldn't have discovered inducing, deducing, and using my common sense.

Master Sulow removed his mask. "Meenore! Young Elodie or Lodie or any other name you prefer!" Holding the mask, he bowed elegantly. "How long have you been watching my wretched attempts?"

Had he truly been unaware of us?

I curtsied. IT inclined ITs head.

"Come! I will not refuse you food today." He led us to the yellow mansion and opened the door. "Please come in, Lodie."

"Elodie."

"Serve us out here, if you please, Sulow. Your mansion is impossible for me, as you know."

I was being protected. I felt embarrassed, as if Master Sulow would guess that Masteress Meenore didn't trust him.

He entered the mansion and returned in a few minutes

with a tray that held a bowl of apples (again), a smaller bowl of dried apricots and walnuts, a sliced honey cake, and a bowl for each of us. He set the tray on the bench in the first row before the purple mansion. Gallantly he motioned me to sit.

I did, and he took his place on the other side of the tray. IT settled ITself before us, positioned to see Master Sulow and his mansioners and to raise a wing between me and an attacker.

The three of us followed the custom of serving one another.

"Tomorrow afternoon we perform the whole of the minotaur tale, not merely Theseus's scenes. It is rarely performed in its entirety, Elodie."

Ordinarily I would have wanted to see the play more than anything, but now I wanted most to find His Lordship—or His Lordship's killer.

IT put an apple in Master Sulow's bowl and ate one ITself, core and stem. "Why more mansioning on the subject of a monster?"

"*More* means more than one, Meenore. We were unable to perform *Beauty and the Beast*."

I burst out, "Your minstrel sang about a giant slayer and a giant. A giant is a monster."

"Young Elodie, my audience is in a mood for monsters. Meenore, would you grill white cheese if your customers preferred yellow?"

"I can turn white to yellow with my flame, and a mansioner as skilled as you can turn anything to anything."

I smiled with pride. How clever my masteress was.

"No one has eaten any walnuts." Master Sulow put two in my bowl and three in ITs.

I passed one back to him.

He cocked his head toward his three apprentices. "One will be a tolerable mansioner if I heckle and hound him ceaselessly. The girl shows promise as a carpenter, which I can always use, but the third might as well be a piece of cheese for all the good he will do me. If you hadn't come, Meenore, I would have sought you out."

My stomach fluttered.

"Why?" IT asked.

"To apologize. I own up when I'm wrong, unlike some conceited dragons."

"I am never wrong." *Enh enh enh.*

"To apologize to Elodie." He turned to me.

My heart fluttered.

"I regret that your improvisation for His Lordship's guests was cut short."

"Th-thank you."

"I should have taken you when I saw your Thisbe. I'll be honored if you apprentice with me."

CHAPTER THIRTY

Lambs and calves!

IT said something and Master Sulow answered, but I didn't hear. Instead, my mind numb with astonishment, I turned to watch the other mansioners, who were laughing among themselves. I counted a dozen of them—young, old, fair, uncomely—because there were roles for all sorts.

My masteress snapped, "I pay her!"

I came to attention.

"Alas, the guild does not allow me to pay an apprentice."

"Then make her a journeyman."

A journeyman? I gripped the bench with the hand that didn't hold my bowl.

Silence fell between them.

But IT had said I was in danger and had to remain with IT. Had IT changed ITs mind?

"I will pay her. And you, Meenore, may sell your skewers here."

This was my soft bed sending me a pillowy dream. I was still in the lair. I could say anything. Real mistakes were impossible in a dream. "Pay me how much?"

"The beginning rate for a mansioner is two coppers a month. The guild will not let me pay less."

From my masteress I would accumulate a single copper in six months.

Quickly he added, "The guild will not let me pay more, either."

Talk of the guild didn't sound dreamlike. "Why are you willing to pay me?" I wanted to hear him say I was that good.

He said so. "The mayor laughed, and I've been trying to extort a smile from him for fifteen years. The women left off looking at Thiel and watched you."

"Lodie has not the temperament of a mansioner."

I thought IT wanted me to be a journeyman.

"Meenore, let me decide that."

Let *me*!

"She is helping me discover what befell His Lordship. I will not release her until we are done."

"And then, Masteress?" I asked.

"Then you may decide." IT knew I wouldn't leave until the count was found or until we were convinced he would never be found.

But then I would leave. I would rather be a mansioner than even a dragon's assistant.

How my spirits rose! I still pitied His Lordship, but I couldn't feel sad. La! as the princess would have said. La! La!

"You may hasten our inquiries, Sulow, by answering a few questions. We visited today for that purpose, not for you to wheedle my assistant away from me."

Master Sulow transferred the tray from between himself and me to his other side, signifying that sociability had ended. "Ask what you like. I'll answer as I choose."

If Master Sulow had had any part in setting the cats on the count, I wouldn't mansion for him.

"When you were in the kitchen waiting to perform, what did you notice?"

"No one wanted to serve His Majesty. One maid destined for him dropped her tray and wept."

"How long did you spend in the hall itself?"

"I was present to hear my minstrel and then again to watch my apprentices set up, and of course I saw Elodie." He stood and sketched a brief bow for me.

I curtsied.

"Thus I was there when the cats stalked His Lordship. I

could have started them stalking myself, but why would I? Elodie could have as well."

I? I?

But I couldn't have. Everyone was watching me. Master Sulow knew that.

"I don't fancy an ogre owning a castle," Master Sulow said, "but he paid me handsomely. Meenore, nothing passed in the hall to show where His Lordship is now."

"Would *you* have liked the count to become king?"

"An ogre in place of a tyrant? The ogre is far more generous."

"Master Sulow," I said, "did Master Thiel catch your eye?"

"Thiel? Yes. While His Lordship was shape-shifting, Thiel slid a silver spoon up his sleeve."

Thieving even then.

"And two wine tumblers as well. But I didn't see him signal the cats."

"Four nights ago," I said, "were you practicing a lion role? Did you roar in the middle of the night?"

"Several nights ago, yes. I don't remember how many."

"Were you practicing in your mansion, master?"

"No. When I'm sleepless, I march above the town and rehearse at full voice."

"More than one person heard a lion that night," IT said. "Have you told anyone of your late rehearsing?"

"No one."

The townsfolk who heard wouldn't have known it was Master Sulow. They would have thought it was His Lordship as a lion. Had Master Sulow set the ogre trap?

He told us nothing else I thought of interest. When IT had exhausted ITs questions, he gave us leave to speak with his apprentices and the minstrel.

The apprentices said they'd been too intent on their preparations to attend to anything else. They claimed not to have been aware of the stalking until the ogre began to vibrate, which they felt before they saw.

The minstrel had been on her way back to the mansions when the trouble began, but she told us about her observations while she sang. "One in the hall hardly watched me. An elderly goodwife kept her eyes on you, young mistress. Whenever you poured for His Highness, she fidgeted and whispered to her goodman, which was rude while I was singing."

"Where did this goodwife sit?" I asked.

The minstrel gave the answer I already knew: She sat in Goodwife Celeste's seat.

CHAPTER THIRTY-ONE

he noon bells were ringing when we left the mansions. I walked upwind of IT. "Masteress, why do you think my temperament is wrong for a mansioner?"

"Sulow spoke to the heart of it. He gives his audience what they want. You will give them what you want."

Was that true of me? For now I hoped only to perform.

"Next we will speak with Master Thiel." IT set off through a field, heading south.

"At His Lordship's castle?" The castle lay to the south. I was eager to go there and learn any news that might be. Perhaps the count had returned.

"Master Thiel will not soon revisit the castle in day-light. By now someone has counted the silver and the plate. Lodie, I have not half the day to walk with you to His Lordship's woods. You must ride."

"But we have no donkey."

"Common sense! Ride on *me*."

"You?"

IT lowered ITself to ITs belly, then rolled onto ITs side. "Keep your cloak under you. My skin grows hotter as I fly. Now climb on."

I balanced myself, one hip against it, one foot on the ground. IT stood and slid me into place with ITs shoulder. I crossed my legs so all of me was on my cloak. If ITs skin was going to be too hot to touch, there would be nothing to hang on to.

I'm not frightened, I told myself, and clasped my hands so tight the skin whitened. IT ran and flapped ITs wings, bouncing me hard while I could still cling to IT, but the moment we were aloft, ITs flight evened.

Mother! Father! Albin! I'm a bird!

The day was calm, but flying made a wind. What power, to create a wind! The air ballooned the princess's cap, lifting it half off my head.

ITs wings pumped. My view flickered. Wings raised, and I saw the landscape, blurred and tinted, through ITs wing segments. Wings down, and my sight cleared. Below lay the count's castle. I leaned over and almost fell.

How reduced the castle seemed from above! I saw it as

if drawn on parchment: six squares for towers on the outer curtain, four circles for the inner towers; big horseshoes for the inner gatehouses, smaller horseshoes for the outer ones; straight lines for the curtain walls, except the front wall, which bulged outward, edged by the meandering moat.

Two people—sparrow size—walked along the inner curtain wall walk, four along the larger outer. Several stood here and there in the inner ward, several in the outer. The search was still in progress. His Lordship hadn't returned, but they hadn't given up hope.

South of the castle the hills rippled higher and higher toward the distant mountains. Below us lay pastures and cleared fields and fields that had not yet been harvested. Beyond was forest, evergreen and autumn orange. I wondered if all I saw belonged to His Lordship.

Approaching the forest, IT flew lower, and ITs wing strokes shortened. My ride became bumpy again. I would have fallen if IT hadn't tilted to save me.

IT landed and ran. I jounced up and down but, luckily, not sideways. Wings still beating, IT careered directly at the woods.

I had seen IT land more neatly than this. IT was toying with me!

So I refused to be frightened. I leaned back and thought about how I'd roll off if we crashed into the trees that were rushing at us. At the last moment IT turned aside, slowed, and stopped. IT lowered ITself and folded ITs wings.

Enh enh enh.

I slid off, stood, lost my footing, and toppled, becoming filthy yet again.

IT furrowed ITs eye ridges. I dusted myself off.

IT whispered, "Kindly mansion Princess Renn's voice, but softly."

Her voice wasn't soft. Still, I tried. "La! Perhaps I can. No, I can do better." I thought about what she might say. "La, Masteress!" I raised and lowered my pitch without increasing my noise. "How brave you are to fly!"

"Please call to Thiel. Not softly."

"What should I say?" I whispered, too.

"Desire him to come to you—to her."

Why? I invented a reason. "Thiel?" I cried, loud enough to be heard a mile away. "Thiel? La! I cannot catch my breath. I have such news! La, Thiel, come!"

"You have set the trap. Now we must wait."

A flock of geese passed overhead. I watched the ground, looking for a mouse. Dead leaves rustled in the woods. I raised my head and saw a shadow among the trees, and then Master Thiel emerged.

"Good day, Masteress Meenore, Mistress Elodie." He sounded as if he'd expected us. "Young mistress, you had only to call me in your own voice and I would have come. You are a treat, however, at imitating Her Highness."

I blushed. It made no difference that I knew him to be a thief. In his presence I had to blush.

"Lodie," IT said, "not far into the woods you will find a sack, guarded by his cat. Please fetch it. If the cat snarls, kick him."

"Pray leave the sack, Mistress Lodie, and don't kick Pardine."

I started into the forest.

"The sack holds a brace of partridges," Master Thiel said. "Are you here to rob the poacher?"

"Return Lodie's copper, answer my questions, and you may keep the partridges."

I turned. "And return Master Dess's cow."

He snapped his fingers, and Pardine pranced by me with a sack in his mouth. I left the woods, too. Master Thiel took the sack, hung it from his belt, and lifted Pardine into his arms. I noticed again his twine ring. If anyone needed an eejis, Master Thiel was the one.

"Young Mistress Elodie, the cow is gone."

Oh. For Master Dess's sake, I hoped she'd been taken to a farm and not eaten.

"Ask what you like, Meenore. I am an honest man."

IT snorted. "Bonay has told me what goods you bring him."

"I appeal to you, Mistress Elodie. My father left me to starve. I think it my duty not to."

I blushed.

"Here is my first question: Why would you *not* set the cats on His Lordship?"

"Rather ask why I would. Why would I hurt someone, even an ogre? I wouldn't. I didn't." He paused. "What would I gain?"

That was the real question with him.

"What would he gain, Lodie?"

I touched the purse at my waist, which still lacked the stolen copper. "Revenge on His Lordship for owning your grandfather's castle. Because you, too, hate ogres and—"

"I hate no one."

I rushed on before his innocent look stopped me. "And you don't want an ogre to be king."

"What else, Lodie?"

Induce. Deduce. *Think.* "His Lordship discovered your poaching and was furious."

"I am never discovered"—he bowed to my masteress—"except by a masteress of discernment."

Enh enh enh.

"I didn't harm His Lordship."

Pink smoke curled up from ITs mouth. "You harmed him. In these woods the beasts were his companions. Now, tell me where you think he would hide and how he would act."

"As a mouse?"

"And after, if a cat didn't eat him."

"As a different animal? My dear Meenore, you should ask Mistress Elodie. Sulow says I have no talent for mansioning."

"I am asking you."

"I can't tell you that, but I can tell you something. I didn't think of it until this morning. Walking here with Pardine, I reviewed the lamentable events of that afternoon, and I remembered seeing Sir Misyur flick his wrist."

No! Sir Misyur loved the ogre. I looked at Masteress Meenore, but ITs expression showed nothing.

"I almost missed it and didn't pay attention then. I was laughing too hard. Mistress Elodie, you and he might have been conspiring to keep us from seeing."

What?

IT said nothing.

"I apologize. You would not conspire. Sir Misyur gestured to the servers to delay the next remove. He could see no one wanted an interruption while you performed. His signal to the cats was in addition to the gesture to the servers. It was slight, but a cat teacher couldn't miss it."

"Plausible," IT said.

Impossible, I thought.

"I have more proof. The lord mayor read the count's will last night. He left everything to Sir Misyur. The news is all over town."

I could hardly take it in. Before I could form a thought,

ITs tail whipped around Master Thiel's waist and ITs smoke turned purple.

"Let me go, Meenore. Ouch! What have I done?"

"You have told His Majesty about Sir Misyur's wrist flick, or you have told someone who will tell His Majesty."

"I thought of it only this morning and I've been here. Let me go."

"You concocted the wrist flick when you heard about the will, and you will make sure His Majesty is informed as soon as you may. Lodie, why will he do so?"

I felt as confused as a mansioner who's entered the wrong tale.

"Your scales are hot!"

"How unfortunate for you. Lodie?"

"Because Master Thiel doesn't want Sir Misyur to inherit."

"And what else?"

I spoke slowly, reasoning it out. "Because . . . neither . . . will . . . His . . . Majesty . . ." I had it! "His Majesty will seize the castle. People will believe Sir Misyur guilty because he had riches to gain." I felt breathless. "Master Thiel will receive a reward for his lie."

"I have not told His Majesty. Whatever you think of me, I cannot. Let me go and I'll say why."

IT freed Master Thiel with a snap so sharp that he spun twice on his heels.

"Do not try to run or I will snatch you up again, and I will not be gentle next time."

Master Thiel regained his balance. "Word is all over town. His Highness is deathly ill, poisoned during the feast. He sickened in the middle of last night."

CHAPTER THIRTY-TWO

Master Thiel smiled. "The news is distressing to His Majesty's subjects."

How unfeeling he was. I shivered. Greedy Grenny was horrible, but I didn't wish him poisoned.

My masteress gripped Master Thiel's arm with a claw. "Who is blamed?"

"Master Jak and the taster are imprisoned."

IT let Master Thiel go. "Lodie, we must leave."

"Then I may check my traps, unhindered?"

"Yes. No." The tip of ITs tail circled his ankle. "Give Lodie her copper."

He produced a copper from his purse. "Pardine couldn't tell how pretty you are, or he'd have left you alone." He bowed.

I didn't blush. I was finished. "Is anyone else ill?" I asked. "Any of the others on the dais?"

"I've been told that Her Highness was a little ill, nothing serious. Her father did not share much of his meal with anyone."

"Gluttony and selfishness to good purpose for once." IT lowered ITself. "Lodie, take your seat."

IT landed in a pasture distant enough from both the forest and His Lordship's castle to be hidden from both. I jumped down.

"I must deduce and induce and use my common sense." IT extended ITself on the ground and closed ITs eyes. Only ITs tail switched slowly back and forth. Wisps of smoke rose from ITs nostrils.

I sat on the browning grass. On the farm at this hour, Father and Albin were likely leaving the apple orchard for their midday meal. Our dog, Hoont, would be dancing between the two men, an apple in her mouth, begging to be chased. At home Mother would be stirring the pottage pot. If I were there, I'd be setting out bowls and spoons.

IT raised ITs head and opened ITs eyes. "Lodie, did you see Sir Misyur pass any delicacies to the king?"

"Do you think he and not Master Jak or the taster poisoned him?"

"Answer my question."

"Several times. Sir Misyur was at the end of the dais

table, and His Highness was in the middle. People picked at the food as the bowl went along. They would be poisoned, too."

"They may have been. Thiel may know only of the king, or he may have chosen to tell us only of the king."

"Sir Misyur rose and went to the kitchen more than once to make sure all was well."

IT shook ITs head. "I'm rarely wrong about a character. I've long believed Sir Misyur a good man."

"He could be a whited sepulcher."

"Indeed. I will now think aloud. If you hear a flaw in my reasoning, stop me."

"Yes, Masteress." I felt both nervous and honored.

"Sir Misyur has served His Lordship for seven years. If he knew he was to inherit, why wait to harm him?"

"Maybe—"

"Do not interrupt. Perhaps Sir Misyur has learned only recently that he was to inherit."

"Maybe—"

"Lodie! Sir Misyur, fearing he would no longer inherit when His Lordship married Her Highness, set the cats on the count. He also surmised that His Majesty would not countenance the inheritance. Wanting to keep his wealth, Sir Misyur resorted to poison. In this conjecture, Master Jak and the taster are innocent."

I nodded. These were horrible speculations.

"Don't nod. Sir Misyur wouldn't behave so reprehensibly."

I agreed but didn't nod.

"Let us suppose someone else expects to inherit and signals the cats, then discovers he or she isn't to inherit. . . ." IT shook ITs head. "Two culprits are possible, but not as elegant. A solution should be elegant, Lodie."

I didn't understand, but I had an idea of my own. "Masteress?"

"Yes?"

"What if Master Thiel wormed his way into King Grenville's good graces with gifts of stolen silver or plate or spices or even"—I pointed back the way we'd come—"a brace of partridges. What if he promised to destroy His Lordship . . . ? The king could seize the castle after the count was gone, no matter who was to inherit. Master Thiel would demand riches, perhaps a title, in exchange."

"Possible."

"What if His Majesty refused to fulfill his side of the bargain? Master Thiel might be angry enough to poison him. King Grenville may have been poisoned not at the feast but soon after."

IT said, "Master Thiel may indeed have poisoned the king. He has the malice for it. Master Thiel is my favorite."

"What about the mauled ox?"

IT said, "Master Thiel may have injured the ox earlier and wanted to be with you for the discovery."

"But you said we interrupted the mauling."

"We lack sufficient information." IT rolled onto ITs side for me to climb on. "We will dine at home and then visit your esteemed goodwife, her goodman, and their children. Are you ready?"

I said I was.

In the lair we set to making skewers. Three were complete when a guard wearing a red cloak appeared in ITs open doorway. Her green scalloped cap signified she served the king.

"Elodie of Lahnt?"

I felt IT tense.

"Yes?"

"You are wanted at Count Jonty Um's castle."

Good news! I hurried to the hook for my cloak. "Masteress, His Lordship is back!" He'd sent for me.

IT said, "Why is she wanted?"

I turned from the hook to the guard.

"For poisoning His Majesty."

My knees weakened and I leaned against the wall. Of course they suspected me. I'd poured for him.

She continued, "And for signaling the cats against His Lordship."

CHAPTER THIRTY-THREE

"You can't be serious!" IT said. "She's a child."

They couldn't suspect me of signaling the cats! "I was performing when the cats began to stalk. An imaginary snake was coming out of my mouth. I was reaching for it with both hands. Everyone saw."

The guard said, "She must come."

"I am a fool," IT said. "Who is her accuser?"

The guard hesitated. "Cellarer Bwat. Her Highness sent for you." Her voice softened. "His Majesty's illness has brought her very low."

"He still lives?"

Silence. Why tell a poisoner whether or not she had succeeded?

I still leaned against the wall. "My masteress has

commanded me to go nowhere without IT. I cannot disobey."

"True. I will accompany Elodie."

"She may not bring anyone with her. Apologies, Meenore. You shouldn't have befriended a spy of Tair."

That's what they thought? "I'm not! I've never—"

"Meenore, you might have deduced what she is." She advanced. "Come."

Three more guards filled the entry.

I pushed myself away from the wall and wrapped my cloak around me. "I've never been to Tair. I grew up on a farm in Lahnt."

She took my arm. "And learned to mansion on a farm?"

She walked me out or else my knees would have given way. I looked behind me. IT held the heel of a loaf of bread in one claw, ITs knife in the other. Green smoke rose from ITs nostrils. Green smoke for bewilderment? ITs mouth hung open, and ITs eye ridges were furrowed.

Could IT believe me a spy? Did IT suspect me of poisoning the king, signaling the cats, mauling an ox?

The guards set a quick pace. The one who'd addressed us, the only female, held my right elbow. Another guard had my left. I staggered along between them.

Mother! Father! Fear pounded in my ears. "If I am deemed guilty, the real poisoner won't be caught."

They didn't slow.

"More people will die." I had no idea if this was true.

What would happen when we arrived at the castle? Would a trial take place immediately?

Who would judge me, with His Highness sick, perhaps dying? The mayor? The princess? Sir Misyur, who might have done everything?

Bells chimed—the three-o'clock bells, not the long tolling that would mark His Majesty's death. I was glad at least that the lair lay at the southern edge of Two Castles and there were no witnesses to my disgrace. But the secret wouldn't be kept. Soon my accusal would be known in town. Eventually word would reach my family, who thought me safely apprenticed to a weaver.

The menagerie lay ahead. If only I could shape-shift.

I stumbled. The pressure on my right arm grew, although I hadn't been trying to break free. The guard on my left complained that they were missing their meal. I had missed mine, too, and was hungry through my fright.

A guard behind me said, "Master Jak will have put something aside for us."

Master Jak? I thought he and the taster were imprisoned. No, of course not. I was the one who would be imprisoned. Master Thiel had lied. Why would he lie about this?

To persuade Masteress Meenore to let him go.

The count's castle rose ahead. I made myself heavy and stopped walking.

The red-cape guard snapped, "None of that!"

"I'll take her." The guard on my left slung me over his shoulder as if I were a sack of wheat.

My head jounced with every step. "I'll walk!" I cried, but he didn't put me down.

Someday I will mansion this, I thought.

Sir Misyur and Her Highness were waiting at the door to the northeast tower when I arrived, along with guards who stood so still they might have been nailed in place. My guard set me on the ground and pushed down on my cap to force a curtsy. I would have curtsied!

Sir Misyur only looked at me dolefully, but Her Highness cried, "*Eh*lodie! How could you have hurt him?"

"I didn't! I wouldn't—"

She slapped me across my face. My head swiveled with the force of the blow.

"La! Didn't I give you my own cap?"

I put my hand up to my cheek. "Please, Your—"

"You will have an opportunity to speak," Sir Misyur said. "Until then, you'll be confined to the tower."

"You'll be comfortable in spite of your crime. I give you a princess's word. You won't suffer."

"Does your father still breathe?" I shouldn't have asked,

274

since they believed I wanted him dead.

No one answered. I was led inside.

As I went in, I heard Sir Misyur say, "A mansioner can easily mansion innocence."

The door thudded shut. I didn't hear a lock turn. What need to lock a guarded door?

Facing me was the door to the donjon, closed now. On my right rose a narrow circular stairway in its own little tower attached to the big one. The stairs were dimly lit by occasional slitted windows.

My left-hand guard pulled on my elbow. He and I advanced together with Mistress Guard in the rear. The other guards remained at the bottom. After climbing once around, we reached a short landing and another shut door. The stairs continued, and so did we to the third and top story. A landing here, too, door on my left. Facing me, a ladder led upward to a trapdoor, which must have opened onto the wall walk.

Mistress Guard lifted the latch and pushed the door open. "In you go." She shoved me inside.

The chamber was large and comfortable. In other circumstances it must have been guest quarters. A fire burned brightly and an oil lamp had been lit, no doubt the princess's doing to keep me from suffering, as if light and heat could lessen my misery. A low door across the room would certainly lead to the privy.

The guards exited. The door groaned as a crossbar was pushed home. On my side, the key to the ordinary lock was in the keyhole, useless because of the crossbar.

Furnishings were a small table, a low-backed chair, a case of shelves that held no more than a sewing box and a clay bowl, a barred window too high in the wall for me to see out of, and a bed, a rich man's bed, suspended from the ceiling by ropes and surrounded by drapes to keep out the cold. For extra warmth, a second blanket lay folded at the foot. I threw myself facedown across the coverlet and wept.

I don't know how long I cried. For a while I seemed made of brine. I wept for the ogre, the king, the ox, the princess, Nesspa. And me. Thoughts of yesterday's happiness were torment. I was unlikely ever to become a mansioner.

More than a few tears were caused by thoughts of my masteress. Why hadn't IT flown with me to the castle? IT could have ripped me away from my captors.

Because IT doubted me. IT hadn't ridiculed Master Thiel's suggestion that I had plotted with Sir Misyur, and IT had called ITself a fool when the guards came, a fool for not deducing that I was the whited sepulcher.

That hurt most of all, ITs disbelief in me.

CHAPTER THIRTY-FOUR

I heard the crossbar drawn back. I wiped my eyes and emerged from within the bed drapes. Two guards entered, their faces as blank as new spoons. One bore a tray on which rested pottage, bread, and a tumbler of cider. My empty stomach growled. The second guard blocked the door and seemed to have come solely to protect the first. From me!

The food bearer placed the tray on the table.

"Thank you."

No answer. They left.

Hungry as I was, I set the tray on the floor and pushed the table to the wall under the window. I climbed up but still couldn't see out. I placed the chair atop the table.

Taking care, I climbed onto the table again and stood on the chair.

Night had arrived, a bright, starry night ruled by a gibbous moon. *Gibbous*—rounded—a word Albin taught me.

The window bars bowed outward, so I could see down as well as out. Directly below me was the outer ward bordered by the outer curtain. The town lay too far to the west to see, but in the distance I made out the shiny black strait.

I climbed down and turned my ladder back into table and chair. The kitchen had given me no knife. How frightened they were! But I had been provided with a bowl of water, so I could clean my fingers before eating. I did so now. Afterward, I broke off a corner of bread, then dropped it back on the tray.

His Majesty had been poisoned. Whoever had done it might still be in the castle. Death by poison would prove me guiltless, but my cleared name would be no use to me.

I set the tray by the door, where it tempted me. If I had to keep looking at the food, I would eat it. I climbed up to the window again, poured out the cider, and tossed the bread and pottage. I hoped a hungry night creature wouldn't dine and die.

We'd had no frost yet, so the crickets still sang, untroubled by the plight of a human girl. A dark shape blew across the sky from north to south, turned and returned, angling my way, trailing purple smoke. My masteress!

My masteress, angry. I gripped the bars. How would I convince IT of my innocence?

IT crossed over the outer curtain and flew lower until IT was level with the tower's second story. ITs right claw held a sack.

Again it wheeled back and forth, coming closer with each pass. I feared IT would break a wing on the tower. But IT whipped around and anchored ITself to the stone. Claw over claw, clinging to cracks, IT climbed to me.

"Lodie? Have you—"

"I wouldn't poison anyone. I'm not a whited sepulcher." I was weeping again. "I love the ogre."

"Have you eaten anything here?"

I shook my head. "Nothing. And I'm not a spy."

"Nothing? No drink?"

"None."

IT smiled. I wiped my streaming eyes and dripping nose with my sleeve and smiled back. I had never seen IT look so happy.

"I couldn't warn you not to eat in the presence of the guards. You believe I suspected you?" ITs smoke tinted pink. "You think me an idiot?"

"No. But you called yourself a fool. I thought, a fool for trusting me."

"A fool for not realizing you would be accused. I never for

a moment believed you to be a spy or a whited sepulcher."

I tried not to sound reproachful. "Where have you been?"

"I found Dess and your Goodwife Celeste. They could tell me nothing about Jonty Um, but both have an understanding of poisons and their antidotes. They're in the king's chamber now, along with the physician, Sir Maydsin, who is worthless in my opinion. Dess slipped out to inform me His Highness will likely live."

Relief swept through me. "Do they think I poisoned the king?"

"Dess and Goodwife Celeste?"

I nodded.

"They didn't say."

"Will the guards release me since His Highness is better?" I shook my head. "No. They won't." His Highness had still been poisoned.

"He'll preside over your trial."

And wouldn't be merciful.

"Whatever sort of monarch he is," IT said, "he will be fair. He wants to discover the true poisoner as much as anyone."

How would he do that? "Masteress, would you bring me a few skewers and a jug of water?"

"I have." IT let go of the tower with ITs right claw and held out the sack, which barely fit between the bars. Something inside jingled.

IT grasped the window bars with both claws. "Climb

down, Lodie. You are too precariously perched."

I did. In the sack, along with the food and drink I found a leather purse—containing two silvers and three coppers.

"Masteress!" I cried.

"Speak softly."

I lowered my voice. "Masteress!"

"It is unwise to be in prison without a full purse. You may succeed in bribing a guard, but do not attempt to bribe more than one at once. Each will not trust the other."

"Thank you!"

"If you don't use the coins, I expect them back."

I was affronted. "I'm not Master Thiel." I pushed my old purse into the new one and hung the new one on my belt.

"Lodie, I can visit you only at night, but I will watch your window at intervals during the day. If you need me, tie your cap to a bar. I'll come somehow."

I nodded while pulling a piece of cheese off its skewer.

"You may hear a lion roar again tonight if the wind is in the right direction. Sulow has agreed to roar."

"Why?"

"Perhaps we can draw out our villain."

"Masteress, why did Cellarer Bwat accuse me?"

"Common sense tells me that he knew someone would be named. He didn't want the someone to be himself or any of his friends among the servants, so he offered you, a stranger."

I wondered whether Sir Misyur or Her Highness had asked him or if he'd come forward unasked.

"Farewell, Elodie. May your sleep be sweet."

"Thank you, Masteress." I wished IT could stay. "Good night."

"Do not climb up to the window unless you must." IT let go of the bars and was gone.

I threw a log on the fire and toasted three skewers. With each bite I took in ITs friendship.

When I finished, I returned the remaining skewers and the half-empty jug to the sack, which I hid between the head of the bed and the wall.

I lay down. Firelight made the ceiling glow orange-gray. For how many nights would I look up at it? For how many years?

Two guards brought my breakfast, one of them a chatty, fatherly sort who informed me that the king had eaten his breakfast and his face was no longer so waxen. Goodwife Celeste, Master Dess, and the physician attended him in turn, although they would depart soon if his improvement continued.

"Her Highness rarely leaves his side, and Sir Misyur comes often as well. Aren't you going to eat?"

"Later. I never wake up hungry."

"Children need nourishment."

I wondered if he might be the poisoner, or if someone had instructed him to see me eat. "It tastes bad unless I'm hungry."

The other guard said, "Let her starve if she likes."

The kindly guard gave up, and they left. As soon as they'd gone, I climbed up to the window. A steady rain poured down. I tossed my breakfast—pottage again—out the window and consumed a skewer. I would need to husband food and water until IT came tonight.

King Grenville's skin had been waxen. Martyr's mint caused waxy skin, and so did false cinnamon. Both were grown in Lepai. False cinnamon tasted enough like the true to go unnoticed. Martyr's mint, despite its name, had no flavor at all.

But false cinnamon acted quickly, and His Highness had been poisoned at the feast. He certainly had been well the next day—well and spiteful enough to paint my face with gravy.

In addition to waxy skin, martyr's mint caused slow and light breathing, stomach bloating, listlessness, no pain. And death.

Enough thinking about poison and death. To distract myself, I passed the morning reciting tales and mansioning every role. When the knock came for the midday meal,

I was bellowing, "Fee fie fo fum, I smell the blood of a Lepai man." Not the most sensible line for one suspected of being a spy for Tair.

The door opened, and there was the princess herself, holding my tray. No guards, but I knew they were outside at the ready.

I curtsied while hoping the thick door had contained my words. "Your Highness . . . beg pardon, I was mansioning. Do you know—"

"*Eh*lodie." The lowest note came last, sorrowfully.

I took the tray and set it on the table.

"I shouldn't have struck you." She smiled. "You've heard?"

I nodded. "His Majesty is better. Your Highness, I didn't—"

"Let's not speak of it. I'm still glad I gave you my cap. La! I do not miss it. And until . . ." She shook her head. "I've always been happy to see your head in it."

"Thank you." I wasn't sure what to say. "I've never had such a fine cap." I remembered my manners. "Please sit." I pulled my chair away from the table for her.

"That's your chair." She sat on the bed. "I'll keep you company while you eat your meal. Lamb stew. Won't you try it? I had mine, lamb stew also, quite tasty."

What excuse could I give her for not eating? I wondered if I could trust her with the truth.

Wait! Why did she want me to know her meal had been the same as mine?

"Your Highness, I finished my good breakfast just half an hour ago."

"La! Breakfast? Hardly enough to feed a squirrel. Come, you must have more now."

Could she be the poisoner?

She couldn't be. She would expect me to share with her.

Oh. My tray had but one spoon.

Still, she couldn't be.

Whatever she was, I had to prevent her from forcing food on me. Mansion! My eyes filled with tears. "You have always been kind to me. I promise to eat as soon as hunger returns."

"I won't leave until I see you swallow a morsel or two, for my own consolation. No one will say we starved a prisoner. La! I'll entertain you while you eat. My father . . ."

She *was* the poisoner. I gripped the table, which seemed to spin. Princess Renn was the whited sepulcher.

CHAPTER THIRTY-FIVE

rincess Renn had come to see me eat, because she knew I hadn't touched my meal last night or this morning. If I had, I would be sick or dead by now. I rinsed my fingers in the water bowl, slowly, slowly. Her mouth moved. I restrained myself from screaming and heard not a word.

What poison would she give me? Something quick, that wouldn't hurt, because she didn't want to cause suffering.

How much would kill me?

I had an idea what it might be, and I couldn't eat a bite. When she paused, I said, "Your Highness, alas, my hunger is banished for now." I shivered. "Do you feel a chill?" I held my hands out to the fire, which was blazing, and leaned in as well to redden my cheeks.

She took my shoulders and turned me. "Are you ill, dear?"

I shook my head. "Only cold, and my throat is sore."

"Food will warm you."

I bit on my cheek, hard. "You are too good, but I cannot choke down any." I coughed and wiped my mouth on my sleeve, taking care that she saw the blood.

Her face relaxed. "La, it *is* chilly."

Oh, my cheek hurt.

She held my hands, which were still hot.

I saw her gold bracelets again, but none of twine. Perhaps she thought she didn't need an eejis.

"*Eh*lodie, my father will be just, and I'll see to it that you don't suffer here. I'll leave you now." She twitched the bed-curtains aside. "I see you have enough blankets to make you warm."

She'd made sure of that. I had guessed right about the poison.

She left.

I sniffed my bowl. The scent was faint but detectable: eastern wasp powder. Rare and expensive, but she was a princess. The poison acted in an hour or two, caused chills, fever, tremors, a tight throat, death. A single swallow would be enough to kill me. But I would feel no sharp pain, no agony. No suffering.

If she was her father's poisoner, too, she would have

used something slower on him, because his symptoms had appeared much later.

I climbed to the window, tied my cap to a bar, and descended for my stew and tumbler. As I was about to tip them out, I realized the danger. Even in the rain, she might come out to look for spilled stew.

I threw the meal into the fireplace and began to pace. My masteress said that one culprit was elegant, but there had to be two in this case. Master Thiel had certainly been the poacher and the thief of castle valuables. I would assume Her Highness responsible for everything else: stealing Nesspa, signaling the cats, poisoning her father.

Why do any of it?

Put myself in their steads. That's what I'd told Master Thiel about mansioning, and I'd thought the words significant. Now I knew the meaning: put myself in Princess Renn's stead. She might poison her father because he was about to betroth her to an infant, and she wouldn't be allowed to say no.

But the new betrothal had come after the feast, and he was poisoned at the feast.

I felt bewildered.

Let the king go for now. Why set the cats on the count?

She told me that the king had betrothed her to the count. Put myself in her stead. Suppose she hadn't wanted to wed an ogre, but she had pretended to love him.

And signaled the cats.

To simplify the task, she stole Nesspa. She must have been horrified when I found him. But then, luckily for her, he needed to leave during the feast.

How had she stolen him?

With treats.

How had she kept him hidden?

The answer broke on me like a mallet on the head: by poisoning him, just enough to keep him docile. When I found him he was alert, but he didn't have to be quiet on the wall walk where no one would hear him. Likely she had dosed the other dogs in the hall, too, and that was why they did nothing to stop the cats.

I had tied my cap to the window only a few minutes ago, but I climbed up to look for IT.

The rain prevented me from seeing as far as I had yesterday, and I didn't see IT.

I climbed down.

She must have lulled the ox with poison, too, then raked its shoulder. Why?

She'd spoken about thoroughness when she tied her cap laces three times under my chin. If she did a thing, she did it more than once, or in more ways than one.

Why?

Think elegantly.

If His Lordship (as a mouse) had been seen being

devoured by a cat, she would have had to do nothing more about him. But when the mouse escaped, she had no certainty, so she mauled the ox and frightened the town into believing the ogre a hungry lion. If he returned in his ordinary form, the people of Two Castles would find a way to kill him.

I wished IT would come.

Now for the king's poisoning.

Perhaps at the beginning she didn't want to kill anyone but an ogre. Causing a monster's death wouldn't be evil, according to her. She didn't intend for Nesspa to die. He would have been freed when she was safe from His Lordship.

But when her father announced her new betrothal, she realized—while I was alone with the two of them—that he would go on making matches for her. She decided that he had to die, too. She couldn't have much daughterly affection for him, horror that he was.

That meant he wasn't really poisoned at the feast. She might even have dosed him while I watched. I shuddered.

How?

The fashion of long, flowing sleeves! Perfect for concealment. Prepared for anything as she was, she could have kept a hidden pouch of poison on her always.

With closed eyes, I recalled the scene. I saw her spear a chunk of sausage on her knife with her right hand. Her left passed over the meat to gather up her right sleeve and keep it from trailing through the food. Likely the poison was in her left sleeve. She sprinkled with her left hand.

I remembered the missing mortar and pestle on the morning of the feast. She might have taken them to grind her poison.

Where was my masteress? As soon as King Grenville recovered enough to do without constant watching over, his daughter would feed him something else. In his weakened state, he would certainly die. Everyone would think he'd merely taken a turn for the worse. Cures for poisoning were uncertain.

IT had to come soon!

I returned to my deducing. Princess Renn must have been behind Cellarer Bwat, my accuser. She had probably hinted to him that I might be to blame, hinted so subtly he thought the suspicion his own.

As I mulled it over, I saw she had reason to fear me. I'd witnessed her dismay when His Highness revealed her new future husband. She had directed me to search the stable when she knew Nesspa was elsewhere. I had discovered the mauled ox. And I was the assistant to a dragon skilled at unraveling mysteries. Thorough again, she thought imprisoning me not enough. She had to poison me, too.

I wondered if His Lordship had seen her set the cats on him. Poor count. If he loved the princess, what a blow that would have been.

Had she poisoned him as well as signaled the cats? I remembered his face had been mottled red and white when the minstrel sang, and he'd swayed when he tried to address everyone after the king announced the betrothal. Also he'd hugged himself as if he were cold just before he shifted into the lion.

Poison might have made him less able to resist the cats.

Again I climbed to the window. Below me a hooded figure rounded the tower, walking slowly, hugging the wall. Even from above I recognized Princess Renn's thin shoulders and awkward gait. She was seeking the remnants of my meal.

A moment ago I'd wanted my masteress instantly. Now IT mustn't come!

With trembling hands, I pulled in the trailing cap laces, untied the knots, and took in the cap.

Then I waited, waited, waited.

Surely she must be gone by now. I peeped out.

She was kneeling on the wet ground, her shoulders shaking. As I watched, she raised her head. I retreated, but not before seeing her red eyes, her tragic expression.

The next time I looked, she was gone. I tied the wet cap back in place. A form, grayed by the weather, flew toward me from Two Castles. Soon IT would pass over the outer curtain. I waved. IT would find a way to save the king.

IT wheeled back and forth as IT had last night, but at a greater distance from me. Why?

Abruptly IT flew straight up.

"Come back!"

IT rose higher, then twisted in the air. While frantically beating ITs wings, IT fell and disappeared behind the outer curtain.

CHAPTER THIRTY-SIX

I gripped the bars. IT must have taken an arrow in ITs belly. I heard myself sobbing as if from far away. Could IT survive the arrow or the fall? I squeezed my eyes tight, making colors swirl behind my eyelids—rather than images of ITs death.

Oh, my masteress, I thought again and again.

I untied my cap and climbed shakily down from the window. Then I sat with my head down on the table-top, but after a minute I stood, refusing to cry anymore. I would hope IT lived, so why cry?

IT couldn't save the king now. I would have to attempt the deed myself.

But His Majesty wasn't worth saving compared with my masteress. How could I save IT?

Master Dess might be able to heal IT if I could get to him.

I hadn't tried to escape while I was relying on my Great, my Unfathomable, my Brilliant Masteress Meenore.

I circled the room, looking at everything. The fire poker. Stand on the table, yell for the guards, and smite them on the head as they entered.

No. The first guard would catch my arm before I could strike. I would only anger them.

Might I mansion myself out of here?

I continued to circle.

When would the princess come to see how sick I was?

Had she already poisoned her father again?

I circled the other way. An idea began to form. I thought it out, although I had no time for all this thinking.

I would say this. If a guard said that, I would say the other. They wouldn't be surprised to see me healthy. Her Highness could hardly have told them to expect me to be ill.

Three more circuits, and I was ready. I wrung out my soaked cap and put it back on, although the dampness was unpleasant. Then I eased the key out of the keyhole and tucked it into the heel of my shoe where I could get at it quickly.

I swallowed over a lump in my throat. Masteress Meenore would want to hear about this, if I did well.

The bottom of the bed draperies had a two-inch hem. I found a dropped stitch and pulled, widening the opening.

I knocked on the door. In a gay tone, I cried, "Hail! Open, if you please!" I leaned my ear against the door but heard nothing. If they ignored me, I was lost. His Majesty and my masteress as well. I called again.

A minute or more passed before I heard the bolt pulled free. I backed farther into the room and clasped my hands pleadingly.

The door opened. The guards had changed since Her Highness had come. Luck was with me—half with me, at least. I recognized one of the guards, a young man who had been posted at a fireplace in the great hall and had watched my performance. I remembered seeing him laugh. The other guard was older, with lines of discontent around his mouth.

"Thank you, masters. Time passes slowly in here." I bit my lip. "And I'm frightened." I truly was. My legs could hardly support me. "So I've been practicing my mansioning."

The older guard folded his arms across his chest.

I smiled up at them both. "But I need help with a mansioner's tale that has four characters. A princess." I ran to the table for my spoon. "Here is my scepter." I flourished it. "A beautiful princess." I batted my eyelashes. The younger guard grinned. The older one settled back on his heels.

"The second character is a witch, who has the princess in her keeping." I pulled a blanket off my bed and threw it around me, making a hooded cape. Rounding my shoulders as a hump, I pulled my cap laces forward to suggest a few strands of chin hair. In a crackly voice I said, "I am the witch."

I wished I could do this quicker, but I had to persuade the guards to forget themselves.

Straightening, in my own voice, I said, "I need two princes. I can't portray them."

The younger guard grinned and said, "I've always . . ."

The older guard sent him a reproving look. My heart sank.

But the young guard came to my aid. "Dure, it's dull enough out there." He indicated the door with his head. "Where's the harm? She can't get past us."

Dure's mouth relaxed.

"Alas, they are impoverished princes, their father being a spendthrift. One prince is as kind and warmhearted as the sun, the other as handsome and brilliant as a star."

This was the first tale Albin had ever taught me, and I was using his exact words, pausing where he used to pause.

"Which would you like to be, masters?"

The young guard laughed. "You be the handsome one, Dure. I'm handsome already."

The older guard shrugged. His voice was like rough rocks rubbing together. "Onnore, you could persuade a hedgehog to fly. I will be the handsome one, young mistress."

I sat in the chair, pulled the blanket onto my lap, and tossed my head prettily. "I am sitting in a castle window, sewing." I held an imaginary needle and pushed it in and out of the blanket. "You ride by on your prancing chargers."

They didn't move.

"Walk past me, please."

They did so, awkwardly.

"With pride. Remember, you are princes."

They threw their shoulders back.

"I am so comely you both fall madly in love with me."

Dure snorted.

"Truly, I am half in love already, little mistress," Onnore said gallantly.

"You both return to stand under my window."

They actually came back.

"Each of you wishes to marry me, so you begin to argue."

Neither one said a word.

I pursed my lips and smoothed the hair on my forehead below the cap. "Why do you think *you* should have me, Prince Dure?"

I watched him think. "Because I am so handsome." He chuckled. "Onnore, you are not half as handsome as I."

"But I am as warm as the sun." He laughed. "I can melt your handsomeness."

"Yet I can outwit you and stop you from melting me."

I let them make a few more arguments. The minutes ticked by.

With each rebuttal they laughed harder.

Finally I cast my imaginary needle over my shoulder and turned the blanket into a hooded cape again. I cackled, "You princelings who love my Soulette, I will not give her to just anyone. The man who can find the magical purse filled with coins . . ." I untied my purse from my belt and shook it so they could hear jingling. I took a silver coin halfway out, then dropped it back in.

There is a saying in Lahnt: *Silver blinds men more powerfully than the sun.*

Dure's mouth dropped open. Onnore rose on his toes.

"That man and no other will have my Soulette." I closed my fist around the purse. In my ordinary voice I added, "Both princes, stand at the door, if you please."

They went willingly and stood with their backs to the door. Dure crossed his arms again, his guarding pose.

"Stand there to prevent my escape. Now close your eyes, so I may hide the magic purse."

They closed their eyes, but I suspected they would open them a slit in a moment. I hid my fist in the folds of my skirt.

Princess Renn would certainly check on me soon. Wait, Your Highness, I pray you. Do not come yet.

Noisily I pulled the chair and table to the window and climbed up but didn't leave the purse there. Next, I hurried to the bed and closed the drapes around me. I lifted the mattress and let it fall, smoothed out the bedding, and then—silently—inserted the purse into the hole I'd made in the drapery.

After slipping out between the bed-curtains, I stamped to the case of shelves, which I moved away from the wall, paused, pushed back. I opened the wooden box, then closed it with a loud click. I dragged the table and chair to the middle of the room, laid a fresh log on the fire, and announced in my witch's voice, "There, my sweetlings."

Master Onnore, who was tall enough not to need the chair, shoved the table against the wall and climbed up. He ran his hand along the windowsill, although he could see there was no purse. He looked back to make sure I hadn't left. Then he peered down, seeking the purse below in the outer ward.

Master Dure stood at the shelves, opening the box, looking in the bowl, feeling under each shelf. He, too, glanced at me after every few seconds. Finally he moved the case of shelves aside and slid his dagger between the floorboards.

Master Onnore rushed to the fireplace and used the poker to assure himself I hadn't tossed the purse in there. He would have been comical if the circumstances hadn't been so dire.

Together they advanced on the bed and drew open the

curtains. After a minute or two of carefully shifting bed-clothes and looking at me, they ripped open the mattress and forgot me in pawing through the feathers. I counted to a hundred, then inched the door open, slowly, slowly, until I had just enough room to slip out, and slid it closed behind me—

And heard the princess from below. "I've come with a refreshment for the poor girl. I will take this one to her as well."

My heart pounded, but I fitted the key into the lock and turned, hearing a quiet clink. Then, key still in my right fist, I lifted my skirt and started up the ladder to the wall walk above the tower.

"La! I can climb stairs unaided."

I saw the glow of a torch on the staircase walls below. With all my strength, I raised the trapdoor, climbed out—

And faced low boots and stout calves.

The guard pulled me up by my armpits. I passed a big belly, saw a red beard, green eyes. "Be still. I've got you."

"Her Highness is hurt!"

Princess Renn cried from below, "La! Help! Oh, la!" She had discovered the locked door.

The guard grabbed my left hand and started down. I bent over but didn't step back on the ladder. Other cries rose from below.

"Come." He let go my hand and reached for my ankles.

I jumped back.

The cries continued, the princess's most shrill of all.

Would he come up for me or go down to her?

He descended. I tossed the key over the battlements and raced away. The rain had become fog. If more guards were on the wall walk, the mist might hide me.

The king's chambers were in the northwest tower, on the other side of the gatehouse wall walk.

Let them not expect me to go there. And let me not be too late.

I didn't think His Highness's trapdoor would be guarded, and it wasn't. Why guard it without a prisoner inside? I raised it a crack. Guards would certainly be posted inside or outside the king's chamber, or both.

Luck was with me. No guards on the landing. I lifted the trapdoor just enough to admit me and then gentled it back into place and stole down the ladder. The king's bed hadn't been in the room I'd visited or on the story below, so it had to be in the top chamber, as my prison bed had been.

The tower seemed to sway. I put my hand on the doorknob to steady myself. I swallowed repeatedly before I knew I could speak.

"La, Father! Here I am. . . ." I turned the knob and opened the door. "La! I have extraordinary . . ."

I ran in. An impression of startled faces. "Your

Majesty . . ." I fell on my knees—and was lifted by two guards the instant my knees touched the floor. They began to drag me out.

"I didn't poison you, but I know who did. She'll do it again."

His Highness held up his hand. "How fortunate I am that prisoners break in to bring me truth." His voice had diminished to a whisper. "Pray tell, who?"

Goodwife Celeste sat on a stool near the king's bed. "Elodie!"

Sir Misyur turned away from tending the fire. "Elodie?"

Master Dess sat in the window recess, stroking a small dog in his lap. A third man, likely Sir Maydsin the physician, held the king's wrist, taking his pulse.

The guards loosened their grips but didn't let me go.

His Highness leaned forward. "Name the lady you wish to put in your place."

Say it! I told myself. He may kill me, but say it! "Has . . ." I had to catch my breath. "Has your daughter given you food today?"

"My daughter?" He laughed. Coughed. Laughed again. "You may release her."

The guards obeyed but remained close.

"Master Dess!" I cried. "Beyond the eastern outer curtain, Masteress Meenore lies wounded. IT may have an arrow in ITs belly."

"Your Majesty . . ." Master Dess bowed and hurried from the chamber.

"Misyur, will you be so kind as to find my daughter, and don't tell her what this is about. This girl is always droll. Renn will be amused. We'll hold the trial here."

Sir Misyur bowed and left.

"My daughter did share with me a delicious rabbit pie." He addressed himself to Goodwife Celeste. "She came after you left me for my nap. She is always welcome, but especially when she brings food."

Goodwife Celeste looked startled.

How much poison in the pie? How soon would it strike?

"Now, while we wait, the girl will mansion the tale with the snake." He waved the guards away. "Give her space."

How could I mansion now? I didn't want to!

Goodwife Celeste nodded at me. I began by turning my cap backward for the bad sister. The imaginary moonsnake oozed slowly from my mouth. How hard it was to concentrate.

When the snake had emerged, I leaped from side to side to get away from it.

The king laughed. The guards laughed. The king coughed. Goodwife Celeste frowned.

After an especially wide leap, I turned my cap to the front to be the kind sister.

"La, Father!" The princess entered with Sir Misyur

and two guards, neither of them Master Dure or Master Onnore. "*Eh*lodie?"

The king patted the bed next to him. "Sit by me. The girl is even more diverting than I thought. She claims you poisoned me."

"La!"

"It is in her left sleeve! You'll see. She tried to poison me, too." Oh no! "She was bringing me—"

"My dear, oblige me by holding out your left arm."

I was frantic. "If the guards eat my meal, they'll die!"

"Make her quiet," King Grenville said.

A guard put his hand across my mouth.

"Father! You mistrust me?"

"I trust you. You are my beloved daughter, but hold out your arm."

She held it out. He rolled up the long sleeve inch by inch. No poison.

CHAPTER THIRTY-SEVEN

It had to be there. What had she done with it?

"The other arm," the king said. "I will be thorough." He revealed her right arm to us all. No poison.

I bit the guard's hand. He squawked and let go. "Her purse!"

The guard covered my mouth again.

The king laughed. "She is so funny. Your purse, my love."

The purse contained only keys.

"That is enough. I am tired of this sport. We cannot keep girls who won't stay in their guarded towers. Tomorrow—"

Keys! I'd put the tower key in my shoe. I bit the guard again, and he let go again. "Look in her shoes! I'm—"

The guard muffled me again.

"Father!"

"Dear, you needn't remove your shoes. Tomorrow the girl will die. Poison will be her—" He coughed and put his bedsheet to his mouth. It came away stained with blood, and blood etched a line down his chin.

The guard dropped his hand from my mouth.

What would she do now?

"Father, are you ill again?" She began to untie his cap, a daughterly gesture.

He turned frightened eyes to Sir Misyur. "Look in her shoes." The inside of his mouth was bright red.

She jumped off the bed and stood.

"Your Highness," Sir Misyur said, "take off your shoes."

She stamped. "I will not."

Sir Misyur nodded to a guard, who approached her.

"You see . . ." She laughed awkwardly. "There is a darn in the heel of my hose. I would not have you see it."

"Beg pardon, Your Highness." The guard knelt at her feet. He lifted her right foot by the ankle.

A pouch was in the toe of the right shoe.

"Let me have it." Goodwife Celeste took the pouch and sniffed inside. "Eastern wasp powder." She looked at Sir Maydsin. "Deadly." She rushed out of the chamber, crying, "I have a remedy. I'll fetch it."

"La!" Her Highness pulled herself to her full height. Her voice achieved extraordinary heights as well. "I was kind enough. . . . I was kind. . . . I am kind. . . ." Her eyes swam, and her nose reddened. She buried her face in her long sleeve. "Alack!"

Sir Misyur told the guards to take the princess to the tower where I had been kept.

"If the guards there ate my food, they've been poisoned, too."

"Send them here," Sir Misyur said.

The princess was escorted out, bent over, sobbing.

"Pardon . . . may I leave to find my masteress?"

Sir Misyur nodded.

A Lepai finch flew in the window and landed between Sir Misyur and me. It fluttered its yellow feathers, then began to vibrate—and grow.

I saw Sir Misyur's smiling face and his tears. I wept and smiled, too.

What brought him back now? Where had he been? *What* had he been?

Sir Misyur removed his cloak and draped it around the ogre as he became himself again. "Welcome home, Your Lordship."

I heard distant barking. Nesspa had sensed his master's return.

"Thank you. Elodie, your masteress wants you."

"Is IT injured?"

"The animal physician is with IT."

I ran out of the room and pelted down the tower steps. The day was ending, and the rain had resumed. With my feet squelching in mud, I raced across the inner ward, between the inner gatehouses and the outer, across the drawbridge, along the moat, around the outer northeast tower. And there IT lay sprawled, ITs belly and legs on a mound of hay, ITs head and neck extending across the ryegrass.

Master Dess sat on the hay mound, dabbing ITs belly with linen.

"Elodie!" IT lifted ITs head. White smoke rose in spirals. "You escaped! I congratulate you."

"Master Dess, is my masteress badly hurt?"

IT began to rise, stopped, and asked Master Dess if IT might.

"Yes, honey, honey. Elodie, I wish all my patients would pull their arrows out with their teeth and then eat them. I stopped the bleeding. Took just a moment."

IT sat up, looking pleased with ITself. "Pine arrows and quartz arrowheads. Quite tasty."

I marched straight to IT and hugged ITs front thigh. Leaning my face into ITs belly, I inhaled sulfur. Lambs and calves, IT stank! Heavenly.

"Mmm," IT said. "Mmm, Lodie. If you must. Mmm."

Finally I stood back. "Her Highness signaled the cats

and poisoned the king and mauled the ox and tried to poison me."

"Honey!"

"The whited sepulcher," IT said. "The poison was secreted on her person?"

"In her shoe."

Of course I bathed before entering the lair. IT toasted skewers for me and then insisted I sleep, despite my protests that I wasn't tired and had much to tell and much to ask.

In the morning IT declared a holiday. After breakfast I sat on a pillow on the floor, and IT reclined on ITs side before me, ITs right arm bent at the elbow, ITs big head resting on ITs right claw—a feminine pose, I thought.

"Did you put out your cap to call me? I hoped to approach close enough to see and then fly off again if all was well."

I nodded. "I was watching when you were struck. I thought . . . I couldn't tell. . . ." If IT had been slain.

"Elodie, I told you to stay out of the window." IT touched my shoulder gently with the flat of ITs left claw. "Princess Renn must have suspected I would come to you. Hence the archers."

In a shaky voice I said, "They would have been considerate if they'd shot straight into your mouth."

Enh enh enh.

"I wonder why His Lordship arrived at the castle when he did."

"There is nothing to wonder at. I found him." ITs smoke curled in a lazy spiral. "Logic took you to the menagerie, Elodie. Logic took me there as well. My first two visits bore no fruit, but two failures did not rule out future success, and indeed His Lordship arrived there last night. I discovered him as an additional monkey and brought him here, where he became himself again. Do you know that he had been poisoned, too?"

"I thought he might have been."

"I didn't know. May I enter?" His Lordship stood in the doorway, carrying a large basket, Nesspa at his side.

My masteress heaved ITself up and invited him in.

The count let Nesspa's chain go, and he ran to me, tail wagging. I patted the top of his big head.

With the help of His Lordship, IT moved the table— His Lordship's bench—back to the hearth. I put pillows on top while he placed the basket on the fireplace bench, now our low table. Then he seated himself carefully and removed delicacies from the basket. I toasted skewers. When all was ready, I perched on my stool at one end of the table. My masteress sat at the other. Nesspa stationed himself at the count's leg.

IT and I had just eaten, but we feasted anyway and shared according to custom, with no danger of poison.

Nesspa was too polite to beg, but hospitality was extended to him, too, from my hand and His Lordship's, but not from my masteress's claw.

I had almost the appetite of an ogre, and this ogre had brought marchpane. Still, I finished before him.

When even he finally put down his knife, I said, "You didn't know you were poisoned?"

"No." His ordeal had not made him more talkative.

"But you were ill?" I asked.

He nodded.

"His Lordship has told me some of this, Lodie. Until last night he was in a mouse hole in his bedchamber wall, at first ill almost to death, then improving slowly."

"Why didn't the poison kill him?" I turned to him. "Kill you, I mean. You were so tiny!"

"I am strong, even when I'm a mouse." He made a fist and held it up.

"Did you run to the menagerie as a mouse?" And no cat caught him?

"As a flea. At the menagerie I became a monkey."

"Your Lordship . . ." I hesitated. "Pardon my questions."

"People don't ask enough questions." He shrugged. "They just guess."

Encouraged, I said, "Can you change whenever you want, to whatever you like?"

"Unless there are cats." He patted Nesspa's head. "Then

I can't resist becoming a mouse."

I had been curious about this ever since I first saw him as a monkey: "Are you yourself inside the animal?"

He stared at the ceiling and said nothing for a minute. "I am thinking." He was quiet again. "Are you yourself inside a dream? The monkey is a happy dream."

IT said, "Mmm," but not ITs usual *Mmm*. This one was softer, a feeling *Mmm*, not a thinking one.

"I wake up inside the beast from time to time, to decide if I want to shift back. When I was the mouse, I was awake because I was sick."

"Your Lordship," IT said, "did you realize Her Highness had signaled the cats?"

He shook his head.

I dared to ask the question I most wanted to know. "Your Lordship . . . er, did you love her?"

He blushed. "I did not."

Good!

He went to the middle of the lair, where he paced in a small circle. Nesspa followed him, whining uneasily. After a few minutes His Lordship stopped and Nesspa nuzzled his legs. "I should not have agreed to the marriage . . . but I wanted to be king so people would learn an ogre can be good." He paced again and spoke while walking. "I liked Her Highness. I thought she loved me. I was grateful." He went to Masteress Meenore. "I am to blame."

CHAPTER THIRTY-EIGHT

nh enh enh. "And I am to blame for lighting the forge of a dishonest smith, although I was unaware of his dishonesty, and Lodie is to blame for allowing herself to be the victim of a thieving cat."

I smiled, but His Lordship looked puzzled.

IT continued. "I suppose that your cook is to blame for preparing food that could be poisoned." *Enh enh enh.* "Perhaps the builder is at fault for building the castle you would eventually hold a feast in."

I don't think His Lordship had ever graced my masteress with his full, sweet smile before, but he beamed it on IT now. ITs white smoke curled into spirals, and I understood what spirals meant—dragon happiness.

"Elodie," IT said, "I have not yet told you all. His

Lordship was with me, as a flea again, when I was shot. He returned to the castle to plead your case after Dess told us where you were."

"Thank you, Your Lordship."

He inclined his head. "I knew you would not poison anyone." He stood. "I must leave. Misyur worries if I am gone too long. Meenore, I owe you payment." He untied a brocade purse from his belt. "What is your fee?"

Promptly IT said, "Ten silvers."

Astounded, I blurted, "So many?"

IT glared at me.

His Lordship counted out coins into ITs claw. "And a silver for—"

IT snapped, "You may give that to me, and I will hold it for her."

I glared at IT.

His Lordship gave my silver to IT. "Come, Nesspa." They left.

"You are my assistant, and you are a child." IT placed the silvers in a stack on the cupboard, then lumbered to the coin basket. "You may have these."

I went to IT and received four coppers, a fiftieth of a silver but more money than I had ever owned and much more than my promised salary. "Thank you." I stacked my coppers next to ITs silvers.

Together we dragged the table back to its place against

the wall. IT stretched out again, and I returned to my pillow near ITs head. "There is more to my tale, Lodie, and more to yours."

I sat cross-legged on the pillow. "What happened after you found His Lordship?"

"He spent the night on my floor. He is no cleaner than a human. In the morning he stayed here while I visited your goodwife and her goodman, who are not thieves but the real spies for Tair. Their trade with the smith provides them enough to live on. They said none of this outright, but the goodwife hinted, and I deduced."

Spies? I chewed on it and felt relief. A spy but not a murderer, a spy who'd saved the king's life with her knowledge of herbs.

"Do we have to tell His Majesty?"

"We have no proof, and I will not reveal them to Greedy Grenny. I believe I persuaded the goodwife that I am *not* moody." IT scratched ITs snout. "Now tell me what ensued after I left you."

I did. IT made me act out my mansioning to the guards, and this time I had to mansion their parts as well. IT *enh enh enh*ed heartily.

However, IT stopped laughing when I mentioned leaving my purse.

"You left the coins I gave you?"

"They may still be there." I sat down again. "There's a

saying in Lahnt. *Gold*—"

"Spare me your quaint sayings. Tomorrow we will go to the castle and reclaim your purse."

"I'd like to apologize to the guards." And learn if they'd eaten my meal and been poisoned.

"They may not wish to hear you."

"And we must find out if His Highness survived." How awful that I hadn't thought about this since leaving the castle.

"Yes, we must. But you have not finished your recitation. What did you do when you were outside your prison door? Surely there were more guards."

I continued the tale. IT continued ITs questions. When I'd finally answered them all, IT said, "By coming to see why you were not dead, Her Highness as much as told you she was the poisoner. She saved you the trouble of deducing."

Indignantly I said, "I deduced! I worked out why and how she did it."

"Mmm. Mmm." IT closed ITS eyes, then opened them. "You did. You did well, Elodie."

I felt as if an audience of a thousand had just clapped for me. IT lumbered to the cupboard, where IT removed a skewer from its bundle. "Perhaps Misyur will make me a gift of the remainder of the arrows that were to be shot at me." IT used the skewer as a toothpick and then ate it. "I imagine you will go to Sulow soon, tomorrow or even a few minutes from now, to become his new mansioner. I suppose you will not delay."

Oh! I hadn't given Master Sulow a thought. "Could I do both, proclaim and deduce and induce and mansion, too?"

"I do not want a sometime assistant. You needn't worry. I will find another."

I had more pride than that. "Who will replace me?" Nastily I added, "Is another cog coming from Lahnt?"

"Ah," IT said, sounding pleased.

Oh. Oh. I was saying I didn't want to be replaced. But I was a mansioner. I went to the lair entrance. A brisk wind blew cloud tatters across the sky. I stepped outside. Cold. I stepped inside. Warm. Outside again.

Master Sulow had no warmth. If he'd been my master when I'd been imprisoned in the tower, he'd likely have left me there.

Pacing back and forth between the rain vats on either side of the lair, I debated with myself.

My masteress said I didn't have the temperament to be a mansioner, and in truth, I'd hated mansioning the moon-snake over and over for the king. But perhaps I'd merely hated the king.

And perhaps there was more than one way to be a mansioner, not simply as a member of a troupe. Since I'd been in Two Castles, I'd mansioned for Sulow, for the court, for the king, and for two bewildered guards.

But in a troupe, mansioners became better at the roles they repeated. Albin said a mansioner finds something new in a part each time she steps into it.

I felt pulled in two. I stopped thinking, wrapped my cloak around me, and stared up at the sky. The princess's cap kept my ears warm.

Her cap! The cap of a poisoner.

I stepped back into the lair, extending my arm and holding the cap in my fingertips. At the fireplace I threw it in.

My masteress reached in and pulled it out before it was even singed. "I deduce you no longer want it." *Enh enh enh.*

"I'd rather go bareheaded."

"Then I suggest you sell it. People will fight to own a cap that once belonged to the poisoner princess. Trade it for half a dozen caps, or I will sell it for you if you like."

"Sell it, please." I wanted nothing more to do with the thing.

IT folded the cap carefully. "I will get a better price than you will. Now read to me. I believe you stopped at *mustard*."

I found the book in the cupboard. IT had marked my place with a skewer. Outside the wind blew. IT rested ITs head on ITs front claws, ITs eyes on me.

Mother, Father, I thought. A lair is my home.

EPILOGUE

I did not go to Master Sulow later in the day, and during the night, while I slept in my cozy bed, my mind made itself up. I awoke knowing that, for now at least, I would remain with Masteress Meenore and mansion when the opportunity arose.

Did I mind? Did the decision feel like a sacrifice?

A little. Very little.

Master Sulow was a mere human. His breath never spiraled or turned green. With IT I would have more adventures than I'd get peering out from under Master Sulow's thumb.

Not only more adventures, more consideration of my ideas and more friendship.

I told IT my decision over breakfast, and ITs smoke

spiraled satisfyingly. "A commonsensical choice. You still have much to learn about deducing and inducing."

In the morning we visited Count Jonty Um's castle. Sir Misyur came to the outer ward to talk to us.

The king would live. Goodwife Celeste had saved him with broth and coarse herb bread. He'd slept a quiet night and was now closeted with His Lordship. Sir Misyur believed His Highness wanted assurance of His Lordship's aid in any war against Tair. I thought the king would be disappointed. The count seemed to be a peaceable ogre.

Princess Renn had company in her tower. Master Thiel had charmed his way into visiting her. I supposed he must be stealing the gold rings from her fingers and the bracelets from her arms.

Master Onnore and Master Dure, the two guards, had not eaten my food. They'd been too occupied in searching for my purse—which they'd failed to find—and then in searching for me.

Sir Misyur dispatched a guard to the chamber, who returned with my purse, its wealth untouched. My masteress gave me back my cloth purse and kept the rest.

In the afternoon IT sold Princess Renn's cap for twelve coppers, and I bought myself a kirtle, an apron, and a pair of shoes, all used, of course, but all in the Two Castles fashion, and my own cap—pink with red roses, hardly faded, embroidered around the crown. My custom went to a mending master on Roo Street, not to the mending mistress on Daycart Way who had insulted me, although I paraded back and forth by that mistress in my new finery. She seemed not to notice.

I had three coppers left from my purchases, which I knew I should save to send home, but I wanted to buy something for IT, who called ITself stingy but had shown me only generosity.

On the wharf I found a boat wright willing to sell me a block of cypress wood for a copper, a kingly sum for a snack, but I paid.

IT was selling skewers, so I headed for the lair to hide my gift. On my way I met Goodwife Celeste again, this time at the baker's oven. When she saw me, she hugged me hard, then held me at arm's length and scrutinized my face.

"You are well?"

I smiled. "Very well."

"Safe?"

I nodded.

She shook her head. "IT should never have sent you to the castle alone. Thoughtless of IT."

Thought*more*, I would say.

She let my shoulders go. "We're leaving shortly, but we'll be back. I'll look for you."

"I'll be happy to see you." And sad to see her go.

She took her loaf from the baker, and I continued toward

the top of town. At the corner I encountered a crier for the king, trumpeting that His Lordship had been a lion only momentarily and only during the feast, and that he had never mauled an ox or any living thing. I saw another crier on the next corner. Greedy Grenny was making amends.

In the lair I hid the wood block, which was as thick as my thigh, under my mattress and brought it out while IT was toasting skewers for our evening meal. I placed the gift on the hearth next to IT.

"For me?" IT dropped three skewers into the fire. Smoke rose from ITs nostrils in a green spiral.

I used the poker to rescue the skewers. "You said you like the taste." IT liked cypress and hated oak. Oh no. Had I gotten that backward?

IT touched the wood with a talon. "For me?"

"For you to eat, if you like, Masteress."

"For me?"

I nodded. "If you don't like, perhaps we can put it in the fire or use—"

"Burn cypress, Lodie?" IT picked up the wood and hugged it. "That would be an outrage." ITs inner eyelids closed while IT nibbled a corner. "Excellent quality. I have not received a gift in . . . forty-two years, and that was a trifle." IT stroked the wood.

I smiled at ITs pleasure.

"You bought this with your cap money."

I nodded, although IT hadn't asked.

"Of course you have no other source of funds. You thought of me." Trailing smoke spirals, IT waddled to the cupboard, opened it, and laid the wood on the top shelf. "I will savor it slowly, or perhaps I will simply save it."

King Grenville never thanked me for saving his life. Maybe because I'd revealed his daughter as his poisoner, he felt no gratitude. Or maybe his gratitude was aroused only by a well-cooked dish.

His criers were believed about Count Jonty Um. The tide of popular opinion had turned. By now everyone knew of Princess Renn's attempts on the lives of her father and her betrothed, and the count was pitied and no longer feared.

But the town's goodwill might have come too late. Other than his visit to us, His Lordship stayed away for the next week. The princess and her father removed to their own castle, where she was again imprisoned.

Soon after their departure, more news broke on the town: Master Thiel was to become Prince Thiel and to marry the princess. He had persuaded the king that he would keep Her Highness from poisoning anyone ever again. The couple would be given a burgher's house to live in, and Pardine would be Prince Cat of the kingdom.

I supposed His Majesty no longer wanted his daughter under his roof, and I doubted they would dine together often. On King Grenville's death, King Thiel would rule.

Sentiment in Two Castles was divided. The victims of Master Thiel's thievery were outraged, the rest pleased.

My masteress told me ITs opinion over a mutton stew I had cooked. "When Thiel is king, he will not send Lepai to war. Until then, if King Grenville expects his son-in-law to lead anyone to battle, he will be disappointed. Thiel loves himself too much to risk even an eyebrow hair."

I thought Princess Renn wouldn't poison anyone again for a while at least. I believed she truly loved Thiel—tall, handsome, and now rich Prince Thiel, whose table manners were excellent. But if he angered her, he had better not eat his meals at home.

A monkey and a dog appeared in our entrance. Nesspa, trailing his chain, trotted to the fireplace where the stew pot hung.

The monkey loped in, chittered, stroked my hair, and smiled his toothy smile at me. I jumped off my high stool and curtsied. The monkey took my masteress's front claw and stroked it.

"Welcome, Your Lordship." From ITs pink smoke I knew IT was enduring the petting.

The monkey ran to the middle of the room and began to vibrate.

When the shift was complete, I asked, "May I give you stew, Your Lordship?" I hoped we had enough.

"Thank you." He piled pillows on the floor and sat on them with his legs under our table. I ladled stew into ITs largest bowl and held a morsel of cheese out to Nesspa. Then I poured tumblers of apple cider for us all.

While we ate and drank, my masteress spoke at length about the making of books.

Finally His Lordship put down his spoon. "I have something to say." His chest rose in a huge breath. "The townspeople have forgiven me for being an ogre. Seven smiled at me today."

"That's wonderful, Your Lordship," I said.

"Yes." He smiled, not the huge, sweet smile that transformed his face but a small smile that mixed pleasure and sadness.

We waited.

"Now I would like to travel."

"Where will you go?" I asked, feeling a lump form in my throat. I was losing Goodwife Celeste, and now I would lose His Lordship.

"To Tair. Several of us live there. Humans are not so clannish in Tair."

Nesspa curled up against the wall next to the cupboard.

"When do you depart?" IT asked.

"Soon. I want you both to come." He blushed. "If you will. An ogre can use someone to induce and deduce and someone to mansion."

I had no fondness for Two Castles, and one way to reach Tair involved crossing Lahnt. I might see my parents and Albin. How heavenly that would be.

Father and Mother would overcome their fear of a dragon and an ogre. They wouldn't be like the people here.

My masteress said nothing.

His Lordship's blush deepened. "I will pay you to come."

IT tilted ITs head. "We will consider your proposition. You will pay handsomely?"

"Yes."

"Lodie?" IT asked.

I nodded.

The next day, while I proclaimed, my masteress and His Lordship conferred in the lair about the coming journey. Two weeks later I had been ITs assistant for a month, and IT paid me my first wages, slowly and solemnly counting the twenty tins into my hand. I slid them into my purse, which jingled delightfully. How astonished Mother and Father would be at this wealth.

But I owed three tins to Master Dess, and I had been tardy in repaying him. I found him in the stables of the Two Castles Inn, tending a lame horse.

"I forgot, honey!" he said when I produced the coins—carefully, although Two Castles was a more honest place now that Master Thiel was with the princess.

"Master Dess, I'm going to Tair."

"Ah." He patted the horse's flank. "The cows in Tair are striped, honey, small for cows, but their milk is sweet as honey. I wish you a safe journey."

The following day His Lordship left his castle in Sir Misyur's trustworthy hands and took with him on the cog only enough valuables to half fill the hold. Much of the rest of the hold was stuffed with ITs hoard.

His Lordship, my masteress, and I stood on the deck along with Goodwife Celeste and Goodman Twah, who had delayed their departure to cross with us. I was glad to know the goodwife had peppermint leaves in her purse.

IT said, with satisfaction in ITs voice, "There are those who keep to their lairs and those who travel. We travel."

The cog master raised the gangplank.

I closed my eyes and imagined the mountains of Lahnt and our valley hidden among them. Home and then away again with my two friends—deducing, inducing, using my common sense, and mansioning.

A TALE of TWO
CASTLES

An Interview with Gail Carson Levine

A Deleted Scene from the Novel

A Discussion Guide for Readers

An Interview with Gail Carson Levine

What was your inspiration for *A Tale of Two Castles*?

I wanted to write a mystery, so I went to the source of many of my books: fairy tales. When I came to "Puss in Boots" I found my idea. Near the end of the fairy tale, the cat, Puss, goes into an ogre's castle and challenges him to shape-shift and says he doesn't believe he can turn into anything as small as a mouse. The ogre, who isn't much of a thinker, takes the challenge and first becomes a mouse and then the cat's dinner. What struck me as the mystery at the core of the story is that there are no witnesses: cat goes in, cat comes out, ogre is never seen again. But we have only the cat's account to explain what happened to him. So I wondered what might really have happened and that became my starting point, although it all got transformed as I wrote. The book shape-shifted on me!

The characters' names in this book are wonderful and oftentimes unusual: Meenore, Jonty Um, the dog Nesspa. How did you come up with them?

The version of "Puss in Boots" that I used comes down to us from Charles Perrault, who was French, so I decided to use the French-ness. All the names can be easily pronounced in French, and some are anglicized (spelled in an English way) versions of French words. Meenore sounds French to my ear. Jonty Um is an anglicized version of *gentilhomme*, French for "gentleman"; Nesspa is a version of *n'est ce pas*, which means "isn't it so?" The main avenue in the town of Two Castles is Daycart Way, after the French philosopher René Descartes. I had fun with the names!

This is the first mystery that you've written. Was your process any different in writing this story than it was in writing your previous novels?

My process wasn't very different. I generally stumble around (in writing) until I find my story. But my thinking was different. In my other novels the drama centers on the main character. For example, Ella in *Ella Enchanted* struggles against her curse. Addie in *The Two Princesses of Bamarre* seeks the cure for the Gray Death. But in a detective mystery, which this is, the drama belongs to the crime victim, in this case Count Jonty Um. So I had to figure out how to interest the reader in both the mystery and Elodie. It's writing on two fronts, which I'd never done before.

Do you like to read mysteries? What are some of your favorites?

I do enjoy mysteries, and I have favorite mystery writers: Tony Hillerman, Lawrence Block, Rex Stout, and Dick Francis. I loved the Newbery winner *When You Reach Me* by Rebecca Stead. And, of course, I adore the Sherlock Holmes stories.

Count Jonty Um can transform into any animal, but he seems most comfortable—most himself—when he shifts into a monkey. If you could shape-shift like him, what animal would you become?

First choice would be to turn into an Airedale terrier, like our dog, Reggie, to discover how it feels to have such a powerful sense of smell and what the world looks like in limited color. And then it would be great to look as adorable as an Airedale does. Second choice would be to be a hive insect, like a bee or an ant, to experience certainty and community that are beyond mammalian understanding. And last, I'd be a hawk flying over the Grand Canyon.

Meenore is a brilliant dragon who places great value in logic and reason, and Elodie learns all about how to induce and deduce. Do you find that you think things through the way Meenore does or do you tend to go by your instincts?

I'm very logical, which helps me with the detail I put in my stories and also helps me keep everything straight. But especially when I get near the end of a book, my instincts kick in. A certain ending just feels wrong, and another feels satisfying. In life I tend to like or not like people based on an emotion rather than intellect.

As an actress, Elodie has a wonderful talent for imagining what it's like to be someone else. As a writer, you create characters and dream up scenes for them all the time. Is it difficult to get inside the head of a character?

Characters reveal themselves gradually over the course of a story. Quirky characters, usually secondary characters in my books, are easier than more ordinary ones. Generally I set up the quirks and then I know how that character will react in most situations. My main character is often harder. The story is revealed through her eyes, and I want her to be clear-eyed so the reader can believe what she relates. But because she isn't odd, she's harder to know. I have to work at it.

We learn that Elodie knows the plays *Pyramus and Thisbe* and *Beauty and the Beast*. What are some other mansioners' tales that she might have been captivated by?

I thought about myths and fairy tales as the source of mansioners' tales. Two of my favorite myths are "Cupid and Psyche" and "Pygmalion and Galatea." A few fairy tales I love are

"East of the Sun and West of the Moon," "Ali Baba and the Forty Thieves," "The Twelve Dancing Princesses," and, naturally, "Puss in Boots." Elodie likes what I like! She performs the beginning of "Toads and Diamonds," which I used as the basis of *The Fairy's Mistake* in my Princess Tales.

The details of life in the town of Two Castles are vividly described—from the clothes that people wear to the food they eat. Even though your book is fiction, these details feel historically accurate. Did you do a lot of research as you wrote *A Tale of Two Castles*?

I did some research, not a ton. For details about the ogre's castle I relied on the Newbery Honor book *Castle* by David Macaulay, and I consulted two books about daily life in the middle ages. For details about the cog that ferries Elodie to the mainland, I went online. But since this is fantasy rather than historical fiction and the kingdom of Lepai doesn't exist, I also dipped into my imagination. For example, Masteress Meenore boils the water in the town wells to purify it, but in the middle ages people didn't know that boiling purifies. They didn't even know that germs existed!

Are there more adventures in store for Elodie, Meenore, and Jonty Um?

Yes! The three of them go to Lahnt, where a theft has taken place that threatens an entire mountain, the mountain where Elodie's parents live.

When she leaves home, Elodie receives a list of seven rules from her mother that ranges from "act with forethought, not impetuously" to "be generous." Do you have any rules to live by? And

what advice might you give to someone who is about to make his or her way in the world?

Those two rules are pretty important. I have to work on the "be generous" one. "Be kind" is another biggie, maybe the major one, and I try to live by it. If not a rule, patience is the virtue a writer has to cultivate, because books take a long time to write and to publish. "Be patient" would be the maxim I'd give someone just starting out. And "Experiment; try things out." You don't have to marry your first career. Let the future surprise you.

A Deleted Scene from the Novel

Originally I thought Elodie would teach Masteress Meenore to read, but I decided not to put it in. Most of my revising is cutting. I want a tight book, and so does my editor. This little bit didn't contribute to the main story, so it went. That's one answer, true but not complete. The rest of the answer is that Masteress Meenore's illiteracy is the tragedy of ITs life. I hoped to write more about IT and Elodie, and I didn't want to resolve this problem in the first book. I think it will be worth waiting for. This is the deleted scene:

ITs mood improved after we supped. IT brought out ITs book about the history of dragons and opened it on the table. I stood on a chair to supervise. IT opened to a page in the middle.

"I do not care about the story, Lodie, until I can read it myself. For now, I want to find *the* word." IT held ITs reading stone against the first line and moved the stone slowly from left to right as I'd taught IT.

I bit my lip when it slid past the first appearance. I bit my tongue, not to *tsk* and give away ITs mistake.

The word appeared again in the third line. IT stopped the stone there. "This word is the same as that." IT moved the stone back to the first line and then to the third. "Yes, they are the same. Same length." Using a knife, IT wrote in ITs pan of dirt, copying, noticing when IT had copied backward, wiping out the mistake with a patch of linen, continuing, until the word was there.

IT looked up at me. I saw ITs throat expand and contract in a swallow. ITs flat eyes were wet. "*Dragon*, Elodie, is it not? That is *dragon*. Tell me."

My eyes were a little wet, too. "Dragon."

IT went to ITs coin basket. "I owe you nine tins, Elodie, but I will give you two more for the two *dragons*. I am very pleased."

So IT paid me, not for what I had done, but for what IT had done. IT paid me when IT was happy. I dropped the coins into my purse one by one. How nice to hear them jingle.

A Discussion Guide for Readers

About the Book:

Twelve-year-old Elodie is sent alone on a journey to make a living as a weaver. But instead she dreams of becoming a mansioner (an actress) and is determined to make her wish come true. Elodie travels to the town of Two Castles and encounters many obstacles, including poverty, thievery, a greedy king, a fire-breathing dragon, and a shape-changing ogre. Throughout her adventures, Elodie learns that dreams can change and friendship can form in the most unexpected places.

Discussion Questions:

1. What do you dream about being when you grow up? What if your parents do not support your choice? Do you think you will pursue it anyway?
2. How does Elodie feel when she leaves home? How would you feel if you traveled alone to a new land? Excited? Anxious? Independent? What would you want to take with you on your journey?
3. Read the "Half Dozen Rules For Lodie" on page 20. Do you think the advice Elodie's mother sends her away with is useful? Why or why not?
4. How do you know if someone is trustworthy? Give an example from your own life.
5. Elodie is determined to become a mansioner and does everything she can to make her dream come true. What goals do you have that you are determined to achieve? What are you willing to do to reach those goals?
6. If you could shape-shift like Count Jonty Um, what would you choose to become? Why? What could you use that

power to accomplish? What might be the disadvantages of shape-shifting?

7. If you misplaced something valuable to you, how would you go about finding it? Have you ever misplaced something valuable and not been able to find it again? What did you do?

8. The author frequently uses animals in this book. Why are animals such an important part of this story? How do animals impact the story line? How would the story be different without the animals?

9. Elodie practices "inducing, deducing, and using my common sense" (p. 249). What does that mean? Do you induce, deduce, and use common sense in your daily life? Think of some instances when these skills are useful.

10. Meenore asks Master Sulow if he would have wanted the count to be king. Master Sulow replies, "An ogre in place of a tyrant? The ogre is far more generous" (p. 255). What does Master Sulow mean by his response? Do you agree with him?

11. Do you agree with Elodie's decision to stay with her masteress instead of pursuing the mansioner's apprenticeship? Why or why not? What would you have done in Elodie's place?

12. If you were King Grenville, would you have released the princess and allowed her to marry? Do you think she and Master Thiel are a good match?

13. Count Jonty Um says, "People don't ask enough questions. They just guess" (p. 312). What does he mean by this? Do you think this is true in today's world? How important is it to you to ask questions in your life?

14. In this story, characters are often judged by their

appearances. The ogre is presumed dangerous because of his size and features, Elodie is considered unworthy because she doesn't have a cap, and Master Thiel is trusted because he is handsome. How does this relate to the saying, "Don't judge a book by its cover"? Do you have a habit of judging books by their covers, so to speak?

15. What do you predict will happen when Elodie travels home to Lahnt with her new companions? If you were in Elodie's place, how would you feel on your journey home? What would you want to have happen when you arrive?

Discussion guide created by Sue Ornstein, a first-grade teacher in the Byram Hills School District in Armonk, New York.